OWNING THE FUTURE

A COLLECTION OF SHORT STORIES

BY

NEAL ASHER

I have a varied collection of short stories in my files and, of course, the temptation is there to dump them on Kindle, take the money and run. However, though I think some of them are great, some aren't, and some are profoundly dated. I am aware that there are those out there, who will just buy these without a second thought, so I have to edit, be selective, and I damned well have to show some respect for my readers. Kindle in this respect can be a danger for a known writer, because you can publish any old twaddle and someone will buy it. Time and again, I've had fans, upon hearing that I have this and that unpublished in my files, demanding that I publish it at once because surely they'll love it. No they won't. A reputation like trust: difficult to build and easy to destroy.

I've therefore chosen stories other people have published here and there, and filled in with those I really think someone should have published. Here you'll find some Polity tales, some that could have been set in the Polity (at a stretch) and some from the bleak Owner universe. Enjoy!

Neal Asher 04/06/18

Stories:

Memories of Earth
I believe I wrote this one as a publicity exercise for Tor Macmillan while they were publishing the Owner trilogy, but then it wasn't used. I subsequently shunted it off to Asimov's and they published it in their October/November 2013 issue. There's also an audible version on Starship Sofa (No. 383).

Shell Game
This appeared in The New Space Opera 2 edited by Gardner Dozois and Johnathan Strahan published in July 2009.

The Rhine's World Incident
First appeared in Subterfuge from Newcon Press in 2008, next appeared in In Space No One Can Hear You Scream from Baen Books in 2013. This is the story where the swarm AI the Brockle makes its first appearance.

Owner Space
Appeared in Galactic Empires published by Gardner Dozois in 2008

Strood
First appeared in Asimov's in December 2004, next in Year's Best SF 10 published by Hartwell and Kramer in 2005. StarShipSofa did an audible version: No. 463

The Other Gun
Cover picture story in Asimov's April/May 2013. This is a backstory for the Rise of the Jain trilogy – it concerns the Client.

Bioship
This appeared in George Mann's Solaris Book of New Science Fiction in 2007

Scar Tissue
Not appeared anywhere at all!

The Veteran
There's an audible version of this on Escape Pod, episode 118, read by Steve Eley – went up there in 2007

MEMORIES OF EARTH

The memories were vague now, still nightmarish, and still after all this time he could not quite piece together the course of events. The Grazen mother had attacked just after they'd established the mining operation down on the surface of the world he had named Malden, just after the first proto-life drops in the ocean and when they were building the first terra-forming bases. It must have been watching for it chose its time well. He'd just started expansion of the Rhine drive vortex generator when the Grazen ovoid slammed into the Vardelex.

The yig worms had quickly penetrated the ship's structure, and moments after that Saul and his crew had been battling for survival both in the physical ship, and in the computer realm most of his mind occupied. They'd grabbed everything they could, including Earth's gene bank, and managed to escape – just four hundred of the nine hundred aboard. The hardware and bioware had been wrecked in his skull, but was just functional enough for him to send the detonation signal to a cache of thermo nukes inside his ship. False daylight had marked their landing on Malden as an atomic conflagration destroyed both the Vardelex and the Grazen ovoid and lit in the night sky.

'It reminds me of Earth,' said Tina Chandra, as she closed up her EA suit and walked up to stand beside him.

Saul snapped out of his reverie and glanced across at her, suddenly angry. Then he calmed himself on a slow wheezy breath, nodded obligingly, suppressing the urge to challenge that. How could the view through this panoramic window possibly remind her of Earth? She'd grown up in the Bangladesh sprawl where the only real available views were of further

1

buildings and the seething manswarm, and no view she could have chosen from cams scattered across their old home would have showed her anything like this. Maybe polar ice or government-owned croplands would have been as uninhabited, but they were in no way comparable. But then, her attitude was usual with many of the survivors and especially the long-sleepers like Tina: whenever they talked of 'Earth' they always talked of a halcyon ideal that had only ever existed when life for humans had not been ideal at all. They certainly weren't referring to the nightmare they had left behind.

Blinking weary eyes Saul returned his attention to the scene before him. The sky looked like nougat, striated in pink-and-white and marbled with pale nutty clouds just above the horizon. The ocean was rose, foaming like fizzy wine on the green and scummy sands lying a kilometre from T-base Six. Between the window and that strand lay the flat rocks of the lava flow the base had been anchored to, and there a solitary planter, like a giant steel beetle made like a Doolittle push-me-pull-you, with heads and manipulators at both ends of its body, was at work. It was pausing at hollows between the slabs to spew part of its load of that scummy sand from the beach, this laced with further organics, minerals and a selection of new genetically modified seeds for salt-resistant plants.

'I still wonder if we did the right thing,' she said.

Saul stooped, his back aching, and picked up his EA suit helmet from the ledge below the window. 'Was there any right and wrong in this?'

'It's like a proto-Earth,' said Tina. 'The algae blooms and micro-fauna we found in the oceans when we arrived would have eventually led to larger life forms there then on land. By seeding the oceans we put our own stamp on it – we probably destroyed something precious.'

2

'Something precious in a few billion years maybe.' Saul shrugged and turned to head towards the airlock. 'And very much dependent on how you define precious. I consider our lives precious and, if we don't do this, we die here.'

It was all he had left really. He'd left most of his mind behind on his ship and now even his viral genetic fix was failing and he was growing old, dying. His legacy would be a terra-formed world the long sleepers could walk out on to begin their lives anew. He felt he owed them that.

Tina followed him. 'But what right do we have to interfere?'

Saul rounded on her. He had intended to remain calm, just run through the final check and not end up in another debate about the morality of what they were doing; not end up going round and round in their discussions of the meaning of it all. He was getting tired of the growing number of 'all sleepers', those who advocated closing themselves up in cold coffins until human civilization reached this far out to release them into some future utopia – giving up, in other words.

'So tell me, Tina, when did you start believing in God?' he asked.

She was taken aback, her mouth opening and closing like those modified trout being bred for the inland lakes. 'I don't believe in God – that's ... primitive.'

'Oh, I see.' Saul gazed at her with pretend puzzlement. 'So what's all this talk about our 'right to interfere'? It strikes me that rights are something granted by someone higher up.' He stabbed a finger towards the ceiling. 'And the only higher ups I've thus far seen in this region of space are the Grazen, and the only right they would grant us is to die quickly rather than screaming in a yig-worm burrow.'

Saul turned and stepped into the corridor leading to the rear airlock of Base Six, pausing for a second to peer into one of the cryogenics rooms, at twenty cold coffins arrayed around the wall. Two hundred days ago he, Tina and seventeen others, had woken in a room just like this on the other side of the base, whilst one occupant had died sometime in the past. His coffin truly earning the term before they took him outside, found some soft ground inland and buried him, thus making a small addition to the terran biomass of Malden. Right there was a demonstration of how far he had fallen. He, who had once been able to clone replacement bodies for people and transfer minds between bodies like computer files, could not keep someone alive in a simple cold coffin.

Upon their arrival on the surface, it had soon become evident that they had two choices: struggle to survive using hydroponics in the enclosed bases, or sleep in the cold coffins from their landing craft, whilst the terra-forming of Malden progressed. He'd chosen the latter and still had enough power to force the decision. So they had rested in cold stasis for a century whilst the oceans began filling with terran life, then the century after that and again and again. Saul had woken many more times than the others, constantly tweaking the plan and ensuring everything kept on track. In Earth years, he was a hundred and seventy now, whilst Tina here was just into her forties.

'Bring your case, we've got work to do,' he said, dragging his gaze away from the cold coffins, and together they stepped into the airlock at the end of the corridor.

Upon waking this time Saul had issued his orders, and the few who had woken with him had set to work assembling and testing the first planter robots and re-jigging the robot factories and auto-maintenance bays, utilizing metals and other materials stockpiled over the best part of two thousand years of automated mining and manufacturing. And now the new system was nearly self-sustaining. Just a little more checking and he would be sure, then it would be time to head back to cold sleep, perhaps, for him, for the last time.

He stepped out of the airlock, gazed across a rocky plain to distant mountains, and noted how the greenery was now predominant. Using the rich-in-organics sand and proto-soil from the coastlines the robots had spread their planting inwards over three hundred kilometres and the blooms from two of the bases had already met up and melded. Within another hundred days, green would rim the entire continental landmass. Also, with the genetically modified algae and seaweeds in the oceans rapidly heading towards critical mass, it seemed likely that, by the end of that time period, there would be enough oxygen content in the air to begin introducing small land-going fauna – though of a highly-modified kind. But they did not need to stay awake for that. He just needed this last check; this last glimpse into a computer world he had once mastered and now found killingly difficult.

'Jason and the others are on their way in,' said Tina.

He glanced over to where she pointed and watched the approaching ATV, with its train of enclosed trailers, worming its way down the rough coast road. Jason Fitch and the other seventeen had finished relocating mining equipment to a copper deposit up the coast. The stats looked good and, hopefully, that operation would be the last tweak they needed. He grimaced, turned away.

The lander lay half a kilometre from the base. Saul gazed at the huge chunk of hardware and again wondered why he hadn't had it taken apart and used, and why he kept the mainframe there rather than relocating it to the base. It wasn't as if there was anywhere they could fly to from Malden now. The wreckage of the Vardelex still created the occasional meteor shower even now. After a moment, he realized he was procrastinating and set out at a vigorous pace for the lander, Tina hurrying to catch up with him.

The lander smelt of time, nostalgia, regret. With Tina dogging his footsteps, Saul walked through the cargo bay then passenger compartment to the control room located behind the cockpit. He entered, gazed around the interior for a moment, remembering his last time in here when he had nearly died, when the medic undertaking Tina's present duties had needed to restart his heart. He walked over and plumped himself down in a chair before the main console, paused reflectively before reaching underneath the console to flick on the power switch, remembering a time long ago when he had thought he would never need to touch a button or a switch again. His mind had been vast back then, when he had been able to individually program a thousand robots all at once, or calculate the vectors of every piece of rubble in a solar system. He had been a demigod who had mastered both mind and matter, who at will could build anything, even including human bodies and minds. Now he was an old dying man. How the mighty had fallen.

The computers booted up all around him, the screen before him scrolling code he had once been able to run in his mind, in fact build in his mind in fractions of a second, but which was now just a blur to him.

'You don't have to do this,' Tina warned.

'Yes,' he said, 'but any other way would require me waking up twenty more people and a further hundred days of computer time.'

Was that really the truth? Surely, that was better than risking his life like this? No, he realized why he did this, why he could never leave it alone: he wanted it back; he wanted back everything he had lost. There was always a chance that the bio-interface in his skull had made new connections, that some of the hardware had self-repaired, that he could once again be the godlike Alan Saul he had been. That was worth the risk, in fact, everything else was worth zero in comparison. He reached up and dug a fingernail into the nub of synthetic flesh covering the teragate socket in his skull, then eyed the coil of optic cable already plugged in at one end into the console before him.

'Get your drugs,' he instructed.

Whilst he sat patiently, she connected a saline drip then began injecting a specially designed cocktail of drugs into the line. The balance had to be just right, the enhancers and consciousness expanders to help him deal with something that had once been so easy, drugs for the shock, for the inevitable cerebral bleeds, to deal with his reaction to the odd compounds his damaged cerebral hardware issued when it powered up. Tina also began attaching monitoring pads, skin-stick scanners, and began to set up her induction cauterizer and heart stimulator. He hoped she would have no need of these, but knew it likely he would suffer near terminal or, final damage, this time.

The drugs kicked in and suddenly the code on the screen began to make perfect sense. Sure, that was the feed from Base Two, where a million species of genetically modified insects were held in chemical stasis. He was ready. Time to plug in. He inserted the optic into the socket in his skull.

It opened to him, all eight bases, all the automated factories, all the robots, all the artificial womb houses, the recombinant factories, the cams and scanners and the assessors of life. He saw it whole, entire, knew there was enough redundancy in the system and that it would work. In a hundred years' time, when sleepers here woke again, they would be able

7

to walk outside and breathe the air. Bees would be pollinating flowers, whole ecosystems of rotifers and nematodes would be building soil, and the planter robots, undergoing an automatic reconfiguration, would be releasing the first land-going reptiles, amphibians and small mammals.

Every sparrow that falls...

Then something else focused its attention on him, something numinous just out of reach, immense and possessing a complexity he couldn't fathom. He had sneeringly asked Tina if she believed in God, yet now in this moment he felt the presence of God was something he could not deny. He remembered, in this moment, that every time he had done this before he had experienced the same feeling, and then, on his return to his failing body, forgotten it all. No ... no there is no God. This was just an artefact, just electro-stimulation of those parts of the brain related to religious experience. This was something people had learnt about more than a thousand years ago back on Earth.

'All good,' he croaked, holding up his thumb to Tina, then found he couldn't get his breath.

The next thing he knew the world died and he was back in a suffering old body with Tina leaning over him to cut his throat, pushing in a tracheotomy tube. He breathed, wished he hadn't, wished she hadn't enabled him to, and then he faded.

Please no, don't let me be alive.

But there was no doubt, because Saul recognized the feel of the pads and straps holding him upright in a cold coffin, the bite of the tubes into his arms, the horrible ache of a body stabbed with a hundred needles, pumped of antifreeze and filled with warm blood, and the saccharin taste the drugs left in his mouth. He opened gummy eyes but couldn't see out of the glass, whose exterior seemed to be crusted with dirt. However, it admitted enough light for him to gaze down at his withered body. No one was here to open the door for him so that meant the automatics had woken him. Something must have gone wrong that required his attention.

He flexed his hands and when he at last felt confident enough, he took a couple of coag plasters from the dispenser, pulled the tubes from his arms and pressed the plasters into place. Next, he turned his attention to the straps, which he struggled with because the easy releasers were jammed. The support pads hadn't retracted too, and he needed to manually wind them back. He slumped in the coffin, grabbing for the door handle on his way down and then spilled out onto the floor.

Something was badly wrong.

The floor was filthy, brown and red debris crunched under his hands, then his fingers closed on something solid. He picked it up and peered at it. It took him a little while to register what he held.

A twig?

Next, with his vision clearing, he gazed with complete puzzlement at the surrounding drifts of leaves, then in astonishment at a creature like a chinchilla, peering at him with beady black eyes before nonchalantly bouncing its back legs off a wall before speeding away. He heaved himself to his feet and on autopilot walked over to a locker, kicking aside leaves, which seemed of a bewilderingly familiar shape, to expose the white mycelia of fungi. He struggled to open the door, meanwhile observing that the coag patches weren't working so well because his arms were bleeding. Finally managing to get the locker open he pulled out his clothing, and it crumbled in his hands.

How long?

No screens of consoles were lit in here and the only sign of any power was a dim light inside the cold coffin, and that fading. He headed over to the door, pulled it further open then stepped out into a corridor strewn with more debris, gazed along it to the airlock, which stood open. At least a hundred years had to have passed else he would have suffocated by now. He advanced, but then stubbed his toe against something, and paused to peer down at a human skull.

'They had everything,' said an eerily familiar voice. 'They had the technology, they had the resources and they had the world I gave them.'

'Who is that?' he snapped, checking behind him.

No one nearby, but then it seemed he was now playing a game with himself, because he just knew the voice lay inside his skull, and it was his own. He walked to the airlock, stepped out and saw that old ginkgo trees now blocked the view of the sea. He paused for a moment and glanced back into the base, but did not have the heart to search it, for he knew it would be empty, and so stepped out into dappled sunlight.

The sky had changed, now pink striated with blue, great puffy blimps of clouds sailing overhead. The walk to the shore was not so far, but by the time he reached it, he was wheezing and his body felt as if someone had beaten it from head to foot. A nail of pain jabbed at his temple, his teeth ached. He was old.

'At first they left you on ice because they thought you might not survive another waking,' said the voice. 'They decided to wait until their medical technology had improved, until they could make you a clone body then figure out the wiring in your skull so as to download you to it. They got there with that tech, but by then were already breaking into factions manoeuvring for power, building up their populations with clones programmed for obedience. It started with the robots, which they sent against each other, then the clones and finally a nasty brain-rotting virus. After that the survivors just couldn't pick themselves back up.'

'They died?' Saul asked, wearily lowering himself to a flat rock to gaze out over the beach and across the ocean.

'No, there's a scattering of tribes in the area,' replied the voice. 'And one of those tribes has even reinvented the bow and arrow.'

Saul's head nodded, he dozed then abruptly snapped awake again. How had time passed so quickly? The sea now lay under twilight before him and the stars were coming out above. He glanced aside at a figure standing just along the beach from him: instantly recognizable with his acid white hair, red eyes and black vacuum combat suit. But, of course, this was as much the real item as old Saul sitting here on his rock. A man, or rather a demigod, who could make a clone of himself and load some portion of his mind to it to serve some specific end, did not himself need to travel down to the surface of the world. He would be there, in that steel sphere on the ocean horizon – that vast ship poised in orbit about Malden.

'So my memories of the Grazen destroying the Vardelex are false,' said Saul, gesturing to that distant ship.

'Of course,' replied the projection of the real Alan Saul, 'we dealt with the Grazen long ago but you and the other's here with you needed the motivation for success, and succeed you did.' The projection waved a pale hand at their surroundings.

Old man Saul, on the beach, glanced around at the trees, down at the strand now scattered with handfuls of glittery shells, out at the sea where something swirled and splashed. Yes, they had succeeded in building a living world, and then just fucked up, as ever.

'Were they clones too?' the old man asked.

11

'No, they were original crew who wanted to get away from me and start something new. I adjusted their memories to give them a greater chance of success.'

What arrogance, thought the old man, recognizing it as his own.

'What now?' he asked.

'You are dying,' replied the projection, 'it's time for you to come home.'

'I'm a piece of you that you want back.'

'In essence.'

Old Saul felt too tired to be angry about that. 'Okay,' he said.

The figure strode towards him, stretching out a hand. The old man reached out to clasp that hand – a symbolic act as his body died and his mind transferred. He immediately found himself falling into the twilight, far and deep, hauled in by something numinous, and dissolving in it.

On the horizon, the giant sphere of the Vardelex seemed to blink like a steel eye, and receded.

ENDS

SHELL GAME

See them tangled in an old cat's Gordian dream but ravelled unravelled each thread a metre long white worm, flattened and ribbed and immortal in the chamber in the tower of breathing sliming machine that is dead alive, half alive. Eye tower, perhaps, in their billion worded language of organic chemistries. Sight, for creatures whose only interaction with the outside, had been through chemical osmosis, touch, heat, vibration. But they are immortal these creatures named Shindles by chemically illiterate man. Procreation is a splitting with no loss of knowledge to this race that is a creature, that is one and billions. Intelligence; the crux. Chemical changes and an increase in heat drove them to pay attention to its source and study beyond the infrared. The Shindles had ever been machine builders, only the machines they built were too worrisomely alive for men or women to identify easily them as such. Complex machines of chemistry of life of death. Machines to dissolve food sources, to convert them into a more easily absorbable form. Glass, fashioned in chemical heat and blown by quickly woven lungs of living thread, filled with concentrated enzymes and acids. Animals dissolved screaming. Man to be dissolved screaming. But no, he understood, for he had touched and tampered with the very roots of life and the woman knew how to give him access here. Greetings: organic chemical heavy in potassium compounds - pleasure source do not eat do not overwhelm do not place in glass vessels. Other source! Recognition. Vast intelligence of worldmind bent on strange machines. The communication lasted for months and man and Shindles reached accord and pursued dual purpose. He gave them a sample of squidlike flesh and together, he and they bent and fashioned with will, and deep knowledge ... and hate. Finally, he departed

13

that place. The contents of the glass vessel in his hand squirming, transparent, small: new Shindles.

I woke up panicking in the middle of the night, or rather what we called night aboard the *Gnostic*, sure that something catastrophic had happened. Then I realized the gravplates weren't fluxing and my present experience was entirely due to the new drinks synthesizer Ormod had installed in the refectory. I settled back to try to sleep again and found myself worrying about the disastrous course of my life, and how it would all probably end the next time some suicidal impulse overtook me – probably when I went to feed our cargo. I got up and took a couple of Alcotox and a sleeping pill chased down with a pint of water, then returned to bed sure I wasn't going to be able to get back to sleep, then seemingly an instant later woke to the sound of the day bell.

As I sat up, the lights in my cabin flared into life – cued to come on at the first sign of movement from me during the day. I peered at my clothes crumpled on the floor and the other general disarray surrounding me, and again contemplated how it had all come to this. At a standard 200 years old, I was now hopefully getting through that watershed for the immortal in which it's possible to drown – that period of their lives when people suddenly decided free-climbing mile-high tower blocks or swimming with white sharks might be a fun thing to do, and I agree, they were.

At age 170 I had safely installed myself in a design job at Bionic Plastics, had enough credit stacked up to afford a flat in New York and a beach apartment on the Dubai coast, and not be too worried if Bionic Plastics kicked me out. I'd also just finished my fourth marriage and had begun contemplating doing the tourist thing and going world hopping. Then suddenly none of it seemed enough, I became bored, terminally bored, just felt like I was no longer alive. The risk taking started then; the usual stuff, though I credit myself as being the inventor of a somewhat risky sport called lava skiing. Then came my great idea: get out of the circuit, head somewhere really remote, and truly experience the alien. I sold up everything, stepped world to world to the very edge of the Polity, the Line, and there spent decades doing some things ... well, let's just say the Grim Reaper must have been sharpening his scythe for a sure harvest. A few years ago, I decided to crew on some cruiser, probably because I had finally started to calm down. I found the *Gnostic* on a world where real coffee and a working coldsuit were the height of culture.

Outstanding.

I'd been on the *Gnostic* for a year now as a standard crewman, which basically meant I got the shit jobs the broken-down robots couldn't manage.

Stepping carefully from my bed, I picked up my discarded clothing and shoved it in the sanitizer, then pulled out some fresh clothes from one of the enormous cupboards in this huge cabin – cupboards that contained empty racks for pulse-rifles. I pulled on monofilament overalls, and took up my armoured gauntlets, visor and stun stick. I followed this routine every morning, because every morning it was feeding time. I stepped out of the cabin to be greeted by the sight of Ormod strolling down the corridor.

The captain of the *Gnostic* was a partial choudapt: the result of a splicing of human DNA and the genetic code of an alien species like giant woodlice kept as pets on a world where they'd gone the full biotech route, even their houses being cysts in giant seaweeds floating in the warm seas. He stood about two metres tall and looked like a heavily built hunchback with segmented armouring over his hump. His wide head lacked a neck and mandibles ran down his jawline to fold up before his mouth. His ears were like those of a bat, eyes pure blue, and a hairstyle the Mohican cut and queue of a Samurai to match the armour, like that of those ancient warriors, he always wore over skin all shades of white, blue and cerise. And I don't think he was entirely sane which, though I seemed to be easing off on the self-destruct, was probably why I had decided to crew for him.

He parted his mandibles over his mouth and grinned distractedly to expose teeth sharpened to points. 'Feed the little darlings?'

'It seems my lot in life,' I replied.

He patted me on the shoulder and moved on up towards the Bridge which, from where we were standing lay about half a mile away. I headed on down towards cargo holds big enough to lose a couple of cathedrals in.

At the end of the corridor, I reached a dropshaft, which for reasons as yet to be explained, had ceased to function five days ago. Grav operated from down below so I necessarily descend a fifty foot ladder affixed to the side, which wasn't so bad going down, but got a bit tiresome on the way back up again. I'd queried the *Gnostic's* AI about this and it at once recited some obscure poetry by William Blake about invisible worms and roses. It seemed I'd gone for the full set, for not only was the captain of this ship singing loony tunes, so was its artificial intelligence. It could perform its main task of operating the U-space engines to get us to the required destination, eventually, but everything else seemed to be falling by the wayside. I often wondered how long it would be before the AI ceased to function at all and stranded us out in the middle of nowhere.

Then again, perhaps all these faults were due to huge

16

structural alterations of the ship, because when I checked records, the *Gnostic* had originally been a trapezoidal Polity dreadnought with external U-space engines. Now it looked like a set of pipes from an ancient church organ with the U-engines located in the smallest pipe. But I could see no reason at all for this other than it might reflect the unstable condition of the mind controlling it.

At the bottom of the ladder, I stepped out of the dropshaft, reached round and hit the manual control for lights, which occasionally came on automatically but on this occasion did not. Star lights, in the ceiling, suffused the massive space of Hold One with an eerie blue glow. From where I stood I could not see the far wall though, to my right an aisle lay open between cargo containers and racks, and from there I could see it, a mile away. Putting on my visor and pulling on my gauntlets I headed to the left where the 'little darlings' were located – a cargo that had been aboard *Gnostic* for two years with seemingly no place to go.

The cargo containers here were stacked two high, each being a box twenty-five feet square and fifty feet long with a chainglass sheet with an access door inset across one end. I climbed stairs leading up to a gantry giving access to the second level of containers to begin my work. Like all the others, the first container had the door set high up because the floor level lay three metres up to accommodate a deep hollow with frictionless sides within the container. Turning on the internal light I carefully peered inside, checking each corner, and around the boxes of perma-sealed food animals and the small handler I used to move their contents. Nothing in sight, but shindles had a tendency to stack themselves up the side of the hollow to throw out their dying, which usually went to find a dark corner in which to expire. When they were in this condition, they were

17

especially dangerous, often unable to distinguish any warm living body from their usual hosts, and anxious to deposit the eggs their kind produced at the end of their short lives. Making sure I had missed nothing, I took up a breather mask beside the door, put it on under my visor, then stepped inside, drew my stun stick and proceeded over to the food boxes.

First, I poked the stun stick between the boxes and down the gap between them and the wall to be sure nothing was lurking out of sight. Sure then I was safe, I opened one circular expanded-plasmel box, a metre across and half that deep, and gazed inside. The first thing that always struck me was the beauty of the shell of these food animals, then the familiarity. They just looked like big flat snails, like ammonites, coloured in iridescent hues. Enclosed in a thin layer of impermeable plastic, these huge molluscs were in a state of suspended animation started by them but chemically maintained. Now I picked up the hand control for the handler and it lifted up on maglev and drifted over. Using the various toggle switches, I had it slide its fork tines under the box and lift it. I then pulled the ravel tag off the box and watched the expanded-plasmel begin to decay, drip to the floor and evaporate. By the time I brought the handler to the edge of the hollow, the box was gone, with only the big mollusc in its impermeable coating remaining. Another ravel tag set that coating expanding into a wet jelly that fell away in clumps while I turned to gaze down into the hollow.

A great tangle of hair-thin almost transparent worms squirmed and writhed below me. It offended my sense of aesthetics that I must sacrifice so large and beautiful a mollusc to keep alive these horrible squirmy little things. However, what remained of my suicide impulse was satisfied on enough levels to counter this: the things were dangerous to feed, and it seemed likely that if Earth Central Security discovered we were keeping them aboard, we would end up facing reprogramming or even a death sentence. Certainly, ECS would take away the *Gnostic* AI for reprogramming, and Ormod would have lost the ship. This was because the one small colony of the creatures we had found, we were regrading to Sentience Level 3, with lots of provisos about hivemind potential. They were intelligent, apparently, and speculation abounded that their ancestors had arrived at their current location in the Polity in some sort of spaceship.

I ordered the handler to drop in the big snail, which was now starting to move. It landed just to one side of the main tangle of shindles and stuck out one big slimy white foot to right itself. It then immediately started heading away just as fast as it could, which wasn't very fast at all. The shindles sensed its presence, all of them orientating towards it, then they flowed onto and around it like syrup, engulfing then beginning to penetrate it.

These shindles were very different from those in the colony discovered. They were much smaller, thinner, and transparent rather than white. Also being of surprisingly long-lived variety, their aim now was not to lay eggs, but to feed on the mollusc from the inside. Usually it took them many years to kill their hosts, but there were many of them and our supply of the big snails limited. It would take about half an hour before the snail started to expire, then in two days' time I would fish out the empty shell for disposal. Intelligent indeed – I just saw squirmy parasites.

I was stepping into the third cargo container when the *Gnostic* shuddered and I felt an odd twisting sensation in my gut. The ship had come out of underspace too early, and it was only an hour later, after feeding the rest of our collection of shindles and returning to the living quarters, that I found out why.

'It seem Gnostic find 'nother wreckage,' said Parsival

She was slender, not particularly pretty, and perhaps the least screwed-up crewmember. At a mere thirty years old, she lay far away from her two-century watershed. She came from an out-Polity world rarely visited by ships and with no connection to the runcible network. She just took the first opportunity that came along. That the opportunity was the *Gnostic* was perhaps unfortunate. Slowly she was beginning to grasp standard Anglic, and that she might have chosen badly, but she had promised to serve aboard for two years and had three months to go.

'Any idea what it is?' I enquired, as I sat down at the refectory table.

'Captain looking,' she replied.

Gnostic, like most ship AIs bearing the name of the ship it controlled, often took little detours to ogle some piece of spaceborn wreckage. I had always thought the wreckage it sought was from the big war that ended just after I was born, the war between the Polity and the vicious crablike Prador, and the one the *Gnostic* had been hurriedly built to fight in. However, I was soon to learn my mistake, though Gnostic frequently found wreckage from that war, it certainly wasn't what it sought.

Pladdick, another crewmember, slapped a plate down in front of me: bacon on toast. Since he, being what passed for the engineering officer aboard this ship, had disconnected the food synthesizer from AI control, after it started providing as with raw eggs and a pile of some granular substance none of us had attempted to eat, we could only program it for one simple meal at a time. We were all eating bacon and toast this pseudo-morning. I studied the others at the table.

Excluding Ormod, the crew of the *Gnostic* presently numbered four. Beside Parsival and myself, there was Pladdick, a squat heavy-worlder who seemed perpetually grumpy, and Shanen, who was a standard format human like me who said too much and who, I ascertained, had reached the stage of life I had reached thirty years back – for my own health I tried to avoid her. All were present at the refectory table. Each of us, when not here or about our tasks, occupied one of the large number of enormous staterooms (previously bunkrooms for troops). These were also always available should anyone want to pay to be a passenger. Ormod often complained about the lack of business from that source, and put it down to the ease and convenience of runcible travel between worlds. He never seemed to notice that passengers quite often packed other ships, and never questioned why such people might want to avoid this ship. However, this trip was unusual since we actually did have a passenger. I glanced round as she entered.

Professor Elvira Mace wore a utile envirosuit, had twinned augmentations and very infrequently ventured out of the computer architecture she had created in them. I knew her to be an expert in some obscure branch of alien computer science, but beyond that knew very little about her. She only communicated when she wanted something, which was not often.

'Why have we left U-space?' she asked as she sat at the table.

'The AI running this ship, if "running" is really the correct term, seems to be looking for something,' babbled Shanen. 'However, it's probably only found another chunk of Prador dreadnought or a space station. Last time Gnostic found a Prador itself still in its armoured spacesuit. It was in suspended animation but our lovable AI roasted it with one of the forward particle cannons.' Shanen gazed around at the others at the table. 'I didn't even know this ship was still armed until then.'

'I see,' said Mace, and turned her attention to the plate Pladdick placed before her.

Shanen did tend to babble, but she wasn't stupid and very often got things right, but not this time.

'A bit of a Lild scout ship,' said Ormod, pointing at the big curved screen before him. Unlike the rest of the ship, the Bridge was small scale: just a few chairs at a horseshoe console all more or less facing a panoramic curved screen.

With Shanen at my side – she had suggested we come up here and find out what was going on, and I agreed because I didn't see anything suicidal about that impulse – I gazed at the screen. The object displayed was a simple curved tube of metal trailing various cables and pieces of charred infrastructure from each end.

Lild? I thought. *What the fuck is a Lild?*

'So what's the big interest?' I asked.

Surprisingly, the AI replied first, reciting the first, two verses of Dulce Et Decorum Est, then the Captain continued with, 'Like the Prador, they built ships in their own shape. The Prador did this out of pure arrogance, but with the Lild it was arrogance based on their religion. Did not God model the galaxy on their form? We just made copies of that form with CTDs inside and left them to be picked up, rescued. It was a dirty trick, but enough to discourage them.'

A CTD being a contra terrene device capable of wiping out anything from a small house to cracking the crust of a world, I surmised that such a ploy would certainly discourage them, whoever 'them' might be. Since having been built too hurriedly during the Prador war, it must have been faults not ironed out then, or some event then, that sent the *Gnostic* AI off the far side of weird. Still believing that this was something to do with that

22

same war, I assumed the Lild must have been a Prador weapon of some kind.

'I never realized you were aboard the *Gnostic* during the Prador war,' I said, testing.

Ormod parted his mandibles and grinned, again in that oddly distracted way. 'I wasn't.' Then, still looking at some point above and to the right of my head. 'Professor.'

I turned to see that Elvira Mace had joined us.

'The data are good,' said Mace. 'You may proceed.'

'So you got the location,' said Shanen abruptly.

Still distracted Ormod said, 'You talk about?'

'The Circoven Line war, as you well know.'

Now the captain actually focused on someone properly, and that focus was rather intense and just a little frightening. After a long drawn out pause, he said quite precisely, 'Most Line wars are named after the Polity worlds involved, but in this case the rule was changed. Probably that was guilt – it should be.'

Shanen grinned, a little crazily I thought and replied, 'ECS had no remit to protect Circoven – the people wanted nothing to do with the Polity.'

Something went click in my mind and I remembered the words 'Circoven' and 'choudapt' being used in conjunction. I was about to ask about this, but now the captain rose out of his seat and drew a hand's length of the Samurai sword he always carried.

'Go away,' he said.

'Why captain, are you threatening me?' Shanen asked, laughter in her expression. For me the suicidal impulse must have been at a low ebb that day, for I caught hold of her arm and dragged her from the Bridge. Once out of there Shanen began to fight me, but the doors slid closed and I heard the locks engaging. After a moment, Shanen seemed to get control of herself.

'Tell me about this Line war,' I said. 'Tell us all about it – I think we need to know.'

'Do you all know what a Line war is?' Shanen enquired.

All but Parsival either nodded or said they did, so Shanen explained for our out-Polity recruit.

'Two hundred years ago we fought an alien race called the Prador. There's still argument now, about how that would have ended had not the old Prador king been usurped by a new leader that no longer wanted to continue fighting. Now that was definitely a full-scale all-out war and fight for survival. Line wars are those border Polity conflicts in which the extinction of the Polity is unlikely, but which could become something worse and require a certain level of resource expenditure. I can't really be any clearer than that without getting into statistics.'

'You sound like a logician,' grumped Pladdick.

Shanen shrugged. 'I was once – you get to my age and there isn't much you haven't done.'

'So, specifically the Circoven Line war?' I enquired.

'Mostly these things are started by out-Polity humans and sometimes AIs, but every now and again something completely new comes on the scene.' She grimaced for a moment. 'The Lild starship consisted of a series of concentric toriods five miles across. It arrived far outside the Circoven system about fifty years ago – this being Captain Ormod's home world: one of those worlds that went the full GM route even so far as them modifying living organisms to excrete wood screws, if you see what I mean.' Quite obviously Parsival didn't, but Shanen continued relentlessly. 'Circoven was out-Polity, and despite constant pressure to join, obstinately refused. The Lild

24

starship divided into six segments. One of them headed for Circoven, where it proceeded to bomb that high-biotech world back into the Stone Age, killing some forty million people, whilst the others headed into the Polity.'

'How is it you know about this stuff and I don't?' I wondered.

Shanen turned to me. 'The Polity is a big place, Strager – a lot of stuff like this goes on that most people just don't get to hear about. But what I'm telling you is all available on the nets.'

'That didn't really answer my question,' I insisted.

'No, but I guess I know more about it because I crewed on *Gnostic's* sister ship, the *Gnosis*.' She shrugged, perhaps embarrassed about the name. 'I was aboard *Gnosis* when the crew departed *Gnostic* shortly after the Line war I'm talking about, when its AI turned very strange and abruptly decided to go independent. I guess it was that that lured me back to crew here.'

Suicide impulse, thought I.

At that moment the ship shuddered in a way I'd never felt before, the table vibrating before us, and we could all hear the distant sounds of things falling followed by a deep hollow boom.

'Gnostic not good,' said Parsival, and whether she was talking about the ship itself or its AI I didn't know.

'Fuck is that?' wondered Pladdick.

'Structure shift,' said Shanen, and we all gazed at her bewildered.

'I'll get to that later.' Shanen waved a hand airily and continued with her story as if nothing important had happened. 'The five segments that headed Polity-wards arrived at a world with a population of four billion, a defensive satellite grid, two ECS dreadnoughts on station and fifty attack ships. Ignoring

25

every warning that could possibly be given they proceeded to try dropping asteroids on that world and seemed unable to fathom why none of the rocks were arriving on the surface. Meanwhile, ECS was able to penetrate their com security and discover a great deal about them, and what we found out wasn't good.'

'Well, if they were bombing without provocation I'd say that was pretty obvious,' said Pladdick.

'Oh it went further than that,' said Shanen, 'much further.'

Just then, we all felt the strange sensation of the *Gnostic* dropping into U-space.

'I guess we're not going to the destination logged,' I said.

'I guess not,' said Shanen, then she told us about the Lild.

As Ormod had stated, they were the beloved of God, the Lild. They were nautiloids and one had to see how the discovery that the galaxy they lived in was exactly the shape of their own bodies might affect them. Arrogance and fanatical belief had become a racial trait. The galaxy belonged to them, having been fashioned for them by their god, so everything belonged to them and they could do with it what they wanted, and what they wanted usually involved subjugation, destruction, death. Religion, a vicious and hardy meme at best, usually collapsed as civilizations became spacefaring, for belief systems initiated when the world was still flat and thunder the bellowing of gods, usually could not survive the realities of the universe and the steady abrasion of science. But this thing about their shape, and the shape of the galaxy, sustained the Lild's vicious faith. When the Lild warship encountered humankind, the nautiloids realized that here was a race competing for the watery worlds they preferred, and knew that this was a test laid before them by their

26

god. The Chosen, as they called themselves, decided in an instant that this irritation called the human race must be exterminated. The holy war lasted one solar month, for though one segment of the warship was successful against Circoven, the remainder did not do so well.

Humans did not seem to understand their position in the galaxy; that they must bow to The Plan. The asteroids the five segments dropped were vaporized by energies the nautiloid theocracy knew nothing of and therefore claimed did not exist. The bombardment continued, sort of. When Polity dreadnoughts like the *Gnostic* moved into position and obliterated two segment ships and numerous smaller vessels, denial of the facts became a little difficult. The remainder ran, the area of conflict, or rather the Polity dreadnought hunting ground, spreading out over many star systems. The dreadnoughts destroyed the five segments and most of the smaller ships, but the one at Circoven managed to enter U-space far enough from detection to escape.

'Doubtless,' said Shanen, 'after that segment's return to the Lild home world, there were some theocratic problems to resolve.'

'You not know?' asked Parsival.

'We not know,' she shot back. 'Throughout the surveillance of the Lild here, the location of their home world remained undiscovered. You see, they had some form of AI running their ships, which, though required for space travel, was never allowed to know anything about where the ships were going or where they came from for longer than it took them to operate the U-space engines. Only the Lild astrogators were allowed to retain that information, and we never got hold of one of them.'

'But Ormod now has the location of the Lild home world,' I suggested.

'Yes, it seems that some Lild, heretics, would steal such information when available and keep recordings. At last, it seems, Gnostic found a scout ship that was flown by one of them.'

'And in eight weeks' time,' Ormod announced over the intercom, 'we'll be arriving right over their home world for some payback.'

The *Gnostic* shuddered again, this time so hard that those on the opposite side of the table from me slammed against it, and my chair shot back and went over. When I did finally manage to regain my feet and look around, I swore. The refectory ceiling was now not very far above my head, and one wall had receded nearly three metres and bowed out. And that was only the start.

The Lild, whose name was a complex infrasound pulse transmitted through its watery home and therefore unpronounceable in any human tongue, but whom we shall call Brian, had ascended to power in the wake of the recent resurgence and subsequent suppression of the Evolutionary Heresy. He was a member of the High Family: that species of the Lild whose shells most perfectly matched the God-given shape of the galaxy and who brutally maintained the faith. Floating in his coral palace below the spiral sea, his beautiful twelve-feet-across shell presently being micro-etched with new star systems by a young Low Family Lild with very nervous tentacles and, of course, its own breather system, Brian contemplated the past and what must be done in the future.

The return of the segment of an expeditionary warship with the news they had actually encountered another star-faring race, had come as a great shock to the theocracy. When the bald facts of the warship's defeat were presented, the Evolutionary

Heresy inevitably reared its ugly head from the scientific quarter and civil war ensued. It was a long and ichorous affair and, after Brian's High Family regained power, many Low Family nautiloids were necessarily staked out over volcanic vents until all elements amidst the Chosen stopped asking questions. Even so, the questions remained and now, with the strength of his forces growing, Brian understood that something must be done.

The humans were another test set directly by God, just like the worms before them, though with the worms the nature of the test had been blindingly obvious. Brian shuddered and the note of the micro-etcher stuttered.

'I hope you have made no mistake,' Brian intoned.

'No, your honour,' the young Lild quavered.

Brian would check later, and if the present star-system being etched on his shell was in any way wrong, the youngster would be punished. Nothing too severe, maybe a crushed tentacle or two.

'You may leave me now,' Brian ordered.

The young Lild shot away, slightly ink-incontinent with fear, and disappeared into one of nearby coral tunnels. Brian jetted out a slow stream of water to set himself drifting across to a chamber wall that seemed a chaotic mass of variegated corals inset with flat areas of utter blackness. He reached out a tentacle and interlaced its numerous wormish fingers around what, in a human sea, might have been mistaken for a brain coral. Pictures now appeared in the blackness.

Throughout the recent resurgence of the Evolutionary Heresy, most of the expeditionary warships had returned. Many had been destroyed in the subsequent fighting when Low Family EH elements used their god-granted scientific knowledge to take control of ships from the tentacles of their High Family theocrat captains, but that was all finished now and new ships were in the process of being built. The worms, Brian recollected, had occupied an area of space eight light-years across including twelve star-systems, and two worlds habitable by them and therefore habitable by the Lild. The war against them had taken a little while to get going, since this was the first intelligent alien species the Chosen had encountered, but once they discovered the horrific nature of these demonic creatures, the war became jihad and they swiftly exterminated the worms. The humans, almost certainly being a larger test set by God, must occupy a larger volume of space and maybe even as many as ten or twenty habitable worlds. This meant the Lild needed to build and crew more ships – a task that would take perhaps another twenty years … Brian felt a moment of disquiet.

The survivors of the expeditionary warship to humanspace were now all dead. Quite obviously none of them had been as strong as required by God for they had fallen into heretical thought and even madness. Whilst being put to the question by the inquisitors, a process usually involving one of those volcanic vents, some of them had even clung to their claims that long-range sensing had revealed human activity extending for *tens of thousands of light-years*. Low Family evolutionary heretics, obviously, since it was only those science officers dealing with the ship minds and U-space mechanics, who made such claims. They also claimed the humans were using impossible weapons – devices employing energies and science that just could not exist in God's universe. It was all quite ridiculous, and Brian became angry at his own disquiet. The humans would go the same way as those disgusting worms: the shindles.

While we were hurtling through U-space it was impossible to get an outside view of the *Gnostic*, had its AI even given us access to any of its external sensors or computer systems. However, all of us possessed our own computer hardware and, with our long and old experience, Shanen and I were able to link into the ship's internal sensors to get some idea of what was going on.

'It looks like this now,' said Shanen, gesturing flipping and image from her hand comp to screen fabric stretched on one wall.

The schematic appeared first as a transparent shape sketched out in blue lines until the comp's program, which we had created together, caught up and filled in the details. The image before us was still recognizable as the *Gnostic*, just. As I stated before, when I boarded the *Gnostic,* I had found out how substantially it had altered its structure so it looked like a set of church organ pipes, though with a large difference in length between each pipe. Now those pipes had drastically curved in towards the smallest pipe, which had completely folded around to become a doughnut shape, though with the centre hole nearly closed up.

'Right,' said Pladdick. 'Gnostic is trying to disappear up his own arsehole.' He was particularly grumpy today because his original cabin had reduced in size by half.

'Gnostic get better,' said Parsival.

'What?' said I, brilliantly.

Parsival pointed to the wall to our right, here, where we had relocated ourselves in Pladdick's new cabin – one that didn't seem to be changing shape as fast as the rest.

'What do you mean, Parsival?' asked Shanen.

She stood and walked over to the wall and we all followed her.

'Here,' she pointed, 'and here.'

This wall had been slowly sliding upwards from the

floor. I noticed that what I had at first taken to be a shelf along that wall was approaching the ceiling, and that up there lay a recess into which it would fit perfectly. I surmised that when that shelf reached the correct position, the wall would lock into place.

'These weren't originally here,' said Shanen.

'Gnostic soon correct shape,' said Parsival.

Of course, she had seen more of this than us during her long strolls about the ship. She kept herself to herself, did Parsival, which was understandable being amidst this crew.

'And of course we don't even have to guess what that shape will be,' said Shanen.

'A series of concentric toroids,' I realized.

'Absolutely correct,' said Ormod over the intercom. 'Gnostic is changing its appearance to match that of a Lild warship – one they listed as missing but which Polity AIs surmise strayed into the Prador Third Kingdom.'

'Why?' I asked, then felt stupid.

'All the better to close right up on the Lild home world,' he replied. 'Now, Strager, I know that recent events have been upsetting, but don't you have a job to do? Don't you all have various tasks to perform?'

'Why the hell should we?' spat Pladdick.

'Why?' wondered Ormod. 'Why because from here I control life-support and if you don't do what you're told it might just start to get difficult to breathe in there.'

Oddly, the dropshaft was functional again, but even while allowing the irised gravity field to assist me I still kept hold of the wall ladder. Hold One had now developed enough of a curve so that I could see the distant wall above the hold's contents, but that would not last much longer, for the ceiling would soon cut off that view. I set off to the left and saw that the cargo containers had shifted, gaps appearing between then, but also noted that this had been prepared for, the gaps exposing hydraulic connections between each container.

As I had a hundred times before, I set about my feeding routine, first checking the interior of each container for escaped shindles then feeding those that required it. It was very noticeable to me that the information I had collected on these creatures was at complete variance to what I had been seeing here. These ones just weren't dying off as fast as they should so perhaps their metabolisms had been slowed down? It was only as I was dropping a snail food animal into the last shindle pit, that the full implications of these creatures being aboard hit me, along, of course, with the fact that Captain Ormod was a survivor of a holocaust on a planet whose entire civilization was based on genetic engineering.

'So,' I said. 'I would guess that you're keeping a close eye on me while I'm down here.'

Walking back from the last container, I paused to remove my gauntlets. 'Now, since I've been looking after these things, I've learned a thing or two about them. They'll occupy their host and take complete control of its nervous system, meanwhile eating it from the inside out and multiplying. I bet you've altered these ones so the Lild will be their favoured hosts. It is a nasty plan, but I just don't see how it can work. The Lild might be theocratic, but they are space-faring, which means they are far from stupid and will possess the technology to prevent the spread of creatures so lethal.'

'You are wrong,' said Ormod, who of course had been watching and listening all the time.

'These creatures are a biological weapon you intend to use against the Lild,' I said. 'Just tell me I'm wrong about that.'

'You are wrong about that too,' he replied. 'The Shindles are salvation for the Lild.'

And he would say no more.

Eight weeks passed, during which I pleaded and threatened but got no response, from either the captain or Gnostic. I went on strike, refusing to go down to feed the shindles, then relented after two days without food or water myself. Also during this time, the *Gnostic* continued to change its shape, to join up the tubes of its structure into a ship consisting of a series of concentric toriods five miles across. One day the food synthesizer abruptly reconnected and started working again, then some of the other automated systems began to come back on. Taking my usual journey down into the hold, I observed that many of the cargo containers not containing shindles had been repositioned and that some of the handler robots down there were now on the move and busy separating out six and opening them. When I tried to get a closer look, a handler – a thing like the bastard offspring of a forklift truck and a praying mantis – moved into my path and would not let me through.

I went off to feed the shindles and again wondered what Ormod meant about salvation. Certainly, being small and threadlike and almost transparent, these shindles were different from those first discovered, but what else had been done to them? Were they intelligent, as Polity AIs now though the originals were? Did Ormod intend them to take over the Lild? I just had no idea.

The next time I went down to feed the shindles the handler robots had dismantled the six containers and used them to build a big shed on the hold floor. Sounds of industry came from inside over ensuing weeks, but there wasn't even a crack I could peer through into the interior. I told Shanen about this, and a few days later I saw her sporting numerous bruises and a bemused expression. Doubtless, to relieve the boredom, she had tried to go up against one of those handler robots. Seven weeks into our journey, I arrived one morning for the usual feeding routine and, only when I actually entered the first cargo container and brought over one of the food snails, did I see something had changed. The pit was empty. Checking all the other containers, I saw that they were empty of their shindles too.

'What are you doing Ormod?' I shouted.

He surprised me by replying. 'I want them hungry.'

Then finally, we arrived.

'Well looky here,' said Shanen.

Ormod had reinstated the availability to us of all the ship's sensors, and we now had a large screen upon which we could observe the Lild home system. With computer programs running to contract distances and highlight stuff, we soon saw a busy place indeed. The Lild home world was larger than Earth but only enough to knock surface gravity up about ten per cent. It was a water world with only a few islands at the poles, and though it possessed no natural satellite like Luna, it certainly possessed plenty of unnatural ones. Big space stations hung in orbit in an even grid, and taking a close look at one of them, I guessed a lot of the visible hardware to be defensive weaponry. Then, far out at a point halfway between this world and the orbit of the next world out – an icy orb about the size of Neptune – we observed the fleet of Lild warships, and warship construction stations, hanging in space like a scattering of huge coins amidst massive slot machines.

'I would guess they're making preparations for something,' I said.

'They are preparing for the extermination of the human race,' said a voice behind and I looked round to find that, after eight weeks, our passenger had rejoined us.

'Professor Mace,' said Pladdick, stepping forward with something nasty in his expression. Like us all, he had been really frustrated about all this but, since he was a heavyworlder, that frustration sometimes resulted in fist-shaped dents in the walls.

Taking, if not her life then her health in her hands, Shanen caught hold of his shoulder. 'Just a moment, Pladdick. I think now is the time for explanations.'

Elvira Mace nodded, and taking a wide circuit around Pladdick, strode up to stand beside the screen. She gestured at the Lild warships. 'Already Gnostic is picking up and analyzing vast amounts of data.' She tapped at the console to bring the home world back onto the screen. 'Much has now been confirmed and we are updated on a lot.'

'Tell me,' I said. 'Why are you involved in this?'

She glanced at me. 'Not all the survivors of Circoven look like Ormod.'

'I see.'

She now gazed at Shanen for a moment. 'You know much about this, having served on the sister ship to this one, but I will reiterate for the rest.'

Shanen nodded obligingly, still a little glassy eyed I noticed, and guessed the last eight weeks had taken her far too close to her boredom threshold.

Mace continued, 'The Lild species is a divergent one with two branches that cannot interbreed. The ruling theocratic elite are those whose shells more closely resemble our galactic spiral. Though somewhat interbred they have managed to retain a grip on power through religious oppression and sheer aggression. The lower class, are a hardier and generally more intelligent branch of the species, but less aggressive. Without any kind of intervention, this state of affairs could continue for centuries. Without any intervention, the Polity will end up with a Lild fleet at the Line in a couple of decades.'

'Wait a minute,' Shanen held up a hand. 'Are you saying that what you and Ormod are doing, whatever it is, has Polity sanction?'

'I am saying that for the present Earth Central Security is looking the other way.'

'Deniability,' said I.

'Precisely.'

'So what are you doing?' I asked.

'I will leave the final explanation to Ormod, but let me continue to outline the situation.' She gave a tight little smile. 'Each Lild warship has a captain and six under-captains should the ship separate into segments. These are all members of the ruling elite branch of the species. However, these often return to the home world where the main concentration of this species lives in tunnels in the seabed corals – a massive cave system with internal water separated from that of the sea itself. You see, for religious reasons they cannot breathe water contaminated by their lesser brethren.'

'I do see,' I said. 'With the defences around that world it would be very difficult to get in to drop a bio-weapon in the sea let alone get one down into those tunnels.'

'You do see.' Elvira smiled. 'Then I leave it to Ormod to explain the whole set-up further. He is awaiting you and Shanen down in Hold One.'

'What about us?' Pladdick gestured to himself and Parsival.

Elvira eyed him. 'I will explain further, but you two are

not anywhere near suicidal enough for what comes next.'

'I'm not sure I like this,' I said, but I was already turning to follow Shanen towards the door. The reality? A week of not feeding the shindles had left me bored and listless, half alive and wondering about my chances of, like Shanen, going up against one of those handler robots with whatever weapons I could fashion, just to find out what they were doing. Yes, I was getting through that damned watershed, but I wasn't through it yet. This meeting with Ormod promised something that stirred me up inside, made me feel alive. I could see the excitement in Shanen's expression as she glanced back at me before stepping out into the corridor. Of course, she was a worse case than me.

This time when I used the dropshaft, following Shanen in, I didn't bother with even checking if the irised gravity field was working or touch the ladder. At the bottom of the shaft, Shanen stepped out into the lit area beyond and swore aloud. I swore too when I saw what awaited us.

'Wonderfully realistic, aren't they?' said Ormod, stepping out from behind one of the six nautiloids standing on the floor, arrayed about a large glass sphere. One of them had a shell ten feet across, whilst the other five were about six feet across, fatter with their spirals running slightly off centre, all of their squid eyes and writhing tentacles glistened realistically. One of them, I'm sure, even winked at me.

'Same ones as you loaded with CTD booby traps?' I suggested.

Shanen shook her head and glanced round at me. 'These are a tad more sophisticated I suspect.'

Of course, I had been forgetting that she had been involved in the same conflict as Ormod and Gnostic.

'Much more sophisticated,' Ormod agreed. 'They wouldn't fool Polity security scanners, but they'll fool most of what the Lild have got, if they're not subjected to too rigorous an inspection.'

'If you could explain,' I suggested.

'Simple, really, having communicated with the Lild High Family, this ship has been directed to a place in the fleet, whilst its captain is to take one segment of the ship to the home world where there is now much excitement. For the captain is to take there the human prisoners he managed to capture.'

Fuck, I thought, clonks and booms resounding all around us as this segment of *Gnostic* detached from the main body of the ship

Brian spun like a coin in his underwater palace, his children, nautiloids merely half a metre across, orbiting around him. He was ecstatic. There had been some controversy concerning the late return of one of the expeditionary warships, but a check of the records showed it to be one that had gone missing out in the general direction of human space. The story the captain of that ship told was long and complex tale of their encounter with a human warship, battles, escapes, damaged engines that took decades to repair and finally a sneak raid for intelligence but with an added bonus.

Brian must honour the captain with an audience and give him a chance to tell his story to the theocratic elite. His adventures would be a salutary lesson to all Lild to confirm their place in the universe, to dispel any remaining doubts raised by heretics, and still harbored by those weak of mind. But, most important of all was that added bonus, for he would bring human captives here for all to see – weak malformed creatures obviously not shaped by God. Air breathers and creatures no better than the leaf eaters dwelling on a few home world islands. A species to be crushed for their temerity in confronting the

Chosen.

Brian spread his tentacles and jetted water to bring his spin to a halt. Playfully batting at his children he sent them whistling on their way to play in some other part of the palace. This was a joyous occasion, for the captain of that ship had already confirmed some of his own suspicions. The expeditionary ship the humans had destroyed had just been plain unlucky having arrived at a place where the humans were strongest. This had been a message direct from God to knock the Lild out of their complacency. However, the good news was that these humans occupied just a handful of star systems, more than the worms, and more worlds, but nothing like what the Low Family heretics aboard that first ship had claimed.

Moving over to his screens, Brian stabbed out a tentacle and manipulated the coral controls. Immediately he obtained a view of the new arrival, one of its segments now detached and heading for home world. Within the day that segment would dock with one of the big military stations and the captain and his humans would be shuttled down to the planet, down through the Spiral Sea and finally to here. There was much to do. Brian began summoning High Family theocrats to the palace.

I gazed around at this compartment obviously constructed in what remained of Hold One. So this was what the interior of a Lild warship should look like. We occupied a coraline tube, with interior segmentation, perhaps just like the interior of a length of straightened-out snail shell.

'So what makes you think we're going to have anything to do with this?' I asked.

Ormod parted his mandibles and grinned spikily. 'It's the time of your life.' He glanced at Shanen. 'Is that not so?'

Shanen nodded agreement. Her face was flushed with

excitement and poised on the balls of her feet she looked ready spring into action at once. I knew that she would do precisely what Ormod wanted for, twenty or thirty years ago, I would have too. Now, however, I was starting to see downsides to risking my life.

'Perhaps you could explain further?' I enquired.

'There are risks associated with having people like you aboard,' he told us. 'So, as I prepared for this I never wanted any more than two of you at any one time. I knew that it is precisely those of your kind who would be inclined to do something like this – those who care so little for their own existence. The Lild Theocrat has been told of two captives so that would be preferable, but one being missing can be easily explained. However, captives are essential because they utterly ensure that the nautiloid who did the capturing, would be immediately summoned down to the ocean floor cave systems.'

'Why not you?' asked Shanen.

That grin again. 'With the assistance of a submind of Gnostic I'll be controlling them.' He gestured to the six robot nautiloids. 'I am also holding some other options in reserve aboard this segment vessel and it would be better for me to be here to control them. Gnostic itself has enough to do back in its present position, and I would rather it focused all its processing power on maintaining the subterfuge there.' He shrugged. 'I'm also a lot more adverse to taking risks than I used to be, back when I was the same age as you and learning to talk to shindles.'

'And this is where I have my problems,' I said. 'The shindles will be the salvation of the Lild, you told me. What are they going to do down there? Take control of the theocrats from within and guide the Lild to enlightenment?'

'No.' Ormod seemed to be enjoying my perplexity. 'The shindles you have been nurturing for so long possess no

41

intelligence at all. You have to understand that like my own people, the Shindles are genetic engineers, but they are ones who engineer their own bodies to create their organic technology – they actually create that technology out of themselves. The worms you fed are just a machine, a tool, a delivery system. I am an accomplished genetic engineer myself, but I could never alone achieve what they achieved with them. However, when the organism concerned is cooperating with you at a molecular level, it does get much easier.'

'I was right, then – they're some sort of biological weapon.'

'Yes and no, but I can assure you that not a single Lild will be hurt or in any way incapacitated by them. They are so small and have been engineered precisely so that their hosts will hardly notice penetration, and as they breed and spread from that host to others, there will be no ill effects, rather a slight euphoria and increased production of sex hormones.'

'Stop playing around, Ormod,' said Shanen. 'You're boring me.'

The captain nodded an acknowledgement, and got to the point, which was both stunning and amusing, and highly immoral, I think. I agreed to be one of the human captives because, to be frank, he'd already lured me in too far for me to just walk away from this, and he knew that though I was less inclined towards risk than Shanen, I still hadn't managed to give it up.

If the sphere had been made of chainglass, had been Polity technology, I would have been fine about it, but it had to be Lild technology and I wondered if the glass was strong enough to survive the pressure down at the bottom of the Lild sea. Ormod assured me it was perfectly safe then went on to add further delightful news.

'You have to strip naked,' he told us.

'Why?' I was hoping at least for a high-spec Polity envirosuit capable of keeping me alive should I end up outside the sphere in Lild seas.

'You're captives,' he explained. 'You have been stripped of everything and simply kept alive for display purposes. You'll also be heavily scanned before being taken down into cave systems. The Lild will be highly-conscious of security, especially when bringing you before the Theocrat.'

'Bit of a shell game then,' said Shanen, as she stripped off the shapeless shipsuit she always wore. I eyed her for a little while and, seeing her finally naked, thought that maybe, if we survived this, I should perhaps set our relationship on a different course. Noticing my regard as she pulled down her knickers, she then flipped them up with one foot caught them in one hand and threw them at me.

'Get out of those rags, old man,' she said, and with a flounce stepped through the hatch into the sphere. The cheek, she wasn't exactly a youngster.

I took off the slip-ons and the worn old envirosuit trousers and the T-shirt that had always been my favoured dress for shipboard life and quickly stepped into the sphere beside her. The thick circular-section glass hatch slid round into position on runners then sank down into its hole like a large bung. We were standing on a two-metre diameter circular floor over the life-support machinery. I sat down with my back against the glass. Then glanced across to where Ormod stood with one hand resting against the biggest ersatz nautiloid, which was now donning some kind of breathing equipment. I realized then that of course, this was to filter the water of the contamination from its lesser brethren.

43

'What about communication?' I called, wondering if I would get a reply.

'Directional sound beam,' Ormod said, his voice seeming to issue from inside the sphere. He slapped his hand against the nautiloid and turned away, heading to a big pressure door in the side of this false Lild ship interior.

'Bit of a shell game?' I said to Shanen, really wishing she would sit down because the sphere did not have the room for her to prowl around. Abruptly she did sit, directly facing me, her legs wide apart. Ridiculous. We were about to head into a seriously life-threatening situation, and I was starting to feel horny. I looked to one side, just in time to see water pouring from vents in the walls into the hold – nautiloid atmosphere.

'Shell game,' Shanen repeated. 'Three wallnut shells and one pea and the mark must guess which shell the pea is under. It's all about distraction and misdirection.'

'Yes, I know,' I said. 'The nautiloids will be mainly focused on us, not on their ostensible kin.' I gestured to the robot nautiloids outside. 'But you understand the humour?'

She just stared at me, a slight smiling twist to her expression as she gently patted her hand against her inner thigh.

'Shell?' I said. 'Shell game.'

'Oh I see,' she said, her present amusement obviously about something else.

As the water level rose over the sphere, it became neutrally buoyant, as did the robot nautiloids. Turning now and reaching down to the floor with their tentacles, two of the smaller ones dragged themselves forwards and took hold of handles positioned below the life support section of the sphere to steady it in the water, just in time, for the whole ship shuddered at that moment.

'We're docked now,' Ormod informed us.

'What are these other options you're holding in reserve?' I asked. This whole operation was poised on a knife-edge and frankly, to go on and butcher a few metaphors, if the shell game did not deceive the squid eye, me and Shanen were fish food.

'Explosive options and particle cannon options. Like, for example, the CTD inside one of the smaller robot nautiloids accompanying you.'

'Ah, you neglected to mention that,' said Shanen.

Current abruptly began moving in the water surrounding us, picking up pieces of detritus, but none the Lild could identify as of human origin. Our two nautiloid handlers turned the sphere until they were facing a big iris door opening at the end of the tube. Now the real nautiloids began to appear, and the water filled with booms, pops and high-pitched squeals. After a moment, I began to feel tightness at the base of my skull.

'Infrasound,' Shanen observed. 'Let's just hope they keep the chatter down to a manageable level.'

The robots propelled our sphere out of the tunnel, through the big airlock, or rather, water lock, and into the interior of the space station, our robot nautiloid captain holding proprietary station above us. While we were in transit, Lild came up close pushing their eyes against the glass, or clinking tentacles, divided at the ends into feather fingers, against the glass right next to us, just like humans trying to get a reaction from fish in a fish bowl. At one point, in a chamber shaped like a heart, they all drew back, our handlers depositing the sphere in a large metal cup, and a rhythmic droning ensued, the sphere slowly revolved so we had to shift around inside it to avoid being tumbled about.

'Scanning,' I suggested, as our handlers returned for us.

'Damn,' said Ormod. 'Don't these fuckers ever stop digging?'

'Problems?' Shanen enquired.

'Oh I've got thousands of hours of nautiloid com and language programs running in each of the robots, so there should be no problem about the Lild discovering they're not nautiloids. The problem is the religious questioning. There're those here who want to find out if these newly-arrived heroes might be guilty of heretical thought. It's depressing.'

At some point, we ended up inside a ship, and I'm just not sure when the transition was made, only knowing for sure when our handlers secured the sphere with long straps and we felt the surge of acceleration taking us out into glaring sunlight. Apparently we were to be on display at all times, for I now saw we had been positioned inside a clear blister on the side of the vessel. I was glad of that – everyone likes a good clear view.

The watery world loomed close very quickly since the station we had just departed sat in low orbit. Within minutes, we were descending through atmosphere and that was when the crowds began to appear.

'Ah,' Shanen exclaimed. 'I did wonder what a sphere like this might be used for – I don't suppose they take so many captives they always have the things on hand.'

The atmosphere outside seemed to fill with bubbles and I saw that glass spheres much like the one we occupied, bobbed out there supported on iron-coloured motors that had to be some form of grav-tech. They were individual transports, each occupied by one of the Lild.

'Just the plebs,' I observed. 'The rulers stay down in their comfy caves.' The nautiloids within the spheres were all the smaller ones, the ones with fatter shells with a slight off centre twist, like the five smaller robot Lild accompanying our captain. But soon we left these crowds behind us.

The sky turned pale green above us and the sea soon lay

clear below: flecks of white across deep jade, large enclosed vessels cruising the surface like submarine conning towers, it evident that most of their bulk lay below the surface. The sun, a blue orb nested in white and silvery clouds, fell into sunset and we fell into twilight then night as our vessel roared and descended into the waves.

Lild again appeared around us, but we could only see them when the eerie green lights on their shells picked them out. As we descended into the depths, I began to notice static constellations of lights then glimpses of fairy castles under the sea, on thick stalks that speared up from the black. Then, abruptly, we were down beside a great artificial cliff and the vessel shuddered, as it no doubt docked.

Our captain and five lackeys came for us then and, rather than take us into the cave system via a docking tunnel, took us outside into the sea towards a large round portal in the face of the artificial cliff. Much booming, twittering and skull-thumping debate ensued. Many of the Lild about us now were the big flatter-shelled ones like our captain. After a little while, the huge portal began to open, but as this happened, the five lesser robot nautiloids abruptly departed, surrounded by some of their larger kin.

'Expected,' said Ormod. 'They're off for a visit to the inquisitors for detailed questioning.'

'Nice society,' said Shanen, shivering abruptly. It was getting cold within the sphere despite the life-support machinery labouring away beneath us. After a moment, she slid across and plumped herself down right beside me resting her legs over the top of mine. I put my arm around her.

'How did you stay alive?' she abruptly asked.

'Luck,' I replied.

'I think I'm going to need help.'

'You got it,' said, giving her a squeeze.

'I hate to break in on this touching moment,' said Ormod, 'but this is it, guys.'

Our robot captain had positioned himself on one side of the sphere while another of the higher status ones took the other. We went in through a series of water locks, whereupon the nautiloids around us began dispensing with their filter gear, and this was, indeed, it.

The wide coralline tunnels within were brightly lit and around us the crowd of big nautiloids grew, just as curious as their kin and prone to clink those divided tentacles against the glass. I turned my head slightly to observe our robot captain, just in time to see the first shindle wriggling from one of the many pores in his shell – a nigh invisible flicker of movement. It then streaked across to the nearest living high-status Lild, hitting a tentacle and rapidly vanishing as it penetrated its new host. The Lild seemed not to notice. Other shindles began surreptitiously to depart our robot, gradually depleting the great compacted mass of them it held inside it.

We were brought into a large chamber occupied by Lild obviously grander than those we'd so far seen, all of them hanging in an artificial quadrate framework which had been decorously fashioned to look a little like some kind of seaweed. Our sphere was deposited on a coralline pillar before the grandest of them all. The Theocrat stood out from all the rest, little pinhead lights gleaming all over his shell. That booming head-achy conversation ensued.

'My captain tells a good story,' said Ormod. 'But judging by some of the questions I'm not sure it is all being believed.'

Shanen and I locked closer together in an embrace: the perfectly image of frightened humans brought before alien captors. I don't know how long this audience lasted, because my head ached intolerably and I did not feel at all well. I even began to wonder if the life-support system was working correctly. Then abruptly the note changed – something else now seemed to be occurring.

'Well, I was hoping you'd be shunted off to one side for later study, where the extraction would be easier,' said Ormod. 'Seems not. Seems the big boss wants to demonstrate to his fellows just how feeble these human creatures are.'

'And how does he intend to do that?' Shanen asked – she looked as ill as I felt.

'He wants to open the sphere.'

'Yeah, that'd do it,' I said.

'Time to get you out of there.'

In the sea above us, the five robot nautiloids that had accompanied our captain, had already released their load of modified shindles into the sea. Now one of them presented a hot and very brief surprise to those questioning it. The CTD detonation caused the cave system around us to shudder and, dislodged from its pillar, our sphere began a slow tumble to the floor. I looked around for our robot captain, spotted him easily, for the soft foreparts of his body had fallen away and a great cloud of thready shindles was rapidly spreading out.

'They'll find out about them,' I had said to Ormod, as he had told me what he intended. 'They'll have the technology to remove them from themselves.'

'But by then it will be too late, the damage will be done, and they won't even know that it's been done until years later.'

A hollow shell now, running on Polity tech, the captain's shell descended and locked onto the sphere. Gleaming manipulators extruded from the cavity inside, as it evacuated its water, and tore away the hatch. We threw ourselves into the

49

space previously occupied by shindles, and I just hoped none of them had remained in there. As instructed, we donned breather masks available inside and assumed fetal positions. Crash foam jetted in, filling the cavities all around us, protecting us, padding us, but we still felt the massive accelerations and I lost consciousness twice. The CTD had of course caused sufficient disruption to cover our escape, but I didn't get to see much of that.

'The problem is that galactic shape of the ruling theocratic elite,' Ormod had told us. 'Those of the Lild who less closely match it are more prone to heresy.'

As we shot from the seas of the Lild home world, two things happened simultaneously. The *Gnostic*, parked amidst the Lild fleet, abruptly accelerated away whilst in orbit of the Lild home world Ormod undocked his segment ship, meanwhile playing a particle cannon over the space station's weapons. Some twenty minutes after that Ormod intercepted our straight up trajectory, then accelerated out towards the *Gnostic*.

'The shindles will spread rapidly, infecting most Lild very very quickly. Of course there'll be huge panic and their doctors will work quickly to find a way to remove them, to kill the infection,' Ormod had continued. 'Then they'll discover something quite strange: this terrible bioweapon seems to cause few ill effects at all. Obviously, inferior humans, allied with some of those shindles who managed to escape the extermination, with this failed attack have proven their inferiority to the Chosen.'

The *Gnostic* dropped into U-space just as Ormod, Pladdick, Parsival and Mace began cutting us out of the crash foam.

'It's so small a thing they do, just a little viral re-programming, but something the Lild just don't have the technology to correct.' Ormod was a man who really enjoyed his revenge. 'The tweaks are right down there in the germ plasm, and every Lild hatched from the egg of one infected by the shindles will not grow as expected, it'll be subtle at first, then blindingly obvious after their first few years. Their shape will no longer be that of a flat galactic spiral, but a long hornlike tube. And they will no longer be the beloved of God.'

Shanen and I waved off the others and headed for her cabin. I'd taken far too many risks lately and she had taken enough to satisfy her self-destructive impulse for a while, for a little while. I'll watch her now, see if I can keep her alive. We're not the chosen of any god and only have each other.

ENDS

THE RHINE'S WORLD INCIDENT

The remote control rested dead in Reynold's hand, but any moment now Kirin might make the connection and the little lozenge of black metal would become a source of godlike power. Reynold closed his hand over it, sudden doubts assailing him, and as always felt a tight stab of fear. That power depended on Kirin's success, which wasn't guaranteed, and on the hope that the device to which the remote connected had not been discovered and neutralized.

He turned towards her. 'Any luck?'

She sat on the damp ground with her laptop open on a mouldering log before her, with optics running from it to the framework supporting the sat dish, spherical laser com unit and microwave transmitter rods. She was also auged into the laptop – an optic lead running from the bean-shaped augmentation behind her ear to plug into it. Beside the laptop rested a big flat memstore, packed with state-of-the-art worms and viruses.

'It is not a matter of luck,' she stated succinctly.

Reynold returned his attention to the city down on the plain. Athelford was the centre of commerce and Polity power here on Rhine's World, most of both concentrated at its heart where skyscrapers reared about the domes and containment spheres of the runcible port. However, the unit first sent here had not been able to position the device right next to the port and its damned controlling AI – Reynold felt an involuntary shudder at the thought of the kind of icy artificial intelligences they were up against. The unit had been forced to act fast when the plutonium processing plant, no doubt meticulously tracked down by some forensic AI, got hit by Earth Central Security. They'd also not been able to detonate. Something had taken them out before they could even send the signal.

'The yokels are calling in,' said Plate. He was boosted and otherwise physically enhanced, and wore com gear about his head, plugged into the weird scaly Dracocorp aug affixed behind his ear. 'Our contact wants our coordinates.'

'Tell him to head to the rendezvous as planned.' Reynold glanced back at where their gravcar lay underneath its chameleoncloth tarpaulin. 'First chance we get, we'll need to ask our contact why he's not sticking to that plan.'

Plate grinned.

'Are we still secure?' Reynold asked.

'Still secure,' Plate replied, his grin disappearing. 'But encoded Polity com activity is ramping up, as is city and sat-scan output.'

'They know we're here,' said Kirin, still concentrating on her laptop.

'Get me the device, Kirin,' said Reynold. 'Get it me now.'

One of her eyes had gone metallic and her fingers were blurring over her keyboard. 'If it was easy to find the signal and lock in the transmission key, we wouldn't have to be this damned close and, anyway, ECS would have found it by now.'

'But we know the main frequencies and have the key, and they do not,' Reynold observed.

Kirin snorted dismissively.

Reynold tapped the com button on the collar of his fatigues. 'Spiro,' he addressed the commander of the four-unit of Separatist ground troops positioned in the surrounding area. 'ECS are on to us but don't have our location. If they get it, they'll be down on us like a falling tree. Be prepared to hold out for as long as possible – for the Cause I expect no less of you.'

'They get our location and it'll be a sat-strike,' Plate observed. 'We'll be incinerated before we get a chance to blink.'

53

'Shut up, Plate.'

'I think I may–' began Kirin, and Reynold spun towards her. 'Yes, I've got it.' She looked up victoriously and dramatically stabbed a finger down on one key. 'Your remote is now armed.'

Reynold raised his hand and opened it, studying with tight cold fear in his guts the blinking red light in the corner of the touch console. Stepping a little way from his comrades to the edge of the trees, he once again gazed down upon the city. His mouth was dry. He knew precisely what this would set in motion: terrifying unhuman intelligences would focus here the moment he sent the signal.

'Just a grain at a time, my old Separatist recruiter told me,' he said. 'We'll win this like the sea wins as it laps against a sandstone cliff.'

'Very poetic,' said Kirin, now standing at his shoulder.

'This is gonna hurt them,' said Plate.

Reynold tapped his com button. 'Goggles everyone.' He pulled his own flash goggles down over his eyes. 'Kirin, get back to your worms.' He glanced round and watched her return to her station and plug the memstore cable into her laptop. The worms and viruses the thing contained were certainly the best available, but they wouldn't have stood a chance of penetrating Polity firewalls *before* he initiated the device. After that they would penetrate local systems to knock out satellite scanning for, according to Kirin, ten minutes – time for them to fly the gravcar far from here, undetected.

'Five, four, three, two … one.' Reynold thumbed the touch console on the remote.

Somewhere in the heart of the city, a giant flashbulb came on for a second, then went out. Reynold pushed up his goggles to watch a skyscraper going over and a disk of devastation spreading from a growing and rising fireball. Now, shortly after the EM flash of the blast, Kirin would be sending her software toys. The fireball continued to rise, a sprouting mushroom, but despite the surface devastation many buildings remained disappointingly intact. Still, they would be irradiated and tens of thousands of Polity citizens now just ash. The sound reached them, and it seemed the world was tearing apart.

'Okay, the car!' Reynold ordered. 'Kirin?'

She nodded, already closing up her laptop and grabbing up as much of her gear as she could carry. The broadcast framework would have to stay though, as would some of the larger armaments Spiro had positioned in the surrounding area. Reynold stooped by a grey cylinder at the base of a tree, punched twenty minutes into the timer and set it running. The thermite bomb would incinerate this entire area and leave little evidence for the forensic AIs of ECS to gather. 'Let's go!'

Spiro and his men, now armed with nothing but a few hand weapons, had already pulled the tarpaulin from the car and were piling into the back row of seats. Plate took the controls while Kirin and Reynold climbed in behind him. Plate took it up hard through the foliage, shrivelled seed husks and swordlike leaves falling onto them, turned it and hit the boosters. Glancing back Reynold could only see the top of the nuclear cloud, and he nodded to himself with grim satisfaction.

'This will be remembered for years to come,' he stated.

'Yup, certainly will,' replied Spiro, scratching at spot on his cheek.

No one else seemed to have anything to say, but Reynold knew why they were so subdued. This was the comedown, only later would they realize just what a victory this had been for the Separatist cause. He tried to convince himself of that…

In five minutes, they were beyond the forest and over rectangular fields of mega-wheat, hill slopes stitched with neat vineyards of protein gourds, irrigation canals and plascrete roads for the agricultural machinery used here. The ground transport – a balloon-tyred tractor towing a train of grain wagons – awaited where arranged.

'Irrigation canal,' Reynold instructed.

Plate decelerated fast and settled the car towards a canal running parallel to the road on which the transport awaited, bringing it to a hover just above the water then slewing it sideways until it nudged the bank. Spiro and the soldiers were out first, then Kirin.

'You can plus-grav it?' Reynold asked.

Plate nodded, pulled out a chip revealed behind a torn-out panel, then inserted a chipcard into a reader slot. 'Ten seconds.' He and Reynold disembarked, then bracing themselves against the bank, pushed the car so it drifted out over the water. After a moment, smoke drifted up from the vehicle's console. Abruptly it was as if the car had been transformed into a block of lead. It dropped hard, creating a huge splash, then sank in an instant. Plate and Reynold clambered up the bank and onto the road after the others. Ahead, waiting about the tractor, stood four of the locals, or 'yokels' as Plate called them – four Rhine's World Separatists.

'Stay alert,' Reynold warned.

As he approached the four, he studied them intently. They all wore the kind of disposable overalls farmers clad themselves in on primitive worlds like this and all seemed ill at ease. Reynold focused on one of their number: a very fat man with a baby face and shaven head. With all the cosmetic and medical options available, one did not often see people so obese unless they chose to look that way. Perhaps this Separatist

56

distrusted what Polity technology had to offer, which wasn't that unusual. The one who stepped forwards, however, obviously did trust that technology, being big, handsome, and obviously having provided himself with emerald green eyes.

'Jepson?' Reynold asked.

'I am,' said the man, holding out his hand.

Reynold gripped it briefly. 'We need to get under cover quickly – sat eyes will be functioning again soon.'

'The first trailer is empty.' Jepson stabbed a finger back behind the tractor.

Reynold nodded towards Spiro and he and his men headed back towards the trailer. 'You too,' he said to Kirin and, as she departed, glanced at Plate. 'You're with me in the tractor cab.'

'There's only room for four up there,' Jepson protested.

'Then two of your men best ride in the trailer.' Reynold nodded towards the fat man. 'Make him one of them – that should give us plenty of room.'

The fat man dipped his head as if ashamed, and trailed after Kirin, then at a nod from Jepson one of the others went too.

'Come on fat boy!' Spiro called as the fat man hauled himself up inside the trailer.

'I sometimes wonder what the recruiters are thinking,' said Jepson, as he mounted the ladder up the side of the big tractor.

'Meaning?' Reynold enquired as he followed.

'Me and Dowel,' Jepson flipped a thumb towards the other local climbing up after Reynold, 'have been working together for a year now, and we're good.' He entered the cab. 'Mark seems pretty able too, but I'm damned If I know what use we can find for Brockle.'

'Brockle would be fat boy,' said Plate, following Dowel into the cab.

'You guessed it.' Jepson took the driver's seat.

Along one wall were three fold-down seats, the rest of the cab being crammed with tractor controls and a pile of disconnected hydraulic cylinders, universal joints and PTO shafts. Reynold studied these for a second, noted blood on one short heavy cylinder and a sticky pool of the same nearby. That was from the original driver of this machine … maybe. He reached down and drew his pulse-gun, turned and stuck it up under Dowel's chin. Plate meanwhile stepped up behind Jepson and looped a garrot about his neck.

'What the–' Jepson began, then desisted as Plate tightened the wire. Dowel simply kept very still, his expression fearful as he held his hands out from his body.

'We've got a problem,' said Reynold.

'I don't understand,' said Jepson.

'I don't either, but perhaps you can help.' Reynold nodded to one of the seats and walked Dowel back towards it. The man cautiously pushed it down and sat. Gun still held at his neck, Reynold searched him, removing a nasty-looking snubnose, then stepped back knowing he could blow the top off the man's head before he got a chance to rise. 'What I don't understand is why you contacted us and asked us for our coordinates.'

Plate hit some foot lever on Jepson's seat and spun it round so the man faced Reynold, who studied his expression intently.

'You weren't supposed to get in contact, because the signal might have been traced,' Reynold continued, 'and there were to be no alterations to the plan unless I initiated them.'

'I don't know what you mean,' Jepson whispered. 'We stuck to the plan – no one contacted you.'

'Right frequency, right code – just before we blew the device.'

'No, honestly – you can check our com record.'

Either Jepson was telling the truth or he was a very good liar. Reynold nodded to Plate, who cinched the garrot into a loop around the man's neck and now, with one hand free, began to search him, quickly removing first a gas-system pulsegun from inside his overalls then a comunit from the top pocket. Plate keyed it on, input a code, then tilted his head as if listening to something as the comunit's record loaded to his aug.

'Four comunits,' said Plate. 'One of them sent the message but the record has been tampered with so we don't know which one.'

Jepson looked horrified. Reynold tapped his com button. 'Spiro, disarm and secure those two in there with you.' Then to Jepson, 'Take us to the hideout.'

Plate unlooped the garrot and spun Jepson's seat forwards again.

'It has to be one of the other two,' said Jepson, looking back at Reynold. 'Me and Dowel been working for the Cause for years.'

'Drive the tractor,' Reynold instructed.

The farm, floodlit now as twilight fell, was a great sprawl of barns, machinery garages and silos, whilst the farmhouse was a composite dome with rooms enough for twenty or more people. However, only three had lived there. One of them, according to Jepson, lay at the bottom of an irrigation canal with a big hydraulic pump in his overalls to hold him down. He had been the son. The parents were still here on the floor of the kitchen adjoining this living room, since Jepson and Dowel had not found time to clear up the mess before going to pick up their two comrades. Reynold eyed the two corpses for a moment, then returned his attention to Jepson and his men.

'Strip,' he instructed.

'Look I don't know–' Jepson began, then shut up as Reynold shot a hole in the carpet moss just in front of the man's work boots.

The four began removing their clothes, all with quick economy but for Brockle, who seemed to be struggling with the fastenings. Soon they all stood naked.

'Jesu,' said Spiro, 'you could do with a makeover fat boy.'

'Em alright,' said Brockle, staring down at the floor, his hands, with oddly long and delicate fingers trying to cover the great white rolls of fat.

'Em alright is em?' said Spiro.

'Scan them,' Reynold instructed.

Plate stepped forwards with a hand scanner and began running it from head to foot over each man, first up and down their fronts, then over them from behind. When Plate reached Brockle, Spiro called out, 'Got a big enough scanner there, Plate?' which his four troops greeted with hilarity. When Plate came to one who had been in the grain carriage with Brockle, he reacted fast, driving a fist into the base of the man's skull then following him down to the floor. Plate pulled his solid-state laser from his belt, rested it beside the scanner then ran it down the man's leg, found something and fired. A horrible sputtering and sizzling ensued, black oily smoke and licks of flame rising from where the beam cut into the man's leg. After a moment, Plate inspected the readout from his scanner, nodded and stepped back.

'What have we got?' Reynold asked.

'Locater.'

Reynold felt cold claws skittering down his backbone. 'Transmitting?'

'No, but it could have been,' Plate replied.

Reynold saw it with utter simplicity. If a signal had been sent, then ECS would be down on them very shortly, and shortly after that they would all be either dead or in an interrogation cell. He preferred dead. He did not want ECS taking his mind apart to find out what he knew.

'Spiro, put a watchman on the roof,' he instructed.

Spiro selected one of his soldiers and sent him on his way.

Having already ascertained the layout of this place, Reynold pointed to nearby door. 'Now Spiro, I want you to take him in there,' he instructed. 'Tie him to a chair, revive him and start asking him questions. You know how to do that.' He paused for a moment. They were all tired after forty-eight hours without sleep. 'Work him for two hours then let one of your men take over. Rotate the watch on the roof too and make sure you all get some rest.'

Spiro grinned, waved over one of his men and the two dragged their victim off into the room, leaving a trail of plasma and charred skin. Like all Separatist soldiers, they were well versed in interrogation techniques.

'Oh, and gag him when he's not answering questions,' Reynold added. 'We all need to get some sleep.'

Reynold turned back to the remaining three. 'Get in there.' He pointed towards another door. It was an internal storeroom without windows so would have to do.

'I didn't know,' said Jepson. 'You have to believe that.'

'Move,' Reynold instructed.

Jepson stooped to gather up his clothing, but Plate stepped over and planted his boot on the pile. Jepson hesitated for a moment then traipsed into the indicated room. One of the troops pulled up an armchair beside the door and plumped himself down in it, pulsegun held ready in his right hand. Reynold nodded approval then sank down on a sofa beside where Kirin had tiredly seated herself, her laptop open before her and connected to her aug. Plate moved over and dropped into an armchair opposite.

'That's everything?' Kirin asked Plate.

'Everything I've got,' he replied.

'Could do with my sat-dish, but I'm into the farm system now – gives me a bit more range,' said Kirin.

'You're running our security now?' Reynold asked.

'Well, Plate is better with the physical stuff, so I might as well take it on now.'

'Anything?'

'Lot of activity around the city, of course,' she replied, 'but nothing out this way. I don't think our friend sent his locator signal and I don't think ECS knows where we are. However, from what I've picked up it seems they do know they're looking for an seven-person specialist unit. Something is leaking out there.'

'I didn't expect any less,' said Reynold. 'All we have to do now is keep our heads down for three days, separate to take up new identities then ship out of here.'

'Simple hey,' said Kirin, her expression grim.

'We need to get some rest,' said Reynold. 'I'm going to use one of the beds here and I suggest you do the same.'

He heaved himself to his feet and went to find a bedroom. As his head hit the pillow, he slid into a fugue state somewhere between sleep and waking. It seemed only moments had passed, when he heard the agonized scream, but checking his watch as he rolled from the bed he discovered two hours had passed. He crashed open the door to his room and strode out, angry. Kirin lay fast asleep on the sofa and a trooper in the armchair was gazing round with that bewildered air of someone only half awake.

Reynold headed over to the room in which Spiro's man was interrogating the local, and banged open the door. 'I thought I told you to keep him quiet?'

Their traitor had been strapped in a chair, a gag in his mouth. He was writhing in agony, skin stripped off his arm from elbow to wrist and one eye burnt out. The trooper in there with him had been rigging up something from the room's power point, but now held his weapon and had been heading for the door.

'That wasn't him, sir,' he said.

Reynold whirled, drawing his pulsegun, then tapping his com button. 'Report in.' One reply from Spiro on the roof, one from the other trooper as he stumbled sleepily into the living room, nothing from Kirin, but then she was asleep, and nothing from Plate. 'Plate?' Still nothing.

'Where did Plate go?' Reynold asked the seated guard.

The man pointed to a nearby hall leading to bunk rooms. Signalling the two troopers to follow, Reynold headed over, opening the first door. The interior light came on immediately to show Plate, sprawled on a bed, his back arched and hands twisted in claws above him, fingers bloody. Reynold surveyed the room, but there was little to see. It possessed no window so the only access was the door, held just the one bed, some wall cupboards and a sanitary cubicle. Then he spotted the vent cover lying on the floor with a couple of screws beside it, and looked up. Something metallic and segmented slid out of sight into the air-conditioning vent.

'What the fuck was that?' asked one of the troops behind him.

'Any dangerous life forms on this world?' Reynold asked carefully, trying to keep his voice level.

'Dunno,' came the illuminating reply. 'We came in with you.'

Reynold walked over to Plate and studied him. Blood covered his head and the pillow was deep red, soaked with it. Leaning closer Reynold saw holes in Plate's face and skull, each a few millimetres wide. Some were even cut through his aug.

'Get Jepson – bring him here.'

Jepson seemed just as bewildered as Reynold. 'I don't know. I just don't know.'

'Are you a local or what?' asked Spiro, who had now joined them.

'Been in the city most of my life,' said Jepson, then shifted back as Spiro stepped towards him. 'Brockle … he might know. Brockle's a farm boy.'

'Let's get fat boy,' said Spiro, snagging the shoulder of one of his men and departing.

Brockle came stumbling into the room wiping tiredly at his eyes. He almost looked thinner to Reynold, maybe worn down by fear. His gaze wandered about the room for a moment in bewilderment, finally focusing on the corpse on the bed.

'Why you kill em?' he asked.

'We did not kill him,' said Reynold, 'but something did.' He pointed to the open air-conditioning duct.

Brockle stared at that in bewilderment too, then returned his gaze to Reynold almost hopefully.

'What is there here on Rhine's World that could do this?'

'Rats?' Brockle suggested.

Spiro hit him hard, in the guts, and Brockle staggered back making an odd whining sound. Spiro, obviously surprised he hadn't gone down stepped in to hit him again but Reynold caught his shoulder. 'Just lock them back up.' But even as Spiro turned to obey, doubled shrieks of agony reverberated, followed by the sound something heavy crashing against a wall.

Spiro led the way out and soon they were back in the living room. He kicked open the door to the room in which Jepson's comrades were incarcerated and entered, gun in hand, then on automatic he opened fire at something. By the time Reynold entered Spiro was backing up, staring at the smoking line of his shots traversing up the wall to the open air-duct.

'What did you see?' Reynold asked, gazing at the two corpses on the floor. Both men were frozen in agonized rictus, their heads bloody pepper pots. One of them bad been opened up below the sternum and his guts bulged out across the floor.

'Some sort of snake,' Spiro managed.

Calm, got to stay calm. 'Kirin,' said Reynold. 'I'll need you to do a search for me.' No reply. 'Kirin?'

Whatever it was, it got her in her sleep, but the sofa being a dark terracotta colour had not shown the blood. Reynold spun her laptop round and flipped it open, turned it on. The screen just showed blank fuzz. After a moment, he noticed the holes cut through the keyboard, and that seemed to make no sense at all. He turned to the others and eyed Jepson and Brockle.

'Put them back in there.' He gestured to that bloody room.

'You can't do that,' said Jepson.

'I can do what I fucking please.' Reynold drew his weapon and pointed it, but Brockle moved in front of Jepson waving those long-fingered hands.

'We done nuthin! We done nuthin!'

Spiro and his men grabbed the two and shoved them back into the room, slamming the door shut behind them.

'What the fuck is this?' said Spiro, finally turning to face Reynold.

The laptop, with its holes...

Reynold stepped over to the room in which Spiro and his men had been torturing their other prisoner, and kicked the door open. The chair lay down on its side, the torture victim's head resting in a pool of blood. A sticky trail had been wormed across the floor, and up the wall to an open air vent. It seemed he only had a moment to process the sight before someone else shrieked in agony. The sound just seemed to go on and on, then something crashed against the inside of the door they had forced Jepson and Brockle through, and the shrieking stopped. Brockle or Jepson, it didn't matter now.

'We get out of here,' said Reynold. 'They fucking found us.'

'What the fuck do you mean?' asked Spiro.

Reynold pointed at the laptop then at Kirin, at the holes in her head. 'Something is here...'

The lights went out and a door exploded into splinters.

Pulse-fire cut the pitch darkness and a silvery object whickered through the air. Reynold backed up and felt something slide over his foot. He fired down at the floor and caught a briefly glimpse of long flat segmented thing, metallic, with a nightmare head decked with pincers, manipulators and tubular probes. He fired again. Someone was screaming, pulse-fire revealed Spiro staggering to one side. It wasn't him making that noise because one of the worm-things was pushing its way into him through his mouth. A window shattered and there came further screaming from outside.

Silence.

Then a voice, calm and modulated.

'Absolutely correct of course,' it said.

'Who are you?' Reynold asked, backing up through the darkness. A hard hook caught his heel and he went over, then a cold and tongue slammed between his palm and his pulse-gun and just flipped the weapon away into the darkness.

'I am your case worker,' the voice replied.

'You tried to stop us,' he said.

'Yes, I tried to obtain your location. Had you given it, the satellite strike would have taken you out a moment later. I planted that locator in the leg of one of Jepson's men – just to focus attention away from me for a while.'

'You're the one that killed our last unit here – the one that planted the device.'

'Unfortunately not – they were taken out by satellite strike, hence the reason we did not obtain the location of the tactical nuclear device. Had it been me, everything would have been known.'

Reynold thought about the holes through his comrades' heads, through their augs and the holes even through Kirin's laptop. Something had been eating the information out of them even as it killed them. Mind reaming was the reason Separatists never wanted to be caught alive, but as far as Reynold knew, that would happen in a white tiled cell deep in the bowels of some ECS facility, not like this.

'What the hell are you?'

The lights came on

'Courts do not sit in judgement,' said the fat boy, standing naked before Reynold. 'When you detonated that device it only confirmed your death sentence, all that remained was execution of that sentence. However, everyone here possessed vital knowledge of others in the Separatist organisation and of other atrocities committed by it – mental evidence requiring deep forensic analysis.'

Fat boy's skin looked greyish, corpse-like, but only after a moment did Reynold realized it was turning metallic. The fat boy leant forwards a little. 'I am the Brockle. I am the forensic AI sent to gather and analyse that evidence, and incidentally kill you.'

Now fat boy's skin had taken on a transparency, and underneath it Reynold could see he consisted of knots of flat segmented worms, some of which were already dropping to the floor, others in the process of unravelling. Reynold scrabbled across the carpet towards his gun as a cold metallic wave washed over him. Delicate tubular drills began boring into his head, into his mind. In agony, he hoped for another wave called death to swamp him and, though it came physically, his consciousness did not fade. It remained, somewhere, in some no space, while a cold meticulous intelligence took it apart piece by piece.

ENDS

OWNER SPACE

Kelly Haden worked herself into a sweat on the training machines positioned in the outer ring of the *Breznev's* spin section, the scars on her arms and chest tightening. She would have preferred to use free weights, but such were not allowed aboard ships like this since a malfunction of the spin section or, for that matter, of the ship entire, could result in heavy lumps of iron hurtling about like chaff. There was also the matter of the weight itself when a lightly constructed training machine like the one she was using could stand in for a few hundred pounds of iron.

Finishing her workout she picked up her towel and headed for the ladder leading up to the inward hatch, but the exercise had not dispelled the taut feeling of frustrated anger in her stomach. She climbed up into the sleeping quarters.

'Feeling better now, Societal Asset Haden?' enquired Longshank from his bunk. He was reading his notescreen again – some esoteric biological text no-doubt. She glanced at him, took in his long grey hair tied back with some confection of coloured beads, at his greywear deliberately altered for individuality: sleeves cut away above the elbow, red fabric from the three Collective flags they found aboard sewn around the collar and waistband. They all did this sort of thing. Kelly had been one of the lucky ones to have found an old Markovian uniform jacket, which she had altered to fit, and had cut off her greywear trousers at just below the knee. It was a form of escape – the only escape for them that seemed likely now.

'No, I don't feel much better, Societal Ass Longshank,' she replied.

What had once been humorous exchange now contained a hint of bitterness.

The inner ring of the spin section was the Bridge. It was without a ceiling and while working at any of the consoles it was possible to see ones fellows upside down overhead. Kelly, being a Ship's Engineer, had been quite accustomed to this sort of thing, but it had taken some getting used to for the other escapees, and the vomit vacuums had seen plenty of work.

'How are we doing?' she asked Traviss, who in the low grav sat strapped into his chair at the centre of a horseshoe of navigation consoles before the projection cylinder.

Traviss was a young hyperactive man who had been in the Collective military until he showed a talent with computers and spatial calculus and was reclassified as a 'societal asset'. Like them all, he had resented the resultant scrutiny from the Doctrinaires. He touched a control and the projection cylinder filled with stars.

'Our sling-shot around Phaeton is taking us nicely out of the system's gravity sink and we'll be able U-jump in sixteen hours.' One of the stars flashed red and a little way out flashed the blue spinning-top icon of the *Breznev*. Between the two, lay three icons representing the Collective pursuit vessels from Handel. They weren't the problem. The problem was a green icon accelerating out from the nearest star to Phaeton. The *Lenin*, though not as close to them as the other ships, it would now easily be able to intersect their course. It was also faster, so there would be no outrunning it.

Traviss continued, 'I calculate that the *Lenin* will be able to knock us back into the real in three days if we continue along our present course.'

The others were gathering around now: Slome Terl, astrophysicist and their paternal figurehead; Olsen Marcos, who was a geneticist and an amateur historian – though that was a pursuit now strictly controlled in the Collective – and Elizabeth

Terl, Slome's daughter and plain physicist in her own right. Of the fifty people aboard, everyone was an expert of some kind, and every one the Collective had reclassified as a 'societal asset', and had subjected to doctrinal scrutiny and control. To say the Collective was ruled would be to deny what it claimed to be, but it *was* ruled, by those who did all they could to skew reality to fit doctrine. The Doctrinaires knew that anyone above a certain intelligence level was a danger, yet also essential for a space-faring civilization, so such people had to be *managed*.

'Space has, by definition, three dimensions,' said Slome. He was old, bald and running to fat, and possessed a mind that sliced through problems like a microtome.

'Somewhat more than that, I would suggest,' said Elizabeth – young, arrogant, and though intelligent, more intent on displaying that intelligence than using it.

'Shut the fuck up, Liz,' said Kelly distractedly.

The girl gave Kelly a superior look then reached up to flick a lock of her bright ginger hair aside. She was pretty too, which Kelly also found annoying.

'Our options are limited,' said Traviss. He touched another control and areas of the cylinder shaded in different colours. Their ship lay within a blue hemisphere that disappeared off-cylinder – the Collective. A red area impinged from above with other discrete red areas scattered below, with one large red hemisphere filling the lower right of the cylinder.

'If you would run through those options,' said Slome, and Kelly got the suspicion that Slome and Traviss had already done so, and had already come to a decision.

Traviss touched controls and numbers appeared in each of the coloured areas. 'Red signifies danger,' he said needlessly. 'Area One is what's left of the Grazen Empire. If we head that way we'll either run straight into their defences or their wormships will catch up with us.' He glanced round. 'And if we're lucky they'll blow us out of space rather than capture us.' They all knew what happened to humans caught by the Grazen.

'Area Two?' Slome prompted.

'Areas Two, Three and Five are asteroid fields,' Traviss explained. 'We would have to drop out of U-space to navigate them.' He highlighted some stars in the Collective adjacent to Area Three. 'Even if we tried to get through Three, which is the smallest, the Collective could send ships from the bases indicated and intercept us.'

'Six?'

'Grazen outposts scattered in an asteroid field and an extended dust cloud.'

'You surprise me,' said Slome.

Kelly interjected, 'Collective problems at home ended that mission. In my opinion, the area wasn't worth taking – nothing there remotely human-habitable and it would have taken years at the cost of many ships. But the Doctrinaires don't let facts get in the way of ideology – there'll be another attack on it.'

Slome nodded then pointed a gnarled finger at the hemisphere of red. 'And that?'

Traviss hesitated for a moment and Kelly knew precisely why. She also knew that Slome's prompting and Traviss's hesitation were just a performance. They both knew where this was leading. Kelly wondered what it was they were yet to reveal.

'That's been under Interdict since before the Markovians. I can't really find out much about it,' Traviss replied.

'But you've found something,' said Slome.

'Yes,' Traviss appeared distinctly uncomfortable with the act. 'That area is classified as Owner Space.'

After a brief almost embarrassed silence, Elizabeth laughed knowingly, then said, 'The Markovians were not noted for their rationality.'

Kelly felt the need to defend Traviss, despite the fact that he and Slome were playing some game. 'Yes, which is why our oh-so-rational Collective slaughtered them.'

Elizabeth shot back, 'The Collective is a doomed ideology, but their rationality is superior to the myth-making and religions of the Markovians.'

'Well, I can always drop you in one of the escape pods if you want to go back,' said Kelly. 'That's supposing the Doctrinaire aboard the *Lenin* thinks you a valuable enough asset to pick up.'

Elizabeth began to bristle until Olsen interrupted heavily, 'The Owner is no myth, though some people's conception of him may stray into the territory of religion.'

Holding up a finger to silence his daughter, Slome turned to the geneticist and sometime historian. 'I heard something about all this when I was a student under the Markovians. Perhaps you could elaborate?'

Olsen shrugged. 'Highlight the Sabalist System would you Traviss.'

Traviss complied, picking out a star sitting just inside the border of the Grazen outpost with the Collective.

'Owner Space extended to here. The Owner apparently ceded the area to us in the pre-Markovian era. The Markovians lost it to the Grazen over a century ago, but we still have a lot of data and biological samples from Sabal itself. Those samples indicate a great deal of adaptation from ancient Terran forms.'

'That was almost certainly our work,' said Elizabeth.

73

'We aren't in that league,' Olsen replied.

'But perhaps we were?'

Olsen shook his head.

'Though I know some of the details, this is the first I've heard about the Sabal connection,' said Slome.

'It's in some very old data files – I did some research,' Olsen replied. 'Those same files were secured by the Collective and I came under the scrutiny of Doctrinaires long before they invented the concept of 'societal assets'. Some of my fellows weren't so lucky.'

'So we are now to believe in immortal super beings?' enquired Elizabeth.

'We don't have to,' said Kelly.

They all turned to look at her.

She continued, 'The Grazen avoid that place. When I was engineer aboard the *Mao* a Grazen scoutship faced us down rather than enter there. We tore it apart. Grazen ships get destroyed if they try to enter that area, and Collective ships get flung out – their drive-systems wrecked.'

'This was when you were fighting for the Collective,' said Elizabeth.

'This was when I was an engineer grovelling in radioactive sludge below the *Mao's* engines.'

Elizabeth did not have much more to say about that – they could all see the shiny scar tissue down the side of Kelly's face, her neck, and disappearing under her jacket.

After an embarrassed silence, Slome said, 'Well, as you say, Traviss, 'limited options'. But we must make a decision.' He turned to Kelly. 'I defer to you on this since without you we would never have escaped the Commutank, and since you have greater experience in these matters...'

Kelly knew that a 'however' was due.

'…however, the Grazen would peel off our skins over a slow fire, while the Collective would peel our minds and we'd soon all become obedient little citizens when they fitted us with strouds.' He gestured towards the viewing cylinder. 'As I see it, when we drop into U-space we should run for the edge of the Grazen outpost where we will be in their territory only briefly before reaching the … Interdict Area.'

Hints, rumours, stories – nothing clear and nothing proven – that's all Kelly had ever heard while in the Collective fleet. The whole, however, had left an impression on her, an idea: the Owner was something to be feared, something even the Grazen feared. Perhaps that was just the fear of the unknown.

'We won't be able to enter there,' she said – not entirely sure of her facts. 'We'll get crippled and flung out and those aboard the *Lenin* will capture us, if the Grazen don't get to us first,' said Kelly.

Slome gave a weak smile. 'Yes, that would have been true.'

'Would have been true?'

Slome gestured to the cylinder. 'Show them the message Traviss.'

Traviss cleared the cylinder, then after a moment brought up a brief text message: 'Escapees from the Collective, Owner Space is open to you. Welcome'.

Traviss said, 'Its source was deep inside Owner Space.'

'Very well,' said Kelly, her spine crawling. 'Owner Space it is.'

Clinging to the handholds, Doctrinaire Shrad gazed at flecked void through the thick portholes of the *Lenin* and ground his teeth. A stupid waste of resources, he felt, specifically himself.

He should have been back with the Central Committee planning the coming attack on the Grazen Empire, not out here chasing after a few assets gone bad. The other Doctrinaires in the Committee had driven him out – those fools with their unsound ideology did not understand precisely how things should run in the Collective. They called his leadership of the previous campaign 'disastrous', and did not understand how working with the old Markovian command structures in the fleet had hindered him. Well he would bring these assets back, strouded and subservient, then return to his place in the Committee and bring to fruition his vision of the New Deal. Meanwhile – he turned from the viewing window – he would have to see about correcting the ideological aberrations he had found aboard this vessel.

Two of the Guard held the engineer, his hands bound behind his back, between them. Shrad pushed himself over and caught hold of some of the masses of pipe work running from the reactor cylinder. Then with an exclamation, he snatched his hand away and had to stop himself by grabbing the shoulder of one of the Guard, who, as ever, just silently maintained his position.

'Those pipes are hot, Doctrinaire Shrad,' observed the engineer. 'If you must grab pipes I suggest you grab the ones painted white.'

'Thank you, Citizen Rand.' Shrad took hold of a white pipe and hauled himself back. 'Now, Citizen, I expect you are wondering why the Guard have detained you.'

'I am overcome with curiosity, Doctrinaire Shrad.'

Shrad could feel his rage growing, but as usual, kept it locked inside. 'I am presuming you understand the ideological concept behind greywear?'

'I do: it being doctrine that all people are equal, all people must also appear so.'

'Yet here you are wearing Markovian overalls.'

It was an unusual contrast: a citizen of the Collective dressed in Markovian overalls, held between two of Shrad's own unit of greywear-clad Guard – men who had once been Markovians.

'I don greywear when I go off-shift. Unfortunately it is not practical in the engineering environment.'

'Are you saying that Committee instructions are wrong?'

'No, Doctrinaire Shrad, I am saying that in the engineering environment I would soil and destroy my greywear, which perhaps the Committee would consider an insult, though of course I don't presume to know what the Committee would think. I just try to do my best for the good of the Collective.'

The words were as correct as they could be in the circumstances, but Shrad could detect a note of forbidden Irony and perhaps Sarcasm. He knew it would be necessary to modify the behaviour of this man.

'Doctrinaire Shrad.'

Shrad turned. 'Citizen Astanger,' he said, feeling an immediate increase in his annoyance. Astanger was a societal asset – a synthesist who under the Markovians would have been called captain of the *Lenin*.

'Is there a problem?' asked Astanger.

Shrad gazed at the man. He was grey-haired, tall and thin, possessed piercing blue eyes and what in another time would have been called a noble face. Shrad had his suspicions that Astanger's ancestry was in fact Markovian – for he possessed a similarity of facial structure to those in Shrad's Guard unit – and that his outer appearance stemmed from the genetic tweaks those rulers had made to their line. It further annoyed Shrad that though Astanger's hair and greywear were utterly correct, he always looked sartorially impeccable.

'This engineer is incorrectly dressed,' said Shrad.

Astanger turned his cold gaze on the man. 'Rand, why are you wearing those overalls?'

'Greywear doesn't give enough freedom of movement Ca… Citizen.'

Ah, thought Shrad, smirking. As he had supposed, this ship being without doctrinal supervision throughout the last five years of the conflict with the Grazen, archaic and politically incorrect behaviour had flourished. Rand had nearly called Citizen Astanger *Captain*.

'Be that as it may,' continued Astanger, 'you knew that wearing anything other than greywear is … ideologically incorrect.' Astanger turned to Shrad. 'As synthesist I suggest, Doctrinaire Shrad, that for the good of this mission Citizen Rand be made to work 120% shifts on 75% rations.'

'That will not be necessary,' said Shrad. He turned to the two one-time Markovians, the two of the Guard – the only ones who wore a slightly different style of greywear in that theirs was armoured. The two men were as stony-faced as ever, each of them bearing a stroud spread like a two-fingered steel hand up the side of one cheek and dividing at the temple to spread two fingers halfway along their foreheads. 'Stroud him.'

Citizen Rand bellowed and began to struggle, but being experienced at this sort of thing, in fact having experienced it themselves, the Guard held him, and one of them quickly slapped a stroud into place. Rand shrieked, and now the Guard released him. For a moment Shrad thought he saw something in the expression of the particular guard who had used the stroud – was he Evan Markovian, or one of the others? Shrad tended to get them confused now. After a moment he dismissed the suspicion – there was hardly anything left inside their skulls of the people they had been.

Writhing like a maggot, Rand tumbled through the air, is face clenched in a rictus of agony, and blood running from underneath the stroud. Then, abruptly, his face went slack, moronic. The probes, about two thousand of them in all, had found their required locations in his brain, in some of those locations killing brain matter and in others injecting certain combinations of neurochemicals. Now the recordings would be playing. The indoctrination process would take about three hours and Rand would be a good citizen afterwards, if he survived – only one in three did. Satisfied, Shrad turned to gaze at Astanger.

'It was foolish of him to flout the law,' said Astanger, still watching Rand and seemingly unaffected by what had happened. He now turned to Shrad, 'As synthesist I will now have to factor in that though we may have gained one good citizen, we have certainly lost one good engineer.'

'Be careful what you say, Citizen Astanger.'

'I am always careful, Citizen Shrad … now, perhaps you would like to come to the Bridge. It would seem that the *Breznev* has now dropped into U-space and is taking a most unexpected route.'

'Unexpected?'

'Well, let me say 'disconcerting' – their choices were limited.'

The ovoid, eight miles long, looked like a furry egg from a distance, but closer to revealed itself to be a loose tangle of yard-wide pipes of a white coralline substance. Yig worms dwelt in the pipes, and were currently extending the perimeter of the nest since it had encompassed another asteroid for them to grind up and digest after the nest's departure from the rookery. The Mother, crouched in the centre of the tangle, with sensory tendrils spread half a mile all around her and engaged into yig-channels, which in turn led to exterior long-range sensors. Like a giant metallized crayfish with an extended body she crouched, fended from hard vacuum by yig-worm opalized shields, tending her domain, cataloguing her additions to the yig-work, and raging.

Five million of her children were dead, and the mother's rage was a terrible thing that she knew might last her for the rest of her millennia. Besides the Misunderstanding, this slaughter had been the worst thing that had ever happened to her. No other Grazen had lost so much, and she felt justified in breaking away from the rest of her kind and fleeing to this outpost. But she knew, deep in her fifth heart, that in Grazen terms she was not entirely sane.

When she saw the distortion of the undersphere that signified the presence of humans, she lashed out – the yig weaving a ripple into the undersphere and directing it along the course she set, and she relished the coming opportunity for vengeance. Human neurology was a simplistic and easily manipulated thing, and it was possible to exact punishment lasting even beyond the death of the neural network that formed the being. She still had some of the murderers with her now – forever shrieking in yig-channels. Only when the ripple was away did she experience a sudden dread. The distortion was so close to *his* realm, and this might lead to another Misunderstanding. She waited, observed the human vessel slam up into the oversphere, then observed it continuing on under conventional drive. She felt a moment of chagrin at her impulsive reaction. The ship would be crippled and flung back out, so there was no rush – it would soon be hers.

Then the other human vessel rose into the oversphere.

The Mother observed it for a little while. She surmised that once it saw what was about to happen to the one ahead of it, it might flee into the undersphere, so sent another ripple to render its undersphere engines inert. Then she began to consolidate a kernel nest for travel. She withdrew her tendrils to the kernel, shifted supplies and the required devices inside, selected specific yig-worms and opalized the kernel. The nest yig opened a path through the outer opalized shields to the oversphere and, clawing space, she shot out, wrapped in her kernel. The second vessel, now limited to oversphere drive, was heading directly *there* too. She travelled slowly, waiting for both vessels to be expelled, and relished the prospect of revenge. Then, in horrified disbelief, she observed the two ships enter *his* realm, unharmed.

Wearing a spacesuit, which gave her a lot more shielding than she had ever been allowed aboard the *Mao*, Kelly clung to a handhold in the drive penny and gazed at one drive unit – a teardrop of polished alloy ten feet long. There were three of them evenly spaced around the circumference of the penny, where bubblemetal beams braced tham at a distance apart precise to one ten thousanth of an inch. The penny was temperature-controlled simply to maintain this accuracy, since variation in temperature would have resulted in disastrous metal expansion. It was all irrelevant now. The drive unit she was studying obviously lay out of true with the rest, and if that wasn't enough, the smoke coiling from a blown-away inspection hatch certainly was.

'What's the problem, Kelly?' asked Slome over the suit radio.

Kelly pushed herself away from her handhold over to the central cleanlock, went through, and out the other side she began undogging her helmet. There were three of them awaiting her in the drive annex – no room for any more: Slome, his daughter and Olsen.

'The problem is,' she replied at length, 'no more U-space drive.'

'What?' said Elizabeth. 'You're saying you can't repair it.'

The girl was really starting to irritate Kelly now. 'A U-space drive is fitted and tuned in the Gavarn station complex. It takes about eight months just to balance it and all the processing power of the complex itself. If I took back what we've got in there,' Kelly stabbed a thumb over her shoulder. 'they'd likely scrap it and start again.'

'Well,' said Slome, listening to his headset, 'it may all be irrelevant now.' He gestured to the ports over to one side, and Kelly pushed herself over, dreading she was about to see one of those shimmering tangles of pipes the Collective called a Grazen dreadnought, but which she thought wasn't an apt description at all. The things had only appeared occasionally during the war, and the Collective had not managed to destroyed one of them. If the Grazen had used them properly, the Collective would have ceased to exist, but you weren't ever allowed to say aloud anything like that aboard the *Mao*. Instead the Grazen had used just those wormships which, though dangerous, the human ships were able to destroy. However, the sight that greeted her eyes was something she had only ever seen in very hazy high-magnification pictures.

'Border post,' said Olsen.

'A what?' asked Elizabeth.

Why was she here? Someone more senior should have been here.

'Something I read about. They were also called death posts, though since we're sailing on past I suppose the description inapt.'

'Or they have been deactivated by whoever sent us that invitation,' said Slome.

It certainly looked a bit like a post, though one with streamlined ovoids attached at each end. It was huge, as Kelly recollected the high magnification scan readout put these objects at two miles high, and there were thousands of them. The Doctrinaires aboard *Mao* told everyone they were the product of the ancient Collective from Earth, betrayed by the humans who took control before the Markovians. No one believed that, too many of the crew had heard the rumours about that entity called the Owner, though of course no one said so.

'That could have been what hit us,' said Elizabeth.

Kelly shook her head. 'I don't think so – that felt like something the Grazen used. Usually, after a strike like that the wormships would be all over us. Maybe they're not attacking because of our location.' She didn't feel as sure as she sounded, but felt the need not to let any of Elizabeth's statements go unchallenged.

Slome was listening to his headset again, nodding to himself. After a moment he said, 'Seems the same thing just happened to the *Lenin*, and now it's heading directly towards us.'

Kelly rested her head against the port. It was quite simple – they'd gambled and lost.

Slome continued, 'We're on the edge of a solar system here – one with a habitable world. Under conventional drive we could be there in eight months.'

'Do we have the supplies for that?' asked Kelly.

'Water and air recyling will last that long, the food will just have to.'

'Then what?'

'We land.'

'I don't see what good that will do us.'

'Would you rather the *Lenin* caught up with us out here? At least down on a planet there's some chance of evading the Guard.'

'Yeah, right.'

The Grazen U-space weapon had knocked out both the U-space drives of the *Breznev* and the *Lenin*, and Astanger had thought they were all about to die. Owner Space would fling them out if they headed that way and, anyway, they would never be able to flee the aliens using conventional drive through realspace. Whether they continued on course after the *Breznev* had seemed irrelevant, but in the end saved them from the Grazen. Owner Space flung out human ships yet it destroyed the Grazen ones. This time it did not do the first, and fear of the second was, Astanger suspected, keeping the Grazen away.

However, their situation was now dire and Shrad's insistence on pursuing those assets and punishing them seemed quite insane. With a Grazen dreadnought sitting in vacuum behind them, reversing their course would have been stupid. Taking some other course out of Owner Space would have taken years under conventional drive, and they just did not have the supplies for that. Heading straight for the same planet to which the other ship was heading seemed the best course available, but still, Shrad was mad as a box of frogs

Citizen Shrad – the one everyone knew was responsible for the war against the Grazen, even if Collective society doctrine classified individual responsibility as an outmoded concept, and opined that there were no leaders.

Shrad had ordered all the strouded, but for the Guard, to stop eating and good little robots that they were, that is precisely what they had done. Now, a month into their slog insystem, some of those people were dying. Astanger felt much regret for their straits, since though the strouding process made good little robots of them, it did not relieve them of suffering – that would have been too much to ask of the Collective. However, all those dying were not crew but non-essential personnel, because those strouded did not have sufficient independence of thought to be essential. They were also, in Astanger's opinion, better off dead. At least Engineer Rand had not suffered death by slow starvation – his stroud had not taken and he died before they could get him to the medbay.

Everyone else was on half rations, except of course for Shrad himself, he being the most *essential* person aboard. Astanger could think of numerous people aboard who were more essential ... the entire crew, for example. And it now seeming likely that there might be no return to the Collective – it struck him as unlikely that a rescue ship would be sent what with Shrad having been black-balled from the Committee – Astanger was attracted to the idea of depriving Shrad of his ability to eat. This was a position he never imagined himself to be in when he had received his military call-up. As a misty-eyed youth, he had known himself to be a member of an advanced and rational political system.

The Collective had taken power before he was born, and he'd been born into a still relatively free society, for it took quite some time for the dictats to actually take effect. The Capital World felt the effects first, and it took some years for them to reach his borderland home world. He grew up with the changes, the indoctrination and propaganda, and the kowtowing to the Doctrinaires. He crewed on Fleet ships still run the old Markovian way and, because of his indoctrination, thought the system bankrupt. As a ship's security officer, he applied the dictats of the new Doctrinaires each ship now acquired. This was probably what accelerated his ascent of the promotion ladder to the position of captain. Then came the war with the Grazen.

As captain, he had a greater overview of events and, though Shrad's propaganda talked of Grazen assaults on Collective worlds, Astanger knew otherwise. It started to nag him, the way Shrad and his lackeys called a straightforward assault on the Grazen a 'defensive manoeuvre'. Plain aggression was couched in terms of Collective-speak, thus the bombardment of a Grazen nest was a 'tactical clearance' and the incineration of a planet-based alien nursery – one of Shrad's 'special projects' – was 'groundwork procedure'. This elicited his dislike of Shrad, the Committee, the Collective and of himself. Being older, and wiser, he began to reassess his life. But what could he do, he was but a small cog in the Collective machine? The introduction of greywear and the gradual dismantling of the Markovian command structure brought about his disgust and contempt, and the strouds finally aroused in him a cold hatred. But, again, what could he do?

Five years before the end of the war, a wormship attack deprived *Lenin* of its Doctrinaire. He spent the rest of the war ensuring the ship didn't get another one. The Grazen withdrew from numerous worlds, then consolidated their nests around the core of their empire – if 'empire' was the correct description of their system of governance, which he frankly doubted. Supplies to fleet ships were low, resources scant. The Committee called it a 'victory of political rationality over animalistic imperialism' and recalled the fleet. Seeing the reality, Astanger counted the cost. The Collective destroyed twenty out of tens of thousands of their nests and burned a nursery world. It lost fifteen hundred and six capital ships, numerous support vessels, and saw ground assault troops exterminated – some of them burned on the nursery world in the common kind of screw-up occurring when military tactics became subject to political control. The total human cost somewhere in the millions, though it was impossible to get an accurate count.

Victory indeed.

But now, here aboard the *Lenin*, he wanted to *do* something. Many of the crew agreed with him – the exceptions being new personnel who had not been aboard during those five years – but they simply weren't enough. The crew complement consisted of fifty-eight people, all, by Committee ruling, unarmed. Shrad had one hundred of the utterly loyal Guard with him, all of them armed with handguns and carbines, and with access to even more powerful weapons than those. It seemed hopeless, and would become more so, in the months to come, as his crew steadily starved.

The Mother retreated to the nest, but could not bring herself to finally return her vessel to its structure. Only partially reconnecting her tendrils into the yig-channels and thus to the nest's long-range sensors, she gazed at the two human ships as they moved beyond the barrier. No reaction, nothing. She could not believe this: every wormship sent through there had been destroyed, the posts had fried *all* the drive systems of every human ship that strayed that way and then flung them back out. Why not now?

She seethed as the two ships made for the nearest world within *his* domain. She gazed at them throughout the months of their journey, her frustration growing at letting two – now they had lost the ability to travel in U-space – so easy targets escape. But she was frightened: there was the Misunderstanding to consider.

Then it started again.

Through long-unused yig-channels she received the news that the humans were preparing for another attack on the Grazen. Spy yigs peppered throughout Collective space reported uncontrolled industrialization and the practical rapine of worlds. They reported massive movements of supplies, ships and human warriors. Apparently, these last were different somehow, and this too was a worrying development. The Grazen had predicted such an effort as a remote possibility when they withdrew to wait, taking a long view of events, for the inevitable collapse of a doomed-to-failure societal experiment. Analysis of this new effort, showed that it would bankrupt the Collective and bring about its predicted collapse early, but that would be no consolation if they hit another nursery world.

Though she had physically separated her nest from the rest of the Grazen, she could not separate herself from her kind's racial will, the purpose, the gestalt that was the Grazen. Whilst others of her kind prepared with cold efficiency to hold the Collective at bay until it collapsed, the Mother raged. She wanted to strike out, to damage, to hurt, and the nearest humans to her were but a few weeks away through the undersphere then the oversphere.

The posts had not touched them, so perhaps they would not touch her? Maybe *he* was looking away, maybe *he* was gone? It was said by some that he took the form of a human, so maybe he was as short-lived as that kind and had died? While with one part of her mind she was so foolishly wishful, with another part, she reasoned that something like *him* would not die and would not be caught with his guard down.

Then came the communication.

Though couched perfectly in the language of the yig-channels, the mother knew its source to be alien. Tracing back through the undersphere to its source she felt a moment of pure dread. *Him?*

But the misunderstanding... was the essence of her reply.

He explained, and she felt a sudden overwhelming joy.

She once again detached her consolidated kernel for oversphere travel and fell away from her main nest. Clawing through vacuum between asteroidal debris until she found clear space, she dropped into the undersphere. Yes, she had always felt that humans must pay for the deaths of her children and the other deaths sure to come, and pay, and pay. However, this was different, this was *personal*.

Kelly gazed at the images displayed in the viewing cylinder. The two probes showed the world ahead to be beautiful, warm and burgeoning with life. Bands of forest rimmed the continents, enclosing prairies and mountain ranges. Vast herds of grazing beasts, sometimes tens of miles across, were visible in flowing patterns across the prairies, cutting swathes of brown through the green. One close view showed a predator – some kind of massive reptile stood up on its hind legs – bringing down one of these grazing beasts. It was just a microcosm of the huge ebb and flow of life spread across the landmasses.

The oceans seemed equally as bountiful. Shoals of fish spumed the sea across areas as large as those landward herds. Giant cetaceans hunted and played, enormous sharks the colour of polished copper cruised shorelines swamped by, either basking amphibians, or swimming mammals come ashore to mate and lay eggs.

Birds and flying reptiles swirled across the sky. Tropical seas gleamed sapphire. Snow-capped peaks glistened pure white. Salmon leaped in a million miles of clean rivers. It all looked so wonderfully natural, an untouched paradise.

'Do you even begin to comprehend the kind of engineering involved in creating something like that?' enquired Olsen.

'If it is engineered,' said Elizabeth dismissively.

'Tell me about the engineering,' said Slome.

'Think of the migratory patterns – it all has to be programmed in. Not only has life been created down there from base genetic imprints, it's been programmed to integrate into the entire artificial environment. And you know, there are things down there that went extinct back on Terra and others that simply never existed.'

'Then perhaps they were here before any engineering commenced…' suggested Elizabeth – playing her preferred Devil's Advocate role.

'No, you see they're suited to their environment.'

'Precisely.' Elizabeth was triumphant.

Olsen shook his head at her and turned to Slome. 'Everything down there is suited to that environment, yet, unless a lot of Markovian records are wrong, that environment was a lot colder about three hundred years ago.'

'Go on,' said Slome, his eyes narrowing.

'This world is not where it's supposed to be – it's much closer to the sun.'

Elizabeth barked a laugh. 'So, this immortal superbeing is also capable of moving worlds? I think it more likely that initial Markovian studies were inaccurate and that inaccuracy simply copied.'

Olsen shrugged. 'That's always possible.'

Kelly continued gazing at the images and compared what she could see to the incompleteness of many Collective worlds where near-Terran environments were maintained by gas extraction and fixing plants, the importation of essential minerals from elsewhere, the re-sowing of certain biologicals, the endless war against alien biologicals – whole industries working to prevent, in human terms, planetary ecological collapse. This world seemed to function perfectly. There was no sign of atmosphere plants or any other support technology, no sign, in fact, of any technology at all … until Traviss spoke.

'I've found something,' he said.

The images in the cylinder blurred for a moment then settled on a high view of a coastline. Traviss focused in by stages, each time allowing the ship's computers to clean up the image presented. The final image was of an estuary where a river cut down into a wide blue bay. On one side of the estuary, on a blunt peninsula, a large building of some kind seemed evident. Squinting, Kelly was also sure she could make out, projecting from a rocky shore just beside a white sand beach, a jetty with what appeared to be a large twin-hulled boat moored beside it.

'Someone living down there?' wondered Slome.

Kelly shivered. The *Owner*?

'I'm getting stuff in infrared and some other EMR,' said Traviss. 'Nothing substantial, but it does seem likely there's someone down there.'

'Can you give us a closer view?' Slome asked.

'If I do, we'll lose this probe – it won't have enough fuel to pull up again.'

'Do so.'

They all stood watching as the probe obviously headed in a course out to sea and down, the view flicking back to the building and clarifying intermittently. The image shuddered for a little while as the probe's stabilisers failed to compensate for its decelerating burn as it curved round and headed back in. Kelly felt both a growing excitement and trepidation, but really did not know what she expected to see. The final views in the probe's life were clear, and puzzling – something so prosaic in so unusual a location. Nestled in rocky slopes scattered with gnarled trees stood a large building, a house, something like the kind of place the Markovians might have used as a country retreat. It sprawled, fashioned of the surrounding stone, with turrets and towers rising here and there, red tiles on the roofs and many baroque windows. Tracks led down from it to the shore, to some wooden buildings from which a jetty projected out into the sea. Moored next to the jetty floated a large catamaran. As the probe sank down towards the sea, she was sure she could discern a figure sitting on the jetty.

'That last image,' said Slome. 'Can you repeat it and clean it up?'

Traviss complied, and they all gazed at a human figure – difficult to tell if it was male or female – sitting on the jetty, fishing, and waving too. No one could think of anything to say about that – it all just seemed too incongruous. They had arrived at a world that had been under interdict for longer than any of them had lived because some dangerous being owned it … then this.

'Give us that first orbital view again,' said Slome.

Once again, they gazed down from upon high.

Slome pointed. 'On the other side of the estuary the forest comes nearly down to the shore. On the side where the house lies it's hilly for a few miles back before levelling into prairie – that's one of the few areas where forest doesn't cover the land to the rear of the shore.'

'No coincidence, I would suggest,' said Elizabeth, now somehow subdued.

'No,' said Slome. He turned and checked each face in turn. 'I suggest we land on that prairie – as close to the house as we can get – then I suggest we go and see who is living there.'

'Is that a good idea?' wondered Kelly.

'I don't know. However, what I do know is that once this ship is down we'll not be able to take it back up again, and I do know that the *Lenin* is not far behind us and will almost certainly land near to us. A Doctrinaire and the Guard will come. If we were to land anywhere else, our only choice will be to run, and keep on running. There,' He stabbed a finger at the projection, 'some alternative might lie open to us.'

'The Owner might save us,' said Elizabeth flatly.

'Or we might be bringing the Guard down on an innocent lone settler,' said Kelly.

Slome shook his head. 'No one is innocent. Haven't you been reading your Committee dictats?'

The *Breznev* headed towards the world tail first, poised on the bright flare of its main drive. Behind the half-hemisphere of the thrust-plate and the conglomeration of fuel tanks, reactor, lithium pellet injectors and ignition lasers, lay the drive penny for the U-space engines. Beyond this stretched a long reinforced framework holding an access tunnel from the now stationary spin section – a cylinder eighty feet wide and a hundred feet long – inside which the escapees were being crushed into acceleration chairs. Next along from the spin section was the giant brick of the storage section and holds, capped off by the heavy re-entry shield and underslung re-entry plate. The ship left an ionized trail past the world's single cratered moon, the four big reaction thrusters positioned at the four corners of the frame holding the spin section, belched chemical flame to force it into an inward curve.

Further brighter ionization in the world's disperse exosphere, sketched the vessel's course around it and deeper towards the thermosphere. When its speed reached a predetermined level, the main drive cut out, and the thrusters flared again turning the ship nose to tail to present its re-entry shield to the steadily thickening air. The flip-over had its usual effect internally, and clamping down on her churning guts Kelly knew the vomit vacuums would again be required. Explosive bolts blew, clamps detached and especially weakened structural members broke where intended, and the entire drive section detached, small steering thrusters slightly altering its course to throw it into orbit around the world. Landing, with a U-space engine and fusion reactor had never been an option.

The re-entry shield smoked as its layer of soft ceramic began baking hard. It soon began to emit a dull red glow, then fire flared out and back from it enclosing the ship, pod-like. It hurtled down, planing on fire, then the thrusters adjusted its course to bring it down on the underslung re-entry plate, and steadily began firing to slow the ship even further. As the ship penetrated cloud, sealed containers positioned all around the spin section opened like buds to spew parachutes. Using a combination of these and the big thrusters it descended on prairie, scattering herds of buffalo, and one herd of unicorns. Grass fires ignited underneath as it finally began to settle, but they were short lived in the spring green vegetation. With a final whumph, and a settling of parachutes all around, it was down.

Her fingers digging into the arms of her acceleration chair, Kelly knew the logistics of relaunch, and knew the *Breznev* would never be leaving this world. And she vowed to become part of the earth here rather than be subject to those who would soon be coming here.

The gas content of the air was breathable, but it might be packed with lethal microbes and biotoxins. They had no way of analysing the air and there weren't enough spacesuits to go around, and no one wanted to walk out there in the cumbersome things anyway. No one wanted to stay in the ship – not when seeming freedom waited outside. Kelly was damned if she was going to wait until Slome and the others came to a decision about what to do next. While they squabbled, she collected all her stuff in a shoulder bag, including her Sancha carbine and her father's antique sidearm, and headed for the airlock leading into the storage and cargo section.

'Not inclined to debate, SA Haden?'

Standing below the ladder leading up to the airlock, Kelly turned to gaze at Longshank. He was carrying a large backpack, had donned large walking boots in addition to his usual attire, and carried his notescreen clipped to his belt.

'Staying inside this ship is not an option – if something out there kills me I would rather that than waiting here for one of the Guard to fit me with a stroud.'

'My thoughts precisely. Anyway, this Owner-constructed world seems eminently human-habitable. Maybe we'll pick up a few bugs along the way, but I doubt there's anything out there we can't handle in usual immune-response way.'

'You seem very confident.'

'No – resigned.'

Kelly mounted the ladder and climbed, stepped up onto the platform and hit the door control as Longshank stepped up behind her. They crammed into the airlock together and after Longshank closed the first door, Kelly opened the second door leading into the forward cargo section of the ship. It opened with a slight hiss of pressure differential. Kelly clamped her nose and blew until her ears popped.

'There's an ATV packed away in here,' she said, while stepping out onto the next platform. She breathed carefully, wondering if anything would affect her right away, since they were now breathing the air of this world, the cargo section being open to the outside.

'Let's walk,' suggested Longshank.

'Where?'

'Where else?'

Many of the pressure-sealed crates in the section were open, their food contents all used up during the trip here. Other crates, once containing a cargo of freeze-dried ration packs destined for a Collective space station, were also empty. Kelly felt a pang of hunger, but it quickly passed – it had been some days since she felt really hungry. They moved past other sealed crates and Kelly hit the control to lower the loading ramp. Its locks clumped open and slowly it began to descend, exposing painfully bright blue sky. It finally hit down on vivid green dotted with blue and pink flowers. The intensity of light and colour hurt her eyes, but seemed to balm something behind them.

'Come on.' Longshank led the way out.

To their right the silvery material of a parachute rippled in a soft caressing breeze. Longshank pointed to where trees dotted a distant slope. 'Just beyond there – a few hills, a bit of a trudge.'

96

As they walked through the thigh-high grass, birds racketed into the sky to scold them and on one occasion, a large flightless bird leapt up from a nest full of brown-speckled eggs and charged away hooting in indignation. On the slope the vegetation was shorter – the grass cropped down by some animal, and large areas covered by mosses or mats of low-growing vines. Kelly stared at the first squat tree they came to and recognized the green orbs it bore as walnuts. Higher on the slope there were almond and olive trees and others she did not recognize.

Weariness soon set in, and Longshank's 'bit of a trudge' became a growing struggle until the splashing of a stream attracted them to a hollow.

'Shall we?' Longshank enquired.

The water tasted delicious and afterwards they ate some of the walnuts, even though they were unripe. An eagle soared above, and short-eared rabbits scattered and observed them from ridges. Eventually they hit a track, and in dry mud Kelly observed the impressions of the soles of a boots little different from the kind she was wearing. The track wound down through a sparse scattering of trees, beyond which she could see the multiple roofs of the house they had observed from orbit, and terminated against an ironwork gate set into a hedge of copper birch. Something like a chrome spider was working along the hedge far to their right, pruning back with multiple gleaming pincers. A simple latch admitted them to perfect lawns and rose gardens.

'Well hello,' said a man, standing up from inspecting a large red rose. 'Goodness me, I haven't had any visitors here in what …' He turned to gaze at a huge gnarled oak standing within its own circular border in the middle of one of the lawns. '…well, since I planted that.'

'Are you the Owner,' said Longshank.

The man, a stocky grey-haired individual with a deep tan and eyes like green chips of glass, gazed about himself for a moment. 'I guess so … sort of.'

Slome gazed about himself, the tightness in his guts increasing, then peered back at the loading ramp as he heard the sound of an electric motor. The ATV – basically an aluminium box able to hold six people and some cargo, suspended on four independent rubber wheels – rolled down onto the grass. Now it was down, the fifty escapees began unloading supplies and placing them in makeshift packs. Slome turned from the scene and peered down at the notescreen Traviss held – now displaying a map of the area. He tapped a finger against forest just back from the peninsula on this side of the estuary.

'There, I think,' he said. 'If they head towards the estuary they could end up trapped against it by the Guard.'

'Peerkin said the same,' Traviss replied, adding, 'They've voted him temporary leader what with his experience of wild environments.'

'Good. They need to go deep and keep under cover – we'll update them on whatever happens at the house and warn them if they need to run.'

'They'll probably run when the *Lenin* comes down anyway.'

Slome nodded.

'So it'll be me, you, Elizabeth and Olsen in the ATV. Anyone else?'

'No, we'll need the space for Haden and Longshank if we have to run.'

Slome was all too aware that that might be the case. Why would this 'Owner', supposing him able, want to help them anyway? He had deliberately remained out of contact with the human race for longer than living memory and, though initially human himself, was supposedly no longer of that kind. Why had the Owner allowed them, and the *Lenin*, through? Maybe the Owner no longer existed, and maybe the individual they had seen from the probe was someone who had come here in the intervening time?

'We're ready,' Elizabeth called.

He glanced over and saw that the steps were now folded down from the ATV and the others climbing aboard. Snatching up his pack, he ambled over and boarded too, taking the seat saved for him by Elizabeth behind the driver, Traviss. They headed away, leaving the other escapees to grab up what they could and head for the hideaway in the forest. Traviss accelerated the vehicle through the tall grass and soon hit the slope, navigating fast amidst the trees and obviously enjoying himself. It took them very little time to come upon a track and within sight of the house.

'Take us around to the front,' said Slome, upon seeing the hedge.

Traviss took them round then down beside a stream, up through an orchard, then onto another track. Visible through the apricot trees to their left stood an arch, to which they headed. This led into a stone courtyard. Traviss parked the ATV before steps leading up to a heavy wooden door. Even as they climbed out from the vehicle the door began opening, and a man stepped out.

'Hello and welcome,' he said.

Slome studied the man and thought he just looked too damned ordinary to be this 'Owner'.

'I have some of your fellows here already,' the man said. 'Come in. Are you hungry?'

The others looked to Slome for guidance and, after a moment, he led the way up the steps and held out his hand. 'Slome Terl. My companions,' He gestured at each in turn. 'are my daughter Elizabeth, Olsen Marcos and Traviss Painter. Who might you be?' Rough calloused hand and a strong grip – the hand of a labourer. The Owner? It seemed unlikely.

The question seemed to puzzle the man for a moment, then he said, 'Call me Mark – that would be best I think.'

'Are you the Owner?' asked Elizabeth – somewhat querulously, Slome thought.

Mark grinned. 'You could say that, and you would be both right and wrong.' Now he looked up. 'Are these with you too?'

Slome abruptly gazed up into cerulean sky, but for a moment could see nothing. Then, the flare of steering thrusters.

'No,' said Slome. 'That is the *Lenin* – a Collective ship containing those who intend to either kill or enslave us. Can you help? Because if you cannot – we had best start running now.'

'Oh I can help,' said Mark. He looked up again. 'Seems they have a shuttle.'

Again, Slome could see nothing for a moment or two, then he discerned a brief glint departing the position of the steering flame and the vague darkness of the *Lenin*. His eyes weren't bad – he'd recently had an optic nerve cellular stimulation and corneal cleaning – he should in fact be able to see better than anyone else here.

'You have good vision,' he commented.

'Positively omniscient,' Mark replied. 'Do come in.'

He led the way into a well-lit entry hall, floored in polished wood and surrounded by statues carved from the native stone. Slome recognized only one of them: the legendary beauty

Alison Markovian. From the hall, Mark took them through double doors into a plushly furnished living area.

'Ancient Earth,' said Olsen. 'I think.'

Slome's gaze fell on Haden and Longshank who were standing by an oval table before the window, steadily working their way through bowls piled with food. On the table platters were heaped with comestibles. As the smell reached his nostrils, his stomach immediately rumbled and his mouth started watering.

'Help yourself,' said Mark.

'Thank you.' Slome led the way over to the table. He wanted to say something to Haden and Longshank, but that want was secondary to his hunger. They all quickly tucked in and when a small amount of food in Slome's shrunken stomach satisfied his hunger he finally turned to them.

'You didn't wait for a decision,' he said.

'Decision about what?' Kelly asked. 'About whether or not to stay at the ship and wait for a Doctrinaire to come along and scrub our brains?'

Slome nodded, turning to glance over his shoulder and note that the man, Mark, had left the room. 'What have you learned about him?'

'Very little. He's been here a long time, or so he claims, but he's equivocating about whether or not he's the Owner.'

'With us too, but he says he can help us.'

'Do you think him capable of helping us?' Elizabeth interjected. 'I've seen no evidence here that he can do anything about the Guard, and that shuttle will be here soon.'

Slome shook his head – he didn't know what to think.

Kelly shrugged. 'Despite his equivocation I trust him. I don't know why.'

'And on that basis we should risk ending up under the stroud?'

Olsen now said, 'I've told you all what would be involved in creating something like this world. The Guard should be nothing to someone that capable.'

In the viewing cylinder, Astanger watched the shuttle descend towards the incongruous house on the planet below. Shrad had taken fifteen of the Guard with him and, perhaps sensing Astanger's intentions had set the rest patrolling or guarding the most critical areas of the ship – twenty of them were here on the Bridge, ever watchful, their damaged minds rendered incapable of suffering boredom. Two of them stood behind each of the crew and four of them were standing watch about the weapons system controls – those consoles now abandoned by Chadrick, the weapons officer.

Now, having flown into low orbit to drop the shuttle, it was time to move the *Lenin* back out. Astanger turned to his Bridge crew.

'Okay, bring us out,' he instructed.

'Where to?' enquired Citizen Grade – the helmsman.

'Precisely to where Doctrinaire Shrad instructed us to wait: the Lagrange point between this world and its moon.' He shot a glance at the two of the Guard standing behind him, then at the two standing behind Grade, and watched them studying the course alterations the man made. Were they even capable of knowing what he was doing? Of course they were. On occasion, he had taken the opportunity to speak to some of them. Though devoid of any social ability, or any understanding of plain conversation, they were intelligent and focused in other almost enviable ways. Good little robots.

And they were an atrocity.

Since Astanger had started questioning *everything*, he also questioned his inculcated hatred and contempt of the Markovians. Shrad's Guard had all once been Markovians, and since Shrad had boastfully mentioned this only a little while ago, Astanger had begun to recognize the bone structure and features of those he had been taught to hate. Now he did not hate them, just felt a huge sadness and pity, but he did hate Shrad. What the man had done, what the Committee had done, had nothing to do with social engineering, nothing to do with making a better world, nothing to do with *doctrine*. Shrad and his kind were rulers substantially less restrained about how they used their power than the Markovians. Only Astanger's self-disgust exceeded his disgust for Shrad and his kind.

As his men bent to their task, Astanger, with bitterness in his mouth, returned his attention to his controls and tried to concentrate on what he had been doing before. In the cylinder, he pulled up a view of the moon. It was a cratered monster over two thousand miles in diameter, and only after scanning the planet below had Astanger now turned his attention to it. As yet he had found no evidence of technology, but there was something odd about the astrogation data that just kept on niggling at him, so, barring some opportunity to disarm the Guard aboard his ship and then incinerate Shrad's shuttle on its return journey, he focused on that sphere.

Now under drive again the *Lenin* headed for the Lagrange still point. The Guard, Astanger noted, seemed rooted to the deck despite the sideways drag of acceleration. On his screens, he decided to call up Markovian data on this sector of space, despite the watchful eyes behind him. Very quickly, he found the first discrepancy: the world wasn't in the right place. He felt a surge of awe, then immediately told himself not to be stupid – the data were obviously wrong. Then another glaring error became evident. According to the Markovians this world should not even have a moon. He speculated about the possibility of it being recently captured in orbit and thus also repositioning the world, but that didn't gel. If such a thing had happened between the time the Markovians recorded these data and now, there would be huge volcanic activity below and other massive damage. Nothing like that evident. But he realized all this was nothing to do with what was niggling him.

Astanger called up the astrogation data again and kept on going through it. He gazed at the position of the Lagrange point and suddenly realized what was bothering him: it was too close to the moon. Now calling up data on a similar orbital set-up within the Collective, he confirmed this, then began to make his own calculations. The moon, he soon realized, must mass considerably less than a sphere of rock over two thousand miles across, yet, the data they had gathered on it showed it to be precisely that.

Abruptly he cancelled out the data on his screens then just called up prosaic stuff about their current trajectory. He leant back and considered some possibilities. Either the scanners were malfunctioning – a not unusual occurrence under Collective rule – or that moon was definitely not what it appeared to be.

He reckoned it was hollow. He also reckoned Doctrinaire Shrad might be heading for a rude awakening. He smiled to himself at the prospect, which seemed the best he could hope for. Then the U-signature detection alarm wiped the smile from his face, and horror bloomed in his chest as the ship's scanners automatically redirected, and displayed the source of that signal in the viewing cylinder.

A Grazen dreadnought had just arrived.

Doctrinaire Shrad crouched behind the perfectly manicured rose bed and watched his men close in on either side of the window, then raising his thumb telescope to his eye, he observed those inside – clicking up the light amplification since the greenish yellow sun was now setting and stars beginning to blink into view on the far horizon.

What were they doing in there, having a party? He had already seen Slome Terl standing near the window picking at a plate of food while talking to the traitor Kelly Haden. It had to be some kind of trap. They must have seen his shuttle coming in to land and known that justice was snapping at their heels. He lowered his telescope. And what about this place?

Shrad could not quite equate the massive technology of those constructs they had passed while heading into 'Owner Space' with this house. He'd thought long and hard about what he had read in secret Collective records and come to some conclusions. Though it was doctrine that those structures were the product of a previous collective from ancient Earth, he was of a sufficiently high rank to know the truth. There had been an Owner who once had contact with the Markovians – though details were sketchy since many records had been destroyed during the 'transition of power' – and during the recent 'victorious conflict' with Grazen, those 'posts' had damaged and repelled human vessels and destroyed Grazen wormships. However, nothing had been heard about the Owner for longer than living memory. It struck him as likely that though the being had once existed, he or it did not exist now. The action of the posts? Automated systems obviously breaking down. He surmised that during the 'transition of power' some high-ranking Markovians had fled out this way and managed to get to this world during some periodic malfunction of the posts. This residence looked distinctly Markovian – like one of those country retreats where Shrad had obtained the base material of his Guard.

He smiled to himself. If he could capture some high-ranking Markovians that could be put on trial the Committee would be much more inclined to send a rescue ship and their 'resources are presently unavailable' and their 'tactical requirements do not permit' would probably change. His discovery about the malfunctioning of the posts also opened up massive new territories to the Collective...

'We are in position,' Citizen One of the Guard informed him through his earpiece.

'Commence action – I repeat: subdue and restrain them. Do not, I repeat, do not kill any of them even in the likelihood of losing Guard strength.'

Raising his thumb telescope again, he now observed one of the Guard beside the window slap something against the glass, then lower his breather mask over his face. The blast disintegrated the window and the men either side now tossed in flash and gas grenades. After the subsequent detonations, and while numb-smoke belched from the house, the fifteen Guard piled inside. Shrad waited for a moment, but though he heard shouting from inside, there was no shooting, then he stood, and pulling up his own breather mask into place, he drew his sidearm and headed over.

Broken glass crunched underfoot, the table had been tipped to one side and food and dishes spilled across a carpet patterned with geometric shapes. Kelly Haden was still fighting, but three of the Guard had her pinned and were cuffing her hands behind her back. Slome Terl just lay there fighting for breath. All six of the figures on the floor wore dishevelled greywear modified in ways that would be a political offence in themselves. All six, then, were escapees – there had to be others here.

Abruptly Shrad realized the smoke was clearing. He glanced up to see it being drawn away into holes in the ceiling – interspersed between the inset lights now slowly growing brighter as it grew darker outside – then returned his attention to the captives as the Guard hauled them up onto their knees. He holstered his sidearm.

'Seven of you, search the rest of this place and bring here anyone you find – stay in contact,' he instructed.

Seven departed, but the eight remaining were certainly enough to keep under control the patently subdued captives. The smoke now all but cleared – it had a short active life anyway – so Shrad removed his mask. He sniffed at the burnt hair smell, realising it came from where the flash grenades had seared the carpet. Then he strode forwards to stand before the six kneeling figures.

'Did you think the Collective could allow its Societal Assets to escape?' he enquired.

None said anything.

'You, Kelly Haden, you betrayed the Collective, stole its property and, as I understand it you killed two of the Guard.'

Haden shrugged and looked away. Shrad gave a muted nod to the guard standing beside her, who stooped and drove the butt of his carbine into her stomach. She groaned and went down with her forehead on the carpet.

'It strikes me as evident that your obvious external ugliness reflects the ugliness inside you,' said Shrad.

'Fuck ... you ... and your little robots,' she managed.

Shrad nodded to himself. 'Under Collective authority I have a choice about what I should do with you. For the murder you committed the sentence should be death, but I have the

107

leeway to make my own decisions in this matter.' He nodded to the Guard. 'Stroud her.'

One of the Guard hauled her up by the hair, while another righted the table and placed a case on the surface, which he opened to reveal twenty strouds lying in the foam packing like a collection of steel prosthetic feet for birds. He took out one of these and placed it in a programming slate – these strouds needing to be prepared as had been the one Shrad had instructed to be placed on the *Lenin's* engineer.

'Going to help us,' spat Elizabeth Terl somewhat hysterically, gazing beyond Shrad.

Slome Terl bowed his head, a look of pain on his face. Shrad turned and saw four of his Guard returning, leading a man into the room – his hands cuffed behind his back.

'Put him with the rest,' he instructed. 'Is there anyone else?'

'We have found no one yet, but there is still much to search,' replied Citizen Five of the Guard.

'Very well. You four remain here.' Shrad now watched as the Guard brought the man over and forced to his knees beside Haden. 'Who are you?' he finally asked.

'My name is Mark,' the man replied calmly.

Shrad felt a sense of victory upon hearing the name. In the back of his mind, he had held the suspicion that his reasoning about this house might have been at fault. Now he felt sure he was right.

'Mark as in Markovian, I've no doubt,' he said. 'How did you come to be here?'

'Well, my mother met my father–'

Shrad gave that muted nod and a carbine butt smacked across the man's mouth. He went over, spitting blood and remained there until hauled back up onto his knees again.

'Was there any need for that?'

'There was.' Shrad turned to the guard who had now prepared the first stroud. 'Go ahead.'

The guard walked over as two others restrained Haden. Abruptly the man, Mark, burst out laughing.

'I fail to see the reason for your amusement,' said Shrad.

'Oh I'm just amused at the rather crude technology. Do you honestly think your Collective will survive after lobotomizing most of it citizens? Do you honestly think its economy and social structure could survive your coming attack on the Grazen? Though of course, that's not something you'll find out about, since the Grazen will stop playing their waiting game ... just like the one that's coming here.'

'Explain yourself.'

'Gladly. Your social system is bankrupt and bound to fail. The Grazen withdrew to their heartlands to await that failure, since it would have been less costly to them than continuing to fight you. Now that they have seen that the Collective is about to attack again, they'll come out fighting, and this time they won't be sending those insentient and easily mass-manufactured wormships.'

'How do you know all this?'

'I'm the Owner – haven't you figured that out.'

The others were now looking at the man with something approaching hope. Shrad felt another sudden doubt of his earlier reasoning. Maybe this man did have some power and, if so, Shrad must clamp down on it fast. The man looked human enough, so a bullet in the brain would soon solve any problem he might cause. And there was also that 'crude technology'. Perhaps that was the better option – even strouded the man could still stand trial for his crimes against the collective will.

The Committee much preferred to put those before the cameras who said what they were told to say.

'You are Markovian scum and a liar. Now tell me about the Grazen coming here.'

The man shrugged. 'They normally keep away. We had a bit of a misunderstanding about a thousand years ago ... or rather they misunderstood what I meant when I said no, keep out, these star systems are mine. I thought I put it to them quite clearly, but apparently not...'

'It's a good act, Markovian, but you're on your knees with broken teeth.'

'Yeah, bastard that.'

'You were saying?'

'Oh yeah ... well, they normally keep out, but the one whose nest you passed on the way in here lost all her children on that nursery world whose bombardment you instigated. She's not happy – especially now the Collective is preparing to attack again. I rather think she would like to have you all screaming in her yig-ware.'

'You babble.'

Even so, Shrad removed his communicator from his belt, and opened a channel to the shuttle uplink. 'Citizen Astanger – report.'

After a short delay: 'Tell your fucking Guard to let us get out of here! And tell them to let Citizen Chadrick back to his weapons console!'

'Give me your situation.'

'Sitting here with our thumbs up our arses watching a Grazen dreadnought approach. It's already fired a ranging shot.'

'Where would you go, given the opportunity to run?'

'Down where you are. If we stay out here we're dead!'

The communicator was slippery in his palm and he felt as if someone was trying to wind his insides around a stick. This should not, could not be happening.

'Put me on … general address,' he managed.

'You're on.'

'Guard…' Could this be some sort of ploy by Astanger? No, Astanger would have called him first. 'Guard, allow Citizen Chadrick back to the weapons console and allow Citizen Astanger to move the *Lenin* out of danger. … Astanger, I will keep this channel open – keep me informed of events.'

'Oh yes, like I'm going to have time for that!'

Shrad lowered the communicator and clipped it back on his belt. This Mark had *known*, and the Markovians had never been above using additional cerebral wiring – it was from the remaining files on that technology that Collective Social Assets had managed to work out how to make strouds. What else could the man control, influence? He turned and pointed.

'Use the stroud on him! Now!'

From his knees, Mark launched himself to his feet, but the Guard brought him down.

'Keep that fucking thing away from me!' he bellowed.

Shrad smiled. He had correctly understood what was happening here; this man was not the Owner but just some Markovian refugee. He fought, but soon the stroud was in place and he was kicking on the floor, his face clenched up in agony as blood ran from underneath the device. Shrad stepped past him.

'So you see your all-powerful Owner,' he gestured dismissively to the prostrate form. 'Now, I can find them of course, but I want you to tell me where the rest of the escapees are. Obviously I don't want to waste societal assets, but I will have each of you strouded in turn if you do not tell me.'

111

'Did your father fuck your mother up the arse to produce you?' asked Haden.

Shrad sighed, then gave the nod to the guard beside her. Nothing happened.

He gave the nod again, but the guard no longer seemed to be paying attention.

'Strike her,' he instructed.

The guard lifted his carbine and gazed down at it, then looked up at Shrad. Tears were pouring from the man's eyes. Abruptly he went down on his knees and slowly bowed his head.

What?

A clattering, then the sound of bodies hitting the floor. Two of the Guard had collapsed, another two went over even as he watched. Others were sinking to their knees like the first, or just suddenly finding somewhere to sit down. Some were crying, others grinning idiotically.

'It is, actually, not a crude technology at all. The Markovians obtained it from the Grazen who, though they would not admit to it, obtained it from an excavation of some ruins left by those I called the jelly people – they were okay, but tended to be a bit impetuous. Anyway, I needed to see one of your strouds from the inside to be sure of the structure. I've U-transmitted the signal now, so every single strouded human being in the Collective just woke up to what has been done to them, or, if the damage is too severe, died.'

It felt to Shrad as if ice was forming down his spine. He reached down, drew his sidearm, turned. The man, Mark, was on his feet facing him. Shrad fired once, the bullet snapping the man's skull back and blowing its contents out behind him. The head slowly swung forwards again, one eye was missing.

'And that completes the deal,' said Mark.

112

Shrad shot him four more times, the shots smashing into the man's chest and knocking him staggering back. Mark grinned, then his legs gave way and he slumped to the floor.

Astanger secured his strap, as the *Lenin* turned hard. The sound of the ship's guns impinged – an accelerating drone – and the power drain momentarily dimmed the lighting.

What happened to the Guard?

Some of them had just collapsed where they stood. One of those nearest him, a woman, was crouching beside a console, clinging with both hands, her weapon abandoned on the floor and sliding away from her. Her expression was one of horrified amazement, yet someone strouded usually didn't show emotion. Another, over near where Chadrick had taken position at the weapons console, was kneeling, his carbine propped upright before him. He seemed to be crying.

No matter. It might be that the *Lenin* would not survive the next few minutes so the condition of those aboard would cease to be of relevance. Again came the detonation of something that got too close before the guns took it out. The ship shuddered, and smoke began crawling through the air from the Bridge exit.

'It's going to be a hard re-entry!' shouted Grade over the racket.

'Go to earpieces and mikes,' said Astanger.

'Okay – I'm on,' replied Grade.

'We've still got to drop velocity.'

'Yup.'

As they slowed into atmosphere they would become a much easier target for the pursuing alien vessel, but Astanger knew that out in space the *Lenin* would end up smeared across vacuum. Collective ships had encountered these dreadnoughts on a few occasions, and been destroyed almost out-of-hand.

The *Lenin* began shaking, and Astanger recognized the muted but growing roar of atmosphere. Inertial forces tried to drag him out of his chair as the ship flipped nose-to-tail. He saw a member of the guard slam into the ceiling above, then lost sight of him in smoke. Someone was shrieking; short jerky shrieks like those you might hear in an asylum, not from anyone in pain. A body slammed down with a wet crunch nearby, then smeared blood across the floor as deceleration dragged it away. Grade had gone for a full emergency landing: not dumping the drive section but decelerating down towards the planet on the drive flame.

'Will you bring us down close to the *Breznev*?' Astanger enquired.

'Within a few miles of it – if we don't get hit on the way down,' Grade replied.

'Chadrick – status?'

'It seems to be holding off, I don't know why.'

I do, thought Astanger. *If it destroys the Lenin then we all die. The Grazen wants us alive to play with. I wonder how long–*

'Captain!' Chadrick shouted.

What now, some weapon he can't stop? Astanger knew that Chadrick must be in some distress to use the old politically incorrect title even if the Guard were down.

'What is it, Chadrick,' he said calmly.

'The moon ... look at the moon.'

What?

Astanger cleared the pursuing alien vessel from the viewing cylinder and trained the ship's scanners on the moon, and just stared in shock even though he had known there was something odd about that satellite. There was a line drawing across the surface, longitudinally. It flickered – an arrow-straight firestorm. On one side of the line was the surface he had earlier viewed, on the other side … on the other side was something else. He saw massive pylons, steel plains, and valleys cutting through either buildings or clustered monolithic machines, transmission or reception dishes the size of calderas, giant throats glimmering with lights and webworks of scaffold, ships bigger than anything he had ever seen gathered in frameworks like bullets in an ammunition clip. It was impossible to take in the vast complexity of it all. The moon was obviously some vast vessel or station.

Owner space?

Yeah, now he knew for certain why it remained so. Whoever had constructed this thing possessed more resources, more plain unadulterated power than entire civilizations.

But how did it affect them, right now, aboard the Lenin? It didn't. If they didn't get down to the surface of that planet soon they would be dead. Moon or otherwise.

'Keep your scanners focused on the Grazen, Chadrick,' said Astanger, then switching to general address, 'When we're down, I want someone to break open the weapons locker. We grab what we can and we get out – that ship will be on us in minutes.'

'What about … the Guard?' enquired Chadrick.

'What about them?'

'I … I don't know.'

'We ignore them.' Astanger took a steady breath. The G-forces were high now and it was becoming difficult to talk. 'Something's got to them … through their strouds … maybe some Grazen … viral weapon.'

115

The muted roar had now become a full-throated one. And the ship was shuddering around them. The Guard were probably irrelevant, since anyone not strapped in an acceleration chair when they began their descent was probably either dead now or suffering from multiple fractures. Maybe he and his crew should be merciful and kill them on the way out. No, they wouldn't have the time.

Blackout.

When consciousness began to fade back in, Astanger realized the roaring he could hear now was only from the engines. He felt the pressure rapidly dropping away from him, and judging by the pull of gravity the ship was coming down at a steep angle. This was going to be bad. The *Lenin* settled with an almighty crash and the drive cut out. Then with a creaking and groaning the ship toppled and slammed down flat on whatever it had landed on. The impact flung Astanger sideways in his chair, but the side-padding absorbed most of the shock. He was now sideways to the pull of gravity. Peering down to the bottom of the spin section he saw a tangle of bodies, blood, and some exposed broken bone where the Guard had ended up. Some of them had landed on Citizen Breen – Astrogation – but she seemed okay because she was pushing them away and unstrapping herself. She climbed through the tangled mass over to the spin section controls and hit the step motor button. The section shuddered and began to turn, and she walked round with it. Step by step it brought sets of acceleration chairs down to ground level, and the crew unstrapped. Astanger released himself from his chair last and eyed the bodies that had tumbled round like stones in a polisher. A few of them were still breathing. One was bubbling blood from her mouth and muttering.

'Okay, let's get out of here.'

116

Those from Engineering had broken open the weapons locker and, when Astanger arrived, were passing out carbines, sidearms and loading up two shoulder-held missile launchers.

'Should we get food?' enquired someone.

'No time,' Astanger replied.

The loading ramp was nearly underneath the ship, but its hydraulics managed to lift the cargo section enough for them to crawl out. Outside a pall of smoke obscured much, and in places the blackened ground was still burning. Checking a notescreen map and positional indicator, Astanger led the way towards the *Breznev*, and towards that house lay. After a few hundred yards, light penetrated – reflected from that awesome terrible moon as it breached the horizon – then a breeze began sweeping the pall aside to reveal a nightmare perhaps a mile to their left.

The Grazen ship.

The thing possessed no aerodynamics, no recognizable engine or drive section, nothing remotely resembling human technology. It was a loose tangle of metre-wide pipes, the colour of charred bone, nearly half a mile across. Within this tangle was a nacreous and vaguely spherical core. Some of the pipes, their mouths open to the air, were moving as if questing for the scent of something. Astanger had a fair idea what that might be.

'No – keep moving.' He slapped and engineering assistant on the back as the man raised, and aimed, a missile launcher at the ship. 'You'll only attract its attention.'

But what was 'it'? Was he talking about the ship itself or what it contained? He'd seen pictures of organic fragments from destroyed nests, but there were so many different kinds of those that no Collective Societal Asset had managed to put together an entire Grazen. He had little idea of what they actually looked like, how big they were, anything, really. The Collective described them as alien maggots – but that politically motivated

117

description, predicated on charred evidence gathered from the bombed nursery world, was not helpful.

'Keep moving.'

Surely, their luck could not hold for much longer.

It didn't.

A sound issued from the Grazen ship – the sighing groan of caves. Astanger glanced back at it and saw some of those pipes inclining towards the ground, coming together then levelling so he could see straight down their throats.

'You two! Hit that!' he shouted at the two carrying the missile launchers.

Both of them turned and went down on one knee, their shoulder launchers bucking. Something was coming down the pipes as the four missiles struck. Red fire bloomed, spraying bony fragments everywhere, but out of that flame a twiggy wheel two metres across rolled at speed towards them.

'Run!'

The thing seemed to hesitate for a moment, then it made its choice. It accelerated up behind one of those with a launcher and slammed down on the man. Astanger skidded to a halt then ran back to look down into a terrified face. Caged in the gnarled and jointed mass, the man struggled. Astanger had heard about this, the man would begin to scream in a moment, for spikes would soon begin easing into his flesh. He drew his sidearm and shot the man twice through the forehead – the only mercy possible. Then looking back towards the ship he saw its core now open and its pipe components snaking across the ground towards them – the whole mass disassembling and turning into a rolling avalanche of alien technology. And within that mass, commanding it, swept along with it, controlling it, came the Grazen itself. Obeying his own command, he turned and ran just as hard as he could.

Kelly guessed it didn't really matter what had happened. Though the Guard were completely out of it, the Doctrinaire still held a gun and she and her companions were still bound.

'Astanger! Report!' Shrad kept screaming into his communicator.

Any minute now, the situation would change. Either this Astanger would report or he wouldn't. Afterwards Doctrinaire Shrad would return his attention to his prisoners, and strouds no longer being an option, he would probably settle the matter with his gun. Kelly knew him. He represented everything she hated about the system she had tried to escape. He was also the one who had led them into the fight against the Grazen, in which many of her friends had died, and quite often because of his incompetence. She strained at her cuffs, but they were still hardened steel and unbreakable. Maybe if she could get to her feet she could kick the weapon out of his hand. Maybe the others…

She turned and looked at the other five. Elizabeth was down on her side, her head in her father's lap. Slome looked ill and anyway, he was old and fat and would probably be no help. That left Traviss and Longshank. Both of them were focused on the Doctrinaire. Kelly caught their attention and nodded her head towards Shrad. Longshank, who was closest, began to ease a leg forwards ready to hurl himself at the man. The sidearm abruptly whipped round, the barrel aimed straight at Longshank's forehead.

'I don't think so,' said Shrad. He lowered his communicator and clipped it back on his belt. Kelly felt herself deflate.

Shrad continued, 'Obviously the *Lenin* has encountered some difficulties.'

The man looked crazy, thought Kelly. No telling what he might do now.

'But difficulties aside you are all still criminals and betrayers of the Collective. Unfortunately it seems the strouds no longer function correctly.' Shrad gazed round at the Guard. Not one of them remained standing. Some were sitting, some sprawled and unmoving, some kneeling with their foreheads against the carpet. 'No matter – this is easily settled.' He focused his attention back on Longshank. 'For your crimes against the collective will, Daniel Longshank, I now excute sentence on you.'

Shrad pulled the trigger. A hollow thunk ensued and the Doctrinaire looked with puzzlement at his weapon. After a moment puzzlement turned to shock. He yelled and flung the weapon away. Tracking its course Kelly saw it bounce on the carpet and begin smoking, then with a multiple crack it exploded, flinging fragments in every direction.

Kelly began trying to get to her feet, then she noticed something: the Guard. Those of them obviously not dead, were now standing. She hadn't even seen them move.

'Citizen Guard One!' said Shrad with relief.

The one he addressed shook his head. 'No … I think … I was…' He gave a puzzled frown, looked to his fellows for a moment, then slowly returned his attention to Shrad. 'There are holes, but he tells me I can fill them. I remember now: my name is Evan … Evan Markovian.'

Markovian.

'Citizen Guard One!' said Shrad, backing up. 'Kill the prisoners! At once!'

Kelly settled back down, the certain knowledge of what would soon ensue igniting a warm glow in her chest.

'Why should I do that?' enquired the Evan – formerly Citizen Guard One.

'I order you to kill the prisoners!'

'No,' said Evan. He glanced to his fellows and from them received nods of approval. After a moment, he reached and pushed at one finger of his stroud with his thumb. The device lifted, and as if removing an irritating scab, he peeled it from his head.

'Do you know what's happening now?' Evan asked. Shrad could only shake his head mutely. Evan continued, 'Tens of thousands of the Guard, all armed and ready for the new assault on the Grazen, have suddenly found themselves.' He smiled. 'I can see the images in my head, and they are beautiful. I see them marching Doctrinaires to the airlocks of ships and expelling them into vacuum. I see them, on Capital World, lining them up to shoot them. Elsewhere, some have had the idea that sterilization is a better option, and yet others are using flamethrowers. And everywhere personal, painful and long drawn-out vengeances are being inflicted.' He paused contemplatively, gazing down at the stroud he held, then he discarded it. 'I think that last option is the one I want for you, Shrad.' He looked up. 'It's going to take you a long time to die.'

Shrad turned and ran.

Get him, get him now, thought Kelly, but the newly awakened Evan Markovian just watched Shrad's departure with amused contempt. Almost without thinking, she brought her hands forward to push herself upright, then stopped and stared in confusion at her wrists. Where were the cuffs? Glancing back she saw them lying in pieces on the carpet. No matter. She pushed herself to her feet, just as Longshank and Traviss were doing.

'Are you going to let him go?' she asked Evan. 'Because I'm not.'

The man still had that look on his face, but he was utterly motionless. Kelly walked over to him. Prodded his chest. He swayed but showed no other reaction. The other Guard were motionless too. What was going on here? Fuckit. She could not work this out right now. But whatever was happening she was not going to let that fucking Doctrinaire escape. She turned, scanning about her feet, then squatted down to pick up a carbine. She checked it over – just to be sure it still worked.

'This cannot be happening,' said Longshank.

What was the man on about?

A hand squeezed her shoulder. In annoyance, she turned, and then shock took over and she found herself dragging herself backwards.

'It's all right,' said the man who had named himself Mark, the man whose brains were all over the carpet nearby and who she'd subsequently seen shot four times in the chest. He turned to glance over at the others and she could see the occiput of his head was missing exposing a gory cavity the size of her fist.

'Conflicts outside my territory are usually of no interest to me, though I keep watch on them, just to be sure they don't come to represent a danger.'

Kelly stared at the back of his head, watching as the hole just filled up and closed. He turned back towards her, and she saw bright pinpricks of light flickering around him, both his eyes were in place, and red points advanced from deep inside to fill them out, turning them into something demonic. The man Mark seemed to be fading into the background, blurring, or perhaps another background was reaching out from somewhere to grab him back. Abruptly the figure before her came back into focus and was no longer Mark. This individual's hair was bone white over a thin face. His simple attire transformed into something more like the inside of a machine than clothing for a human being. Trying to focus on him, Kelly realized she was looking into something … else.

Around him, indefinable engines lurked at the limit of perception; gathered and poised like a planetoid moments before impact. Vast energies seemed to be focused upon this one man, like a mountain turned onto its tip.

The Owner – Kelly had not the slightest doubt now.

'But I don't like conflicts upon my border. I find them … disturbing.' He nailed her with viper eyes. 'This Collective you fled is one of the most unsavoury regimes I've seen in some time. It would have died, but meanwhile it was stirring up the Grazen, who represent an altogether a different danger.'

There was a coldness here – an indifference to human suffering. Yet, he had saved them. Why did he do that? Kelly suspected he had done so simply because the difference between saving them and not saving them was miniscule to him. She also felt he could annihilate them in a moment, at a whim.

'How can they be a danger to you?'

He paused contemplatively, then said, 'Human speech – I have to slow myself down so much for it, have to hone down a fragment of myself for its purpose. The word should not have been danger but inconvenience. They inconvenienced me once before. They call it 'the Misunderstanding'. It resulted in me losing the biosphere of one of my worlds.'

'What did they lose?'

'Half of their race … but that was long ago when I was more impulsive.'

Had he used the right words then?

'What about them?' Kelly pointed at the Guard.

'They are healing slowly – it's better to take them offline during the process. I used them to set Shrad running, just as I am using the rest of their kind to bring down the Collective.'

He talked about human beings as if they were components in a machine.

'Yes, Shrad,' said Kelly pointedly, gripping her weapon with more determination, but not yet ready to turn away from this being.

He looked at her as if he did not understand, then it seemed the penny dropped. 'I see, Shrad. You want to kill him.' He turned towards the shattered window. 'Walk with me.' Glancing at the others, he instructed, 'All of you.'

They stepped out of his house and began crossing the rose garden. His walking, she saw, seemed okay at a brief glance, but closer inspection revealed that his feet weren't touching the ground. Kelly strode at his side, the others attentive all around.

'My god,' Olsen suddenly exclaimed.

Kelly glanced at him and saw he was gazing up and to her left. She glanced there, taking in the starlit darkness and the rising moon. It took a moment for it to impinge what she had just seen and she looked again. That was no moon.

'My ship,' stated the Owner.

His ship. Fucking hell.

'I don't like problems close to home,' he went on. He glanced at Kelly and she thought: *He's more human now.* Perhaps he had refined that *fragment* he was using for communication.

'The Grazen are an inconvenience. A Grazen Mother who is grieving and half-mad could become something more than that, especially when she positions herself right on my border.'

124

'The one that's coming?' Kelly guessed.

'The one that is already here.'

His presence muted Kelly's sudden fear. 'Here?'

'Yes, here to find a cure for her ill, and a kind of justice.'

Abruptly, Slome interjected, 'Is vengeance a cure?'

The Owner gazed at him and Slome turned pale at what he saw, but the Owner nodded. 'Yes, for that mindset, and for the human mind too, though humans would like to deny their own nature.'

Vengeance?

Then Kelly understood.

Leaning against the trunk of a gnarled olive tree Astanger caught his breath and gazed in horror at the thing poised on the slope below them. So this was a Grazen. He saw a giant crayfish head from which extended many wiry tendrils, many of them spearing away to connect into the writhing tangle of pipe-things, whose black-etched moon-shadows now surrounded him and his crew. Unlike a crayfish, it did not seem to possess a jointed exoskeleton, but a slick and tough-looking red and brown skin. At the extremities of the multiple limbs arrayed down its long body it possessed things like hands, or feet, with digits arrayed in rows under flat pads. Its tail was not a flat fish tail, but a long rattish thing coiled around its already coiled body. And the Grazen was the size of a space shuttle.

It had stopped, why had it stopped? Was it toying with them now?

'What do we do now?' asked one of the crew.

Astanger wanted to reply, *We die, probably very slowly,* but didn't think that would help much. He gazed down at the sidearm he clutched and wondered if it would be best to use it on himself now, or to wait until the monster sent one of those twiggy things for him.

Movement behind.

He looked upslope and saw the pipe-things withdrawing into the surrounding trees. Did it want them to run again? Had the chase thus far not been satisfying enough for it? Then he saw the figure hurtling towards them down the moon-silvered grass, and after a moment recognized the Doctrinaire. Obviously, things had gone badly at the house – perhaps the Guard with Shrad had collapsed like those aboard the Lenin. Shrad must have used the tracer on Astanger's communicator, and had come here because he thought he would be safe. Astanger felt like laughing, but knew it would come out hysterical.

When he saw what was waiting, beyond Astanger and the crew, Shrad came to an abrupt halt.

'Astanger! This way!' Shrad gestured imperiously.

Astanger just rested against his tree watching the pipes moving in quietly behind the Doctrinaire. It was a small satisfaction to know that the man would be suffering a similar fate to them all.

'Come on!'

He started to gesture again, but then must have heard something. Turning, he saw one of the pipes rising up behind him, throated darkness bearing down on him. He fell back to the ground and scrambled downslope, managed to gain his feet and break into a run. The pipe, like a confident python, came down and slowly writhed after him, then halted ten yards out from the first of the crewmen. Shrad kept running until he was up beside Astanger. Horrified, he stared downslope at the Grazen, then he turned on Astanger.

'What the hell do you think you are doing Citizen Astanger! You should've warned me! You should've run!'

Shrad's holster was empty. Astanger gazed his crew, at Breen, Chadrick, Grade and others who now gathered round. He read the contempt and hatred they felt for the Doctrinaire. Transferring his gaze to his own weapon, he swung it to one side in a leisurely motion then brought it back hard across Shrad's face. The man went down and lay moaning, clutching at his cheek.

'He's unarmed,' said Astanger to the others. 'Instruct the others not to give him a weapon and not to give him a bullet when the time comes.'

'Astanger!' Shrad was glaring at him from the ground.

In measured tones, Astanger said, 'If you speak to me again I will shoot you in the kneecap.' He returned his attention to the alien.

The Grazen seemed to be agitated – if he was interpreting correctly its jerky movements and the way it was reaching out with its insectile hands to touch the surrounding tangle. It had deliberately made a gap to let Shrad through, to get them all together in one place, so why was it not now attacking? Was it waiting for others to come this way? How likely was that? The Guard were screwed, so it seemed unlikely to him that they would be coming after Shrad. Maybe the escapees, since their ship lay beyond the Grazen?

The ground shuddered and someone swore. What now? Astanger looked to where many of the crew were now gazing, as the shuddering of the ground increased. The moon was on the move, the glare of some titanic drive behind it. Slowly it shifted from its location above the horizon, and grew visibly brighter. Astanger had no doubt it was moving into a position overhead.

'Please, you must listen to me, Astanger,' said Shrad.

The man was crouching, desperate-looking. He hadn't even noticed what was happening in the sky – it probably didn't fit his ideology.

'Do go on,' said Astanger, almost too stunned to care anymore.

'If we make a concerted attack on the creature itself it'll lose control of those … things. We should be able to fight our way through – get to the ship.'

Astanger considered that. They'd fired eight missiles at the creature and every one of those eight missiles had impacted on opalescent shields that abruptly sprang into being. Bullets just bounced off the thing. Missiles into the tangle of pipework had shattered it, but the pipes just discarded the shattered sections, melded back together and carried on. Now they were all out of missiles and had depleted the rest of their ammunition. He'd seen the others passing bullets to those who had run out. The bullets weren't for the Grazen. Astanger had four bullets left in his sidearm. He could spare one. He raised his weapon and fired once. Shrad went down yelling, clutching the mess of bone and blood that had been his kneecap. Astanger returned his attention to the alien.

Why was it holding back? Did it understand that its prey would suicide when it made its final assault? Was it trying to figure out a way of capturing them alive?

'Captain Astanger,' said Grade – no longer worried about using a politically incorrect form of address.

Astanger turned to see the man pointing upslope. Looking there, he saw a group of people approaching. He recognized greywear, then after a moment recognized some of the escapees. There was one other with them – something odd about him. Two of the pipe things reared back and the group passed between. Now Astanger could see the other individual

128

more clearly. He seemed to be walking in a kind of hollow in the air and around him, metallic things seemed to hover on the edge of visibility. Pale, white hair, eyes that seemed to open into the Pit. Astanger knew at once who this person must be.

The group arrived, the escapees warily watching the crewmen, who moved aside. Finally, they reached Astanger. The Owner glanced down at Shrad, then raised his gaze to Astanger.

'*Captain* Astanger,' he said, then his mouth twisted in a cruel smile.

The moon now glared overhead, and the shuddering of the ground became a muted vibration, like the running of some vast engine, and one Astanger knew was shaking this whole world. That inconceivably gigantic vessel up there was his. Astanger was glad when the … man turned his attention towards the Grazen.

'The Mother,' the Owner intoned.

Astanger looked in that direction too and to his horror saw that the Grazen was lining up some of those tube mouths, and that in them he glimpsed twiggy insectile movement. He stepped back, brought his sidearm up to his chest.

'That won't be necessary, *Captain*.'

Yeah, right.

One of the things spat out, rolled along the ground towards them, its pace leisurely. Astanger stepped back again, heard the sounds of weapons being cocked. The twiggy wheel slowed to a halt over Shrad. Folded down into a kind of leggy cone.

'Astanger!' Shrad screamed.

It hesitated, wavering back and forth. The Owner gestured, and then the thing fell on the Doctrinaire. Shrad began yelling incoherently. Astanger gazed down at him without

129

sympathy, then abruptly jerked his head up as the pipe that had fired the thing began to snake across the ground towards them. Now Shrad began screaming. The twigwork was extruding spikes like clawed fingers and slowly easing them into the man's flesh. He was struggling, but thus encaged had nowhere to go. Astanger noted that the wounds did not bleed. He guessed that would be too easy.

The pipe reached Shrad and fibres speared out, glimmering like spider silk in the moonlight, from the seething multi-jawed face of something inside. The fibres attached all around the cage, dragged Shrad in. His screams disappeared up inside the pipe, becoming hollow and echoey.

'He ordered the bombing of the nursery world,' one of the escapees said.

Astanger glanced at her, recognized Kelly Haden. Then he understood the implication of what she was saying. *The Mother*, he realized.

But it wasn't over. The other pipe-mouths were still there with those things still inside and ready to roll. Astanger was all too aware that though he personally did not take part in the bombing of the nursery world, he was part of the fleet that did, and if he had been ordered to take part, he would have. The things began to ease out.

'It's been the best it could be,' said Grade. The man brought his carbine up underneath his chin and pulled the trigger. Nothing happened.

The Owner glanced at him. 'Hasty,' he said, then returned his attention to the Grazen Mother. 'Must I destroy you?'

Around him, the metallic objects seemed to gain a greater solidity. He held out a hand to one side almost in sad

130

entreaty. Astanger whinced. It felt almost as if he was standing too close to a fire, yet what he was feeling was not exactly heat.

'Withdraw, now,' said the Owner.

Like the heads of tubeworms, the twiggy wheels abruptly retracted out of sight. Movement all around. The pipes were all pulling back towards the Grazen and she began retreating downslope. She, and all her weird technology gathered into a rolling wave falling away from them, then it all began to clump around her, opalescent shields flicking on in intervening spaces, gradually blotting her from sight. With a thrum that transmitted through the ground the whole mass began to rise, then with a sighing groan, it shot up into the sky.

'Thank you,' said Astanger.

The Owner held out a hand for silence, stillness, as he still gazed up into the sky. After about a minute, he returned his attention to them all.

'These,' he gestured to the escapees, 'you will not harm. Their ship is now fully functional and you will all return on it.' He paused for a contemplative moment. 'Your Collective is collapsing. At my request the Grazen will not attack what remains.'

'I have no love of the Collective,' said Astanger.

The Owner nodded, and Astanger reckoned he had no need to say that for it was probably why he was still alive. He noted that though the ... machines around the Owner were now plainly visible, he and they seemed to occupy some encystment in reality, something excised.

The Owner said, 'Leave now. You have one day to get beyond my border.'

A star of darkness flickered within that encystment, and all it contained seemed to be stretching away. Astanger knew that somehow it connected to that vessel hovering above them like the steel eye of some vast god.

'Build something better this time – you have been warned,' the Owner told them.

The encystment retracted into the star, disappeared.

Astanger guessed it was the best they could hope for.

'Well, Societal Assets,' said Astanger to the escapees, 'we'd best find the rest of your people and get out of here.'

'Fuck you,' said Kelly Haden. 'I'm not a 'Societal Asset' and I don't take orders from you!'

Astanger held up his sidearm, reversed it and held the butt out to her. 'Then you must choose who you do take orders from, or choose to give them yourself.'

Really, it was the best they could hope for.

ENDS

STROOD

Like a Greek harp standing four metres tall and three wide, its centre-curtain body rippling in some unseen wind, the strood shimmered across the heath land, tendrils groping for me, their stinging pods shiny and bloated. Its voice was the sound of some bedlam ghost in a big empty house: muttering then bellowing guttural nonsense. Almost instinctively, I ran towards the nearest pathun – the monster close behind me. The pathun's curiol matrix reacted with a nacreous flash, displacing us both into a holding cell. I was burnt – red skin visible through holes in my shirt – but whether that injury was from the strood or the pathun I don't know. The strood, its own curiol matrix cut by that of the pathun's, lay nearby like a pile of bloody seaweed. I stared about myself at the ten by ten box with its floor littered with stones, bones and pieces of carapace. I really wanted to cry.

'Love! Eat you! Eat you! Pain!'

It could have been another of those damned translator problems. The gilst – slapped onto the base of my skull and growing its spines into my brain with agonising precision – made the latest Pentium Synaptic look like an abacus with most of its beads missing. Unfortunately, with us humans, the gilst is a lot brighter than its host. Mine initially loaded all English on the assumption that I knew the whole of that language, and translating something from say, a pathun, produced stuff from all sorts of obscure vocabularies: scientific, philosophic, sociological, political. All of them. What had that dyspeptic newt with its five ruby eyes and exterior mobile intestine said to me shortly after my arrival?

'Translocate fifteen degrees sub-axial to hemispherical concrescence of poly-carbon interface.'

133

I'd asked where the orientating machine was, and it could have pointed to the lump on the nearby wall and said, 'Over there.'

After forty-six hours in the space station, I was managing, by the feedback techniques that load into your mind like an instruction manual the moment the spines begin to dig in, to limit the gilst's vocabulary to my feeble one, and thought I'd got a handle on it, until my encounter with the strood. I'd even managed to stop it translating, what the occasional patronising mugull would ask me every time I stopped to gape at some extraordinary sight, as 'Is one's discombobulation requiring pellucidity?' I knew the words but couldn't shake the feeling that either the translator or the mugull was taking the piss. All not too good when I really had no time to spare for being lost on the station – I wanted to see so much before I died.

The odds of survival, before the pathun lander set down on the Antarctic, had been one in ten surviving for more than five years. My lung cancer, lodged in both lungs, considerably reduced those odds for me. By the time pathun technology started filtering out, my cancer had metastized, sending out scouts to inspect other real estate in my body. And when I finally began to receive any benefits of that technology, my cancer had established a burgeoning population in my liver and colonies in other places too numerous to mention.

'We cannot help you,' the mugull doctor told me, as it floated a metre off the ground in the pathun hospital on the Isle of Wight. Hospitals like this one were springing up all over Earth like Medicins Sans Frontieres establishments in some Third World backwater, and they were mostly run by mugulls meticulously explaining to our witchdoctors where they were going wrong. To the more worshipful of the population, the name 'mugull' was wrong for, 'alien angels like translucent

134

mantis rays'. But the contraction of 'mucus gull' that became their name, is more apposite for the majority, and their patronising attitude comes hard from something that looks like a floating sheet of veined snot with two beaks, black button eyes, and a transparent nematode body smelling of burning bacon.

'Pardon?' I couldn't believe what I was hearing: they were miracle workers who had crossed mind-numbing distances to come here to employ their magical technologies. This mugull explained it to me in perfect English, without a translator. It, and others like it, had managed to create those nanofactories that sat in the liver pumping out DNA repair nanomachines. Now this was okay if you got your nactor before your DNA was damaged. It meant eternal youth, so long as you avoided stepping in front of a truck. But for me there was just too much damage already, so my nactor couldn't distinguish patient from disease.

'But ... you will be able to cure me?' I still couldn't quite take it in.

'No.' A flat reply. And with that, I began to understand, and began to put together facts I had thus far chosen to ignore.

People were still dying in huge numbers all across Earth and the alien doctors had to prioritise. In Britain, their main targets were the wonderful bugs tenderly nurtured by our national health system to be resistant to just about every antibiotic going. In fact, the mugulls had some problems getting people into their hospitals in the British Isles, because over the last decade hospitals had become more dangerous to the sick than anywhere else. Go in to have an ingrown toenail removed; MRSA or a variant later, and you're down the road in a hermetically sealed plastic coffin. However, most alien resources were going into the same countries as Frontieres' went: to battle a daily death rate, numbered in tens of thousands, from new air-transmitted HIVs, rampant ebola, and that new tuberculosis that can eat your lungs in about four days. And I don't know if they are winning.

'Please … you've got to help me.'

No good. I knew the statistics and, like so many, had been an avid student of all things alien ever since their arrival. Even stopping to talk to me as its curiol matrix wafted it from research ward to ward, the mugull might be sacrificing other lives. Resources again. They had down to an art what our own crippled health service had not been able to apply in fact without outcry: if three people have a terminal disease and you have the resources to save only two of them, that's what you do, you don't fudge it in an attempt to save them all. This mugull, applying all its skill and available technologies, could certainly save me, it could take my body apart and rebuild it cell by cell if necessary, but meanwhile, ten, twenty, a thousand other people with less serious, but no less terminal conditions, would die.

'Here is your ticket,' it said, and something spat out of its curiol matrix to land on my bed as it wafted away.

I stared down at the yellow ten-centimetre disk. Thousands of these had been issued and governments had tried to control whom to, and why. Mattered not a damn to any of the aliens; they gave them to those they considered fit, and only the people they were intended for could use them … to travel offworld. I guess it was my consolation prize.

A mugull autosurgeon implanted a cybernetic assister frame. This enabled me to get out of bed and head for the shuttle platform moored off the Kent coast. There wasn't any pain at first, as the surgeon had used a nerve-block that took its time to wear off, but I felt about as together as rotten lace. As that did wear off, I went back onto my inhalers, and patches where the bone cancer was worst, and a cornucopia of pills.

On the shuttle, which basically looked like a train carriage, I attempted to concentrate on some of the alien identification charts I'd loaded into my notescreen, but the nagging pain and perpetual weariness made it difficult for me to concentrate. There was an odd a mix of people around me as you'll find on any aircraft: some woman with a baby in a papoose; couple of suited heavies who could have been government, Mafia, or stockbrokers; and others. Just ahead of me was a group of two women and three men who, with plummy voices and scruffy bordering on punk clothing – that upper middle class lefty look favoured by most students – had to be the BBC documentary team I'd heard about. They confirmed this for me when one of the men removed a prominently labelled vidcam to film the non-human passengers. These were two mugulls and a pathun – the latter a creature like a two-metre woodlouse, front section folded upright with a massively complex head capable of revolving three-sixty, and a flat back onto which a second row of multiple limbs folded. As far as tool using went, nature had provided pathuns with a work surface, clamping hands with the strength of a hydraulic vice, and other hands with digits fine as hairs. The guy with the vidcam lowered it after a while and turned to look around. Then he focused on me.

'Hi, I'm Nigel,' he held out a hand, which I reluctantly shook. 'What are you up for?'

I considered telling him to mind his own business, but then thought I could do with all the help I could get. 'I'm going to the system base to die.'

Within seconds, Nigel had his vidcam in my face, and one of his companions, Julia, had exchanged places with the passenger in the seat adjacent to me, and was pumping me with ersatz sincerity about how it felt to be dying, then attempting to stir some shit about the mugulls being unable to treat me on Earth. The interview lasted nearly an hour, and I knew they would cut and shape it to say whatever they wanted it to say.

When it was over, I returned my attention to the pathun, who I was sure had turned its head slightly to watch and listen in, though why I couldn't imagine. Perhaps it was interested in the primitive equipment the crew used. Apparently, one of these HG (heavy gravity) creatures, whilst being shown around Silicon Valley, accidentally rested its full weight on someone's laptop computer – think about dropping a barbell on a matchbox and you get the idea – then, without tools, repaired it in under an hour. And as if that wasn't miraculous enough, the computer's owner then discovered its hard disk storage had risen from four hundred gigabytes to four terabytes. I would have said the story was apocryphal, but the laptop is now in the Smithsonian.

The shuttle docked at Eulogy Station and the pathun disembarked first, which is just the way it is. Equality is okay, all things being equal; reality is that they've been knocking around the galaxy for half a million years. Pathuns are as far in advance of the other aliens as we are in advance of jellyfish, which makes you wonder where humans come on their scale. As the alien went past me heading for the door I felt the slight air shift caused by its curiol matrix – that technology enabling other aliens like mugulls, creatures whose home environment is an interstellar gas cloud not far above absolute zero, to live on the surface of Earth and easily manipulate their surroundings. Call it a force field, but it's much more than that. Another story about pathuns demonstrates some of what they can do with their curiol matrices.

All sorts of religious fanatic lunatic idiotic groups immediately, of course, considered superior aliens the cause of their woes, and valid targets. Only a week into the first alien walkabout, therefore, did the first suicide bomber tried to take out a pathun amid a crowd. He detonated his device, but an invisible cylinder enclosed him and the plastique slow-burned – not a pretty sight. Other assassination attempts met with various suitable responses. The sharp shooter with his scoped rifle got the bullet he fired back through the scope and into his head. The bomber in Spain just disappeared along with his car, only to reappear, still behind the wheel, travelling at Mach four down on top of the farmhouse his fellow Basque terrorists had made their base. Thereafter attempts started to drop off, not because of any reduction in terrorist lunacy, but because of a huge increase in security when a balek (those floating LGAs that look like great big apple cores) off-handedly mentioned what incredibly restraint the pathuns – beings capable of translocating planet Earth into its own sun – were showing.

From Eulogy Station it was then, in alien and my own terms, just a short step to the system base. The gate was just a big ring in one of the plazas of Eulogy, and you just stepped through it and you were there. The base, a giant stack of different-sized disks nine hundred and forty kilometres from top to bottom, orbited Jupiter. After translocating from some system eighty light-years away to our Oort cloud, it had travelled to here at half the speed of light whilst the contact ships headed to Earth. Apparently, we had been ripe for contact: bright enough to understand what was happening, but stupid enough for our civilization not to end up imploding when confronted by such omnipotence.

In the system base, I began to find my way around, guided by an orientation download to my notescreen, and it was only then that I began to notice stroods everywhere. I had only seen pictures before, and as far as I knew, none had ever been to Earth. But why were there so many thousands here, now? Then,

139

of course, I allowed myself a hollow laugh. What the hell did it matter to me? Still, I asked Julia and Nigel when I ran into them again.

'According to our researcher, they're pretty low on the species scale and only space faring because of pathun intervention.' Julia studied her notescreen – uncomfortable being the interviewee. Nigel was leaning over the rail behind her, filming down an immense metallic slope on which large limpetlike creatures clung sleeping in their thousands: stroods in their somnolent form.

Julia continued, 'Some of the other races regard stroods as pathun pets, but then we're not regarded much higher by many of them.'

'But why so many thousands here?' I asked.

Angrily she gestured at the slope. 'I've asked, and every time I've been told to go and ask the pathuns. They ignore us, you know – far too busy about their important tasks.'

I resisted the impulse to point out that creatures capable of crossing the galaxy perhaps did not rank the endless creation of media pap very high. I succumbed then to one more 'brief' interview before managing to slip away and then, losing my way to my designated hotel, ended up in one of the parks, aware that a strood was following me.

Sitting in the holding cell I eyed the monster and hoped its curiol matrix wouldn't start up again as in here I had nowhere to run and, being the contacted species, no curiol matrix of my own. The environment of a system station is that of the system species, us, so we didn't need the matrix for survival, and anyway, you don't give the kiddies sharp objects right away. I was beginning to wonder if maybe running at that pathun had been such a bright idea, when I was abruptly translocated again, and found myself stumbling into the lobby of an apparently ordinary looking hotel. I did a double take, then turned round and walked out through the revolving doors and looked around. Yep, an apparently normal city street, but for the aliens on the road and in the air, and but for Jupiter in the sky. This was the area I'd been trying to find before my confrontation with the strood: the human section, a nice base for us so we wouldn't get too confused or frightened. I went back into the hotel, limping a bit now, despite the assister frame, and wheezing because I'd lost my inhaler, and the patches and pills were beginning to wear off.

'David Hall,' I said at the front desk. 'I have a reservation.'

The automaton dipped its polished chrome ant's head and eyed my damaged clothing, then it checked its screen, and after a moment it handed, or rather clawed, over a key card. I headed for the elevator and soon found myself in the kind of room I'd never been able to afford on Earth, my luggage already stacked beside my bed, and a welcome pack on a nearby table. I opened the half bottle of Champagne and began chugging it down as I walked out onto the balcony. Now what?

Prior to my brief exchange with the mugull doctor, I'd been told my life expectancy was about four weeks but that, 'I'm sure the aliens will be able to do something!' Well they had. The drugs and the assister frame enabled me to actually move about and take some pleasure in my remaining existence. The time limit, unfortunately, had not changed. So, I would see as much of this miraculous place as possible … but I'd avoid that damned park. I thought then about what had happened.

The park was fifteen kilometres across, with Earthly meadows, and forests of cycads like purple pineapples tall as trees. Aliens were everywhere, a lot of them strood. And one, which I was sure had been following me before freezing and standing like a monument in a field of daisies, started drifting towards me. I stepped politely aside, but it followed me and started making strange moaning sounds. I got scared then, but controlled myself, and stood still when it reached one of its tendrils out to me. Maybe it was just saying hello. The stinging cells clacked like maracas and my arm felt as if someone had whipped it, before turning numb as a brick. The monster started shaking then as if this had got it all excited.

'Eat you!'

Damned thing. I don't mind being the primitive poor relation, but not the main course.

I turned round and went back into my room, opened my suitcase, found my spare inhaler and patches and headed for the bathroom. An hour later, I was clean, and the pain in body had receded to a distant ache I attempted to drive farther away with the contents of the minibar. I slept for the usual three hours, woke feeling sick, out of breath, and once again in pain. A few pulls from one inhaler opened up my lungs, and the other inhaler took away the feeling that someone was sandpapering the inside of my chest, then more pills gave me a further two hours sleep, and that I knew was my lot.

I dressed, buttoning up my shirt whilst standing on the balcony watching the street. No day or night here, just the changing face of Jupiter in an orange-blue sky. Standing there, gazing at the orb, I decided I must have got it all wrong somehow. The aliens had only ever killed humans in self-defence so somehow there had been a misunderstanding. Maybe, with the strood being pathun 'pets', what had happened had been no more than someone being snapped at by a terrier in a park. I truly believed this. But that didn't stop me suddenly feeling very scared when I heard that same bedlam ghost muttering and bellowing along below. I stared down and saw the strood – it had to be the same one – rippling across the street and pausing there. I was sure it was looking up at me, though it had no eyes.

The strood was still waiting as I peered out of the hotel lobby. For a second I wished I'd had a gun or some other weapon to hand, but that would only have made me feel better, not be any safer. I went back inside and walked up to the automaton behind the hotel desk.

Without any ado I said, 'I was translocated here from a holding cell, to which I was translocated after running straight into a pathun's personal space.'

'Yes,' it replied.

'This happened because I was running away from a strood that wants to eat me.'

'Yes,' it replied.

'Who must I inform about this ... assault?'

'If your attack upon the pathun had been deliberate you would not have been released from the holding cell,' it buzzed at me.

'I'm talking about the strood's assault on me.'

Glancing aside, I saw that the creature was now looming outside the revolving doors. They were probably all that was preventing it entering the hotel. I could hear it moaning.

'Strood do not attack other creatures.'

'It stung me!'

'Yes.'

'It wants to eat me!'

'Yes.'

'It said "eat you, eat you",' I said before I realized what the automaton had just said. 'Yes!' I squeaked.

'Not enough to feed strood, here,' the automaton told me. 'Though Earth will be a good feeding ground for them.'

I thought of the thousands of these creatures I had seen here. No, I just didn't believe this. My skin began to crawl as I heard the revolving doors turning, all of them.

'Please summon help,' I said.

'None is required.' The insectile head swung towards the strood. 'Though you are making it ill, you know.'

Right then I think my adrenaline ran down, because suddenly I was hurting more than usual. I turned with my back against the desk to see the strood coming towards me across the lobby. It seemed somehow ragged to me, disreputable, tatty. The pictures of these I'd seen showed larger and more glittering creatures.

'What do you want with me?'

'Eat … need … eat,' were the only words I could discern from the muttering bellow. I pushed away from the desk and set out in a stumbling run for the lift. No way was I going to be able to manage the stairs. I hit the button just as the strood surged after me. Yeah, great, and how did he die? Waiting for a lift. It reached me just as the doors opened behind. One of its stinging tendrils caught me across the chest, knocking me back into the lift. This seemed to confuse the creature, and it held back long enough for the doors to close. My chest grew numb and breathing difficult as I stabbed buttons, then the lift lurched into progress, and I collapsed to the floor.

'Technical Acquisitions' was a huge disc-shaped building like the bridge of the star ship *Enterprise* mounted on top of a squat skyscraper. Nigel kept Julia, Lincoln and myself constantly in camera, while Pierce kept panning across and up and down – getting as much of our surroundings as possible. I'd learnt that quantity was what they were aiming for; all the artwork was carried out on computer afterwards. Pierce, an Asian woman

144

with rings through her lip connected by a chain to rings through her ear, and a blockish stud through her tongue, was the one who suggested it, and Julia immediately loved the idea. I was just glad, after Julia and Nigel dragged me out of the lift, of the roof taxi to get me out of the hotel without my having to go through the lobby. Of course, none of them took seriously my story about stroods wanting to eat people; they were just excited about the chance of some real in your face documentary making.

'Dawson's got a direct line to the head honchos here in the system station,' Lincoln explained to me. For 'head honchos' read pathuns, who, after their initial show and tell on Earth, took no interest in the consequent political furore. They were physicists, engineers, biologists, and pursued their own interests to the exclusion of all else. It drove human politicians nuts that the ones, who had the power to convert Earth into a swiftly dispersing smoke cloud, might spend hours watching a slug devouring a cabbage leaf, but have no time to spare to discuss *issues* with the President or Prime Minister. Human scientists though, were a different matter, for pathuns definitely leant towards didacticism. I guess it all comes down to the fact that modern politicians don't really change very much, and that the inventor of the vacuum cleaner changed more people's lives than any number of Thatchers or Blairs. Dawson was the chief of the team of human scientists aboard the system base, learning at the numerous feet of the pathuns.

'We get to him, and we should be able to get a statement from one of the pathuns – he's their blue-eyed boy and they let him get up to all sorts of stuff,' Lincoln continued. 'According to our researchers he's even allowed access to curiol matrix tech.'

In the lobby of the building Lincoln shmoozed the insectile receptionist with his spiel about the documentary he was doing for the Einstein channel, then spoke to a bearded individual on a large phone screen. I recognized Dawson right away because my viewing had always leant towards that channel Lincoln and Julia had denigrated on our way here. He was a short plump individual with a big grey beard, grey hair, and very odd-looking orangish eyes. He's the kind of physicist who pisses off many of his fellows by being better at pure research than they, and being able to turn his research to practical and profitable ends. Whilst many of them had walked away from CERN with wonderfully obscure papers to their names, he'd walked away with the same, and a very real contribution to make to quantum computing. I didn't hear the conversation, but I was interested to see Dawson gazing past Lincoln's shoulder directly at me, before giving the go-ahead for us to come up.

How to describe the inside of the disk? Computers and big plasma screens stood on rows of benches while machine tools were everywhere. People were gutting alien technology, scanning circuit boards under electron microscopes, running mass spectrometer tests on fragments of exotic metal. Macrotech that looked right out of CERN loomed here and there, while other people were walking, talking, waving light pens. The place had an air of industry and excitement. On Earth, a lot of alien technology was knocking about, and a lot of it turned to smoking goo the moment anyone tried to open it up. It's not that they don't want us to learn; it's just that they don't want us to depopulate the planet in the process. Here, though, things were different: under direct pathun supervision, the scientists and technicians were having a great time.

Lincoln and Julia began by asking Dawson for an overview on everything that he and his people were working on. My interest was held for a while as he described materials light

146

as polystyrene and tough as steel, a micro tome capable of slicing diamonds, and nanotech self-repairing computer chips, but after a while I began to feel really sick, and without my assister frame I'd have been on the floor. Finally, he was standing before pillars with hooked over tops, gesturing at something subliminal between them. When I realized he was talking about curiol matrices, my interest perked up, but it was then that Lincoln and Julia went in for the kill.

'So, obviously the pathuns trust you implicitly, or are you treated like a strood?' asked Julia.

I stared at the subliminal flicker, and through it to the other side of the room, where it seemed a workbench was sneaking away while no one was watching, until I realized I was seeing a pathun sauntering across, all sorts of equipment on its back.

'Strood?' Dawson asked.

'Yes, their pets,' interjected Lincoln. 'Ones whose particularly carnivorous tastes the pathuns seem to be pandering to.'

I tracked the pathun past the pillars to a big equipment lift. Took a couple of pulls on one of my inhalers – not sure which one, but it seemed to help. I thought I was imagining the bedlam moaning. Everything seemed to be getting a little fuzzy around the edges.

'Pets?' said Dawson, staring at Lincoln, as if he'd just discovered a heretofore-undiscovered variety of idiot.

'But then I suppose it's alright,' said Julia, 'if the kind of people fed to them are going to die anyway.'

Dawson shook his head then said, 'I was curious to see what your angle would be – that's why I let you come up.' Now he turned to me. 'Running into a pathun's curiol matrix wasn't the best idea – it reacted to you rather than the strood.'

147

It came up on the equipment lift, shimmering and flowing out before the observing pathun. Now now Fido. Came round the room towards me. There were benches to my left, so the quickest escape route for me was ahead and left to the normal lifts. I hardly comprehended what Dawson was saying. You see, it's all right to be brave and sensible when you're whole and nothing hurts, but when you live with pain shadowing your every step, and the big guy with the scythe just around the corner, your perspective changes.

'It bonded and you broke away,' he said. 'Didn't you study your orientation? Can't you see it's in love?'

I ran, and slammed straight into an invisible web between the two pillars – a curiol matrix Dawson had been studying. Energies shorted in through my assister frame, and something almost alive connected to my gilst and into my brain. Exoskeletal energy, huge frames of reference, translocation, reality displayed as formulae, and me with a pencil and rubber. There is no adequate description. Panicked, I just saw where I didn't want to be, and strove to put myself somewhere else. The huge system base opened around me, up and down in lines and surfaces and intersection points. Twisting them into a new pattern, I put myself on the roof of the world. My curiol retained air around me, retained heat, but did not defend me from harsh and beautiful reality, it in fact amplified perception. Standing on the steel plain I saw that Jupiter was truly vast but finite, and that through vacuum the stars did not waver, and that there was no way to deny the depths they burned in. I gasped, twisted to a new pattern, found myself tumbling through a massive swarm of mugulls, curiols reacting all around me and hurling me out.

It's in love.

Something snatched me down and, sprawled on an icy platform, I observed a pathun, linked in ways I could not quite comprehend to vast machines rearing around me to forge energies of creation. The curiol gave me a glimpse of what it meant to have been in a technical civilization for more than half a million years. Then I understood about huge restraint. And amusement. The pathun did something then. Its merest touch shook blocks of logic into order, and something went click in my head.

Eat you! Eat you!

Of course everything I had been told was the truth. No translator problem; just an existential one. What need did pathuns have for lies? I folded away from the platform and stumbled out from the other side of the pillars, shedding the curiol behind me. Momentarily doubt nearly had be stepping back into the matrix as the strood flowed round and reared up before me: a raggety and bloody curtain.

'Eat,' I said.

The strood surged forwards, stinging cells clacking. The pain was mercifully brief as the creature engulfed me, and the black tide swamped me to the sound of Julia shouting, 'Are you getting this! Are you getting this!'

Three days passed, I think, then I woke in a field of daisies. I was about six kilos lighter, which was unsurprising. One of those kilos was pieces of the cybernetic assister frame scattered in the grass all around me. Nearby the strood stood tall and glittering in artificial sunlight: grown strong on the cancer it had first fallen in love with then eaten out of my body, as was its nature. It's like pilot fish eating the parasites of bigger fish – that kind of existence: mutualism. I had been sent as a kind of test case, by the mugulls who were struggling with human sickness, and after me, the go-ahead was given. The strood are now flocking in their thousands to Earth: come to dine on our diseases.

ENDS

THE OTHER GUN

As the bathysphere landed I fought to regain my humanity, even though my latest communication with the Client had been some hours ago. Talking to that entity was always a bizarre and confusing experience, and one I never wanted to get used to. Every time, afterwards, I felt like a new occupant of my old and battered body. I blinked, remembering the lack of eyelids, held up my hand to clench and unclench it and remembered a lack of fingers, or at least fingers like these, then, with the bathysphere settling, reached out and pressed a thumb against the door control.

The twenty foot wide circular door thumped away from me, releasing from its seals to allow in a waft of vapour and a smell like rotting vegetables, turned its inner locking ring to unlock then slowly hinged down, first exposing a yellow sky bruised with brown clouds.

'Don't take anything for granted,' I said to my companion.

'I never do,' sighed Harriet, her voice as always surprisingly gentle from such a large mouth full of so many teeth.

I glanced at her and wondered how the people of this colony would react to her. Harriet was a Mesozoic era dinosaur, a troodon in the style of those dinosaurs from one of the paleo-history fashions when feathers were out and colourful skin was back in. She was jade on her upper surfaces, mustard yellow below and her back mackerel patterned with hints of navy blue. To add to her gaudy appearance, she had painted her claws gold, wore a variety of silver and gold bangles, and neck rings. It gladdened me that in recent years she'd lost interest in applying eye-shadow. She now stood up on her toes and extended her long neck to raise her sharp reptilian head, which was first at a level with mine, to peer over the door at the landscape lying beyond, and blinked bright slot-pupil eyes.

'Tasty,' she said, which was often her response to heavily muscled humans. She then clicked her fore-claws in frustration and ducked back down. This probably meant the humans concerned were armed.

The door finally came down to rest on boggy ground mounded with heather-like plants and nodular mosses, stabbed through here and there with black reeds. The colony raft sat about a mile beyond, a structure a mile wide and bearing some resemblance to an ancient aircraft carrier. Members of the Frobishers, who were the family I had come to trade with, stood between the bathysphere door and the vehicle they'd come over in – a swamp car with cage wheels. Four heavies clad in quilted body suits and rain capes stood out there, three of them carrying light laser carbines and a fourth holding something that looked suspiciously like a proton weapon. Before these stood a woman, clad much the same as them but studying an ancient computer tablet. This must be the woman I had come to see, scourge of the Cleaver family and a character with growing off-world interests. I moved forwards, raindrops spattering against my crocodile-skin jacket and thick canvas trousers, my heavy boots sinking into the boggy ground as I stepped off the door.

'Madeleine Frobisher?' I enquired.

She was already looking up, studying both me and my companion warily. I advanced towards her and held out my hand, trying to ignore the laser carbines tracking my progress. 'I'm Tuppence.'

She didn't offer her hand in return, instead nodding towards the bathysphere behind.

'Novel form of transport,' she opined.

I lowered my hand and turned to look back. The spherical craft was shifting – adjusting its gravmotors to pull itself back up out of the soft ground. Those motors were far too inefficient to support the entire weight of the craft and send it airborne, not because of their decrepitude, for even though they were centuries old they still functioned as they always had, but because the prador made them when they had only just begun inventing the technology. The craft's main method of ascent and descent attached to its crown: a wrist-thick stent-weave diamond-filament cable that speared upwards to disappear into the bruised sky. Hundreds of miles of it attached at its further end to a giant reel in the underbelly of the *Coin Collector* – an ancient prador tug that once bore a very different name under previous ownership.

'It is,' I replied, 'but it serves.'

'And what is this?' Madeleine gestured to Harriet.

Pointing to my troodon companion, I replied, 'Let me introduce Harriet, who by her appearance you would not realize was once an exotic dancer on Cheyne III.'

Harriet dipped her head in acknowledgement. 'Pleased to eat you.'

'She of course means, "pleased to meet you" since her artificial vocal chords sometimes struggle with the shape of her mouth.' I eyed Harriet. The changes her brain had undergone, having been compressed in that reptilian skull, were a worry. Though at that point, I couldn't figure out whether or not that 'pleased to eat you' was just a little joke at my expense.

'Is she … alien?'

I turned back to Madeleine. 'Harriet is just the result of an extreme desire for change using adaptogenic drugs, zooetics and nanodaption, and is, if you were to stretch the term almost to breaking point, a human being.'

153

'She will remain here,' said Madeleine.

I shook my head. 'She comes with me – that's not negotiable.'

'Then our negotiations are over before they have truly started.'

'Very well,' I smiled at her congenially. 'I have to admit to being disappointed, but if you're going to grandstand by setting pointless conditions...' I shrugged and began to turn back to my bathysphere. I was halfway back up the ramp door before she relented.

'Oh, if she must,' she finally said.

I turned back to see her waving a dismissive hand, this all obviously being a matter of no consequence.

'It's just that there's little room in the ATV,' she added.

'That's not a problem. Harriet is more than capable of keeping up on foot.' I gestured to her vehicle as I returned to her. 'Shall we?'

She held up one hand. 'I do hope you've brought payment and are not wasting my time.'

'Of course,' I replied. 'Twenty pounds of prador diamond-slate, etched sapphires to the value of one million New Carth Shillings and the fusion reactor parts you detailed.'

'Good.' She nodded.

Catching her speculative glance towards the bathysphere, I remembered to send the signal to close the door, and heard it groaning shut as I followed two of the heavies up the steps leading inside the swamp car. Within, seats lined the two sides with plenty of room for Harriet to squat between, but I didn't point this out. The heavies sat down, silent and watchful, while Madeleine sat beside the driver who was obviously another of the Frobisher line. This weedy looking individual bore similar facial features as the rest in here but also had a wart growing in precisely the same position on each of his eyelids – a sure sign of interbreeding. He started up the car – a hydrogen turbine engine by the sound of it – and set it into motion. I stretched up to look out of the narrow heavily scratched plastic windows to see Harriet bounding along beside the vehicle, then settled down patiently. Within five minutes, we were in the shadow of the family raft then driving up a ramp and parking, the engine winding down to silence.

'So where did you find the artefact?' I asked as I followed Madeleine out into a crammed tube of a swamp-car park.

'It's been here in our raft for as long as I can remember,' she replied, 'but only when one of my people studied your broadcast was it identified ... that was about ten years ago.'

'Solstan?'

Madeleine paused, glanced round at me. 'I haven't heard that expression in a while ... no, it's maybe seventeen solstan years ago.'

I grimaced. I'd been chasing rumours about the elements of the farcaster in the Wasteland for twenty years now and found nothing. I often wondered if they truly existed because why, as the Client claimed, would the Polity AIs have ordered it broken up and scattered? If they had truly considered it such a danger, why hadn't they destroyed it completely? I also often considered the unlikelihood of Polity AIs ridding themselves of such a potentially potent weapon, because that seemed very unlike them. But I could only obey and keep on searching, meanwhile slowly plotting my route to freedom.

Harriet had now re-joined us, panting but probably invigorated by the run. The armed escort closed in all around, seemingly a lot more confident now. I wondered if this indicated that they were thinking of doing something stupid. Past experience of trades like this, told me they probably were, and knowing the Frobisher's history did not make me optimistic.

Confirmation came just a minute later as Madeleine led the way up steps so worn the plating was gone to expose closed-cell bubble-metal. Concentrating on my footing with my body's eyes, I also looked through other eyes at the two swamp cars that had just pulled up by my bathysphere. I then watched some Frobishers unloading a heavy atomic shear from one of them, and wondered if this family had become so interbred, they had lost intelligence. It would be interesting to see what would happen when the atomic shear hit the prador alloy of the vehicle. The metal might not be the kind that armoured their war ships, but it was very tough, and the defence system might be old, but had proven effective on many occasions.

'So what's its condition?' I asked, to keep up the pretence. Of course, by the data package Madeleine had sent there had been a good chance that this could have been the real deal, but not now.

'I can't really say. It produces the power signatures you detailed and it's of the shape you described.' Madeleine shrugged. 'Hopefully you know your stuff and will be able to tell me.' She then added, 'But we still get the agreed first payment.'

'Of course,' I said.

I did know my stuff, perhaps more so than she would want. A century of research, experimentation and of perpetual mental updates of the latest research in the Polity, had made me an expert in many fields. I would also recognize a fake, which as I had been at pains to stress during my broadcast across the Wasteland, would result in no payment at all and quite likely some extreme response.

The stairs terminated in a long hall lined with heavy doors, each with a barred window. No doubt at all that this was a prison. Madeleine led the way across to one of them, punched a code into a panel beside it and the door popped open.

'We keep it here for the security.' She gestured me inside.

Without hesitating, I stepped through, Harriet coming in behind me. It was obvious what would happen next, and I was glad that they had not yet tried violence. I walked up to plinth at the centre of the cell and gazed at the object resting under a dome of chainglass. A curved chunk of white crystal lay there, rather like the sepal of some huge flower, but with a disc-shaped plug at its base from which protruded hundreds of micro-bayonets for data and power. I pinged it, and received a facsimile of the supposed power signature of a farcaster element, but I could immediately see the joins. I peered at it closer, ramping up the magnification of my eyes and probing with a spectroscopic laser. The crystal was plain white quartz cut and polished to the required shape, while the base plug was just a not very good mock-up made of bonded resin. I turned as if to address my host, but the door slammed shut.

'Disappointing,' I said.

Harriet was also peering at the object. She gave it a dismissive sniff then turned to face me.

'No good?' she enquired eagerly.

'Another fake,' I said. 'The Client will not be pleased at all.'

Harriet opened her mouth and licked her long red tongue over her white teeth. Evidently, *she* wasn't displeased.

Through my other eyes – the cams on the bathysphere I'd linked to via my internal transceiver – I watched the Frobishers apply their atomic shear to the door. The door reacted by lifting off its seal then slamming down, smashing the shear and its two operators into the ground, then lifting and dropping slowly above the mess as if like a beckoning hand it was inviting the rest to try again. One of them decided to fire some kind of explosive inside, but the door whipped up to send it bouncing back and it detonated by one swamp car, blowing off one cage wheel. The bathysphere defence system then decided to stop playing. Two hatches opened in the ring girdling the vehicle above the door, extruded two Gatling cannons and began firing. The two cars, their liquid hydrogen tanks soon peppered with holes, exploded, but by then all the humans had become bloody smears across the boggy ground.

'Stupid,' I said, then landed a heavy boot squarely in the centre of the cell door. The force of my kick buckled the floor underneath my other boot and the door tumbled clanging into the space beyond.

'Can I?' asked Harriet, stepping from one clawed foot to the other. 'Can I now?'

She had slipped into childlike eager pet mode again. Was that what she was destined to be or was it just a deliberate pose?

'Off you go,' I conceded, and she shot through the opening, her claws leaving scratches in the metal floor.

She'll get herself killed one day, I thought, *but not today.*

All the Frobishers had seen was a big and slightly ridiculous lizard, easy to kill with their weapons and only capable of using the natural weapons with which she had been endowed. I agreed, for I knew that with her long claws she wasn't even capable of picking up a gun let alone firing one. However, Harriet had survived and prevailed during many encounters like this one. I put this down to the fact that she had been a canny and experienced bounty hunter in her time and that, though her intelligence had, apparently, dropped a few tens of IQ points, she hadn't lost that edge.

I stepped back from the door and pulled open the studs in my canvas trousers, peeled back a patch over my right thigh, and watched the skin there etch out a frame and pop open. Next, I reached inside my leg and took out a heavily redesigned QC laser, held it in my right hand and plugged its superconducting power cable into the socket in my right wrist. After a pause, I looked down to a similar patch over my left thigh. I hesitated, then decided otherwise.

No, not today, not the *other* gun.

I stepped up to the plinth, straight-armed the chainglass dome and sent it clanging like a bell across the cell floor. I then extended my other arm and fired the laser, the beam invisible until vapour from the burning artefact etched it out of the air. Playing the high-energy-density beam over the thing, I watched the quartz shatter into hot fragments and the supposed base plug slump into molten ruin, then took my finger off the trigger. The momentary fit of pique had cost me time, and I'd wasted more than enough of it on this world and in the Wasteland entire.

I grimaced, stepped out of the door to the sounds of distant screams and the cracking and sawing of laser carbines.

The *Coin Collector* was a pyramid of brassy metal, its edges rounded and measuring a mile long, the throats of its fusion engines nearly covering one face and possessing enough drive power to fry a small moon. As the giant reel inside its EVA bay, which lay a quarter of a mile up from the fusion engines, wound in the bathysphere, I turned to watch Harriet clumsily using a suction sanitizer on her body to clean off all the blood now she'd licked off everything she could reach with her tongue.

As the bathysphere drew closer to the ancient prador tug, I considered the debacle below. The Frobishers had been utterly unprepared for Harriet and utterly unprepared for me. Harriet had torn into them quickly, leaving the route to the car park scattered with body parts, and had been munching on the same when I had arrived there. More Frobishers had turned up while I was stealing a swamp car and they had managed to get off a few shots before my QC laser fire drove them back and before Harriet finished off the stragglers. I had then taken one of the cars out and set it on automatic before abandoning it. A proton blast had turned it to wreckage about half a mile out, but by then we were well beyond it and soon safe inside the bathysphere. Still, the Client would not be pleased and I did not look forward to that.

I peered down at the holes burned through my jacket and into the artificial parts of my body, which was most of its parts. My sight was slightly blurred, my other senses dull and my right arm wasn't working properly. It seemed likely that as well as structural damage there might be some problem with my smart plasm component. This meant I would have to go into a mould and level two consciousness for nerve reintegration, which also increased the likelihood of the Client communicating with me. This annoyed me intensely, as did the Frobisher's ludicrous attempt to rip me off.

Had Madeleine Frobisher really thought she could just lure me down, capture me, break into my bathysphere and steal the payment I had brought? Had she completely neglected to factor this ship up here into her plans? Then again, perhaps she *had* factored it in. Perhaps her aim had been not only theft of the payment but seizure of my ship as well. How naïve. I stood, walked over to one of the array of hexagonal screens and human consoles plugged into prador pit-controls and made a call.

'Madeleine,' I said, the moment her face appeared in one of the screens. 'That was really a rather silly thing to do.'

'You destroyed the artefact,' she replied. 'Why did you do that? It's something you've been hunting down for ages.'

Odd, I thought, she seemed genuinely puzzled. Working the controls, I called up a view of the Frobisher colony raft from a remote I'd dropped on the surface before descent.

'As you should be well aware, the item you showed me wasn't genuine,' I replied. 'It has not been sitting in your raft over the ages, but was recently made there.'

'It was not!'

'Whatever. Your subsequent attempt to imprison me and break into my craft demonstrated your intent.'

'My intent was to ensure you had brought payment. It was you who started killing my brothers!'

'Weak Madeleine, very weak.' I paused, a suspicion nagging at me. I relayed an instruction to the *Coin Collector* for a search of the area surrounding the colony raft. 'So, if you didn't make the thing, where did you really get it from?'

She gazed at me for a long moment, perhaps realizing her predicament and understanding that lies would not help now. Meanwhile the search produced results: a group of Cleavers watching from around an ancient tripod-mounted holocorder mounted on a platform fixed to a swamp car. This could not be a regular activity of the Cleavers for surely they would have automatic systems in place to keep watch on their enemies.

I further worked some controls to bring up an image, from orbit, of the Cleaver colony raft as Madeleine replied, 'We stole it from the Cleavers. We found out they were bringing in something valuable from the North and ambushed them.'

I glanced round at Harriet, who had moved with eerie silence to stand at my shoulder.

'Squabbling children,' she said, in one of her moments of clarity.

So it seemed, and a plot by the Cleavers to put the Frobishers in my bad books, nicely exacerbated by Madeleine Frobisher's greed and intent to extend her off-world interests. I'd been dragged into a silly feud, my time had been wasted, my body had been damaged and the Client would be pissed off. However, before I could further consider what the Client's reaction would be, the bathysphere arrived with a shuddering crash in its docking cage. I would find out soon enough, I decided.

'Goodbye, Madeleine,' I said, and cut the connection.

The bathysphere door opened into an oval tube twenty feet across and ten high. Everything aboard the *Coin Collector* was of a similar scale – this tube apparently matching the size of burrows made by prador yet to grow into huge father-captains and lose their legs in that process. The interior was plain metal, the lower half roughened with fingertip size pyramidal spikes for grip, tubes of varying sizes branching off for the different iterations of prador children. Its design was obviously an old one made long before the prador started designing the décor of their ships to match their home environment and long before the father-captains dared to come out of their lairs. As I strode into it, the human lighting from induction blisters grew brighter, revealing a group of about twenty thetics marching in perfect synchronization across a junction. I headed over to a parking platform for various designs of scooter, Harriet pacing at my side like some faithful hound.

I mounted a gyroscope balanced mono-scooter, engaged its drive, and using the detached throttle and steering baton guided it from the platform and up along the tunnel to the end where a steep switchback took me up another level. Harriet followed me all the way, still hound-faithful for, except on the odd occasions when I allowed her to let her instincts reign, she never left my side. Five levels later I arrived at a massive oval door, dismounted and walked towards it. With a loud crump, it separated diagonally and the two halves revolved up into the walls, whereupon I entered a small captain's sanctum packed with human equipment plugged into the ancient prador controls. As I approached the consoles, with their hexagonal screens above, they abruptly came on to show me the views I had been seeing in the bathysphere. I stared at them for a long time, utterly certain now of what was to come, then I turned away.

Now it was time for me to deal with my injuries and the inevitable upbraiding from the Client – a prospect I did not relish at all. I walked over to a case against one wall, a thing that looked very much like an iron maiden, woodenly stripping off my jacket as I went. I tossed the jacket into a bin beside it, then struggled with my boots, trousers, shirt and undergarments – a thetic would collect them later and clean and repair them. Naked, I opened the front door of the case to reveal a human-shaped indentation inside, turned round and backed into it, Harriet watching me like a curious puppy. I closed up the lid and immediately I felt the bayonet connections sliding into my body, then everything began to shut down.

Next, I gazed from old dying eyes, reality broken into thousands of facets easily interpretable to a distributed mind, even though the dimensions it could perceive were beyond reason to a human one. However, the facets were going out. Pheromone receptors were stuttering too, and synaesthetic interpreters churning nonsense. Meanwhile, down below, the hot tightness came in peristaltic waves and something was snapping open. In hot orange vastness, I screamed chemical terror and shed. Nerve plugs and sockets parted and a mass of dry chitin fell, a hollow waspish thing bouncing amidst many of the same, doubled iridescent wings shattering like safety glass.

Then all was clear again with new eyes to see. Thirty-two wings beat and pheromone receptors began receiving again, while the synaesthetic interpreters turned the language and code of the Client into something I could understand. The creature rose up, a hundred feet tall, opened its beak and with its new black tongue tasted the air of its furnace.

'You have failed again,' it said.

As the Polity knew to its cost, the prador were vicious predators not prepared to countenance other intelligent entities in their universe. What it did not know, until a year into the start of the war when it seemed that humanity, the Polity and its AIs faced extinction, was that the prador were already practiced in the art of extermination.

I was working in bioweapons – the natural place in the war for a parasitologist and bio-synthesist – trying to resurrect a parasite of those giant crablike homicidal maniacs, when I was abruptly reassigned. I later learnt that others resurrected the parasite, and that assassin drones made in its shape delivered it as a terror weapon. They sneaked aboard prador ships or into their bases, and injected parasite eggs – prador Father-Captains extinguished by the worms chewing out their insides.

Once I boarded the destroyer ferrying me to my destination, along with a large and varied collection of other experts, I got the story. Before the prador encountered the Polity, they had encountered another alien species whose realm encompassed just three or four star systems. Being the prador they had attacked at once, but then found themselves in a long drawn-out war against a hive species who even in organic form approached AI levels of intelligence, and who quickly

164

developed some seriously nasty weaponry in response to the attack. The war had dragged on for decades but, in the end, the massive resources of the prador Kingdom told against the hive creatures. It was during this conflict that the prador developed their kamikazes, and not during the prador-human war, and it was with kamikazes that the prador steadily annihilated the hive creatures' worlds. However, one of these multifaceted beings – a weapons developer no less – managed to steal a prador cargo ship and get out through the prador blockade. And now, this creature, which the AI's referred to as the Client, wanted to ally itself with the Polity for some payback.

My memories of my time with the Client are vague. I'm sure we worked together on bioweapons while other experts there worked on the more knotty problem of delivery systems, and other weapons arising from the Client's science. A bioweapon capable of annihilating every prador with which it came into contact was perfectly feasible, but getting it into contact with enough of them wasn't so easy. Though the prador fought under one king to destroy the Polity, they were often physically isolated. The father-captains remained aboard their ships only coming into physical contact with their own kin, many prador wore atmosphere-sealed armour perpetually, while others had been surgically transplanted into the aseptic interiors of their war machines. A plague would not spread and, to be effective, must be delivered across millions of targets. This seemed impossible, until the farcaster...

U-space tech has always been difficult. A runcible gate will only open into another runcible gate and a U-space drive for a ship is effectively its own gate. Open-ended runcibles had been proposed, developed, and had failed. Without the catcher's mitt, there at the other end nothing without its own integral U-space drive could surface from underspace. It couldn't work. It wasn't possible.

Except it was.

Because of the vagueness of my memories of the time, I am assuming that the AIs developed the farcaster. The device could, using appalling amounts of energy, generate an open-ended gate. It was possible to point this thing anywhere in the prador kingdom, inside their seemingly invulnerable ships, even inside the armour of individuals, and send something. But there was a problem: the energy requirement ramped exponentially with the size of the portal. To send something the size of a megaton contra terrene device, would require the full energy output of a G-type sun for a day, even if the iteration of the farcaster we had, could use that amount of energy, which it couldn't. This was completely unfeasible and, if we could have utilized such massive amounts of power, we could have directed in a much more effective way. However, there were other possibilities. The output of a stacked array of fifty fusion reactors could deploy the device as it stood, and it was possible to open microscopic portals – ones that though small were large enough to send through something like a virus, a spore or a bacterium.

Working together, the Client and I made something that could kill the prador. I don't know precisely what it was – the vagueness of my memories was due to the accident that destroyed most of my body, for it had also destroyed part of my mind. We were ready. We had our weapon and we had our delivery system. But things had changed in the intervening years. The prador had begun to lose and even as we lined up the farcaster for its first tests, the old prador king was usurped and they began to retreat, and to negotiate. The AIs put a hold on our project, then they cancelled it, seizing the farcaster and breaking

166

it into separate elements, which they cast away all across known space.

What happened then? The war ended, apparently. I never knew because my remains were clinging to life in one of the Client's growth tanks as it fled into hiding aboard the *Coin Collector*. Apparently, there had been some contention about the breaking up of the farcaster during which some unstable weapons activated. I don't know. I just don't know.

Consciousness returned to me while I was alone aboard the *Coin Collector*, my mind somehow enslaved, my task to search out and recover the elements of the farcaster, and to one day take them to the Client, when it allowed me to know its location, so it could have its revenge against the prador at last. I waited patiently for that day, for I wanted revenge too and I wanted freedom, and I knew the only way I could have them, would be to finish the job the prador started so long ago.

The Client had spoken and now, with my connection to it renewed and affirmed, or maybe some parts of my mind reprogrammed and updated, I had no choice but to obey. As I stepped out of the repair cabinet and donned newly cleaned and repaired clothing, I felt sick, bewildered by my human form, and still wishing I could change the past.

'Time to finish this now,' I said.

'Finish it?' Harriet perked up.

I did worry about her love of mayhem for it seemed her main interest now. Once she had been an 'exotic dancer' who used various reptiles in her act and then, like many such people for whom appearance is all, she acquired an accelerating addiction to change. First had been changes of skin colour and the addition of snake eyes, then scales, claws and numerous internal changes, adaptogenic drugs and enhancements, and change thereafter for its own sake. At some point the jobs she took to supplement her wealth, displaced the dancing and she became a full-time bounty hunter, and she further adapted herself to that work. I had employed her to hunt down a rogue war drone said to possess some strange piece of U-space tech which just might have been part of the farcaster, but as it turned out wasn't. The drone fried her, leaving not much more than her brain and a bit of nerve tissue. I managed to get her out, in an ab-zero stasis bottle and thence to a hospital in the Graveyard. I didn't hold out much hope for her. Had we access to a Polity hospital her chances would have been better but, since quite a few of her bounties were paid upon delivery of a corpse, or parts thereof, she couldn't return to the Polity. But the next time I saw her I got a bit of a shock.

Her change into a troodon dinosaur had been out of a catalogue that explored the 'limits of the feasible' apparently, and she was idiotically delighted with it. They'd shoe-horned her brain into this reptile body, where it didn't seem to fit right. They'd turned her into something like an upgraded pet that could speak, but didn't possess the hands to do anything more complicated than tear at meat. I felt responsible, and so allowed her to stay at my side.

'Yes, finish it,' I said, the feeling that I occupied some nightmare form slowly receding as I worked the controls, targeting both colony rafts and the Cleaver watch post, then pausing to study the only weapons option.

The Frobishers and Cleavers were nasty and certainly deserved some sort of response, but there had to be innocents amidst them. What I was about to do sickened me, but I simply had no choice ... or did I? I now struggled against my own mind, because my instructions did offer me some leeway, and I opened com channels covering all the radio and microwave frequencies

168

the two families used, and set the equipment for record and repeat.

'This is a message from Tuppence aboard the *Coin Collector* for all Frobishers and Cleavers,' I said. 'You have both wasted my time and threatened my life.' And now the unscripted bit, 'You therefore have one hour to abandon your colony rafts and watch stations. At the end of that hour I will destroy them all.' I paused while a knife of pain lanced through my skull, then faded as I selected the single particle cannon for the chore. The pain returned as I set a timer for firing, then continued with, 'Perhaps, after this, those of you who might be innocent in this matter will carefully consider your choice of leadership. That is all.'

'You are being merciful?' Harriet enquired.

I stepped back from the controls, the pain redoubling in my skull, and slumped into an acceleration chair. I was aware that I had gone, if only a little, contrary to my orders, and now, somehow, I was punishing myself. Paralysed, I watched lights flashing and icons appearing on the screen indicating increasingly desperate attempts from both families to get in contact with me. Ever so slowly, the pain faded – just a small punishment for a minor infringement, and not the agony that could leave me crippled in hell for days on end. The leeway around my orders enabled me to do such things, enabled me to do many things. I rested a hand on my thigh – the one containing the *other* gun.

'Yes, maybe I'm getting old,' I finally managed to rasp in reply to Harriet.

Realizing there would be no immediate action, Harriet paced around the room for a while, before coming back to stand beside my chair, her head dipping as she nodded off into one of her standing dozes.

169

A quarter of an hour later I observed swamp cars, ATVs, heavy crawlers and people on foot, loaded down with belongings, abandoning both rafts. A further half hour passed, and as the end of the hour approached, I heaved myself out of the chair, my head still throbbing with post punishment pain, and approached the controls. The last minutes counted down, the last seconds, and then the particle cannon fired – any effects here on the ship unfelt.

The side view of the Frobisher's raft showed a beam as wide as a tree trunk stabbing down, its inner core bright blue but shrouded in misty green. Molten metal and debris exploded out from the impact point then, when the beam cut right through the raft to the boggy ground below, the whole thing lifted on an explosion, its back breaking and the two halves heaving upwards on a cloud of fire and super-heated steam, before collapsing down as the beam cut out. Another screen showed those on the watching swamp car just gone – a smoking hollow where they had been, while the Cleaver's raft was now just as much a mess as the Frobisher's, though viewed from a different perspective. Harriet was at my side of course, watching with fascination, before turning away in disappointment.

'Tank.' I turned now to face precisely such an object over the far side of the sanctum: a cylindrical tank much like one used for fuel oil or gas, but covered with an intricate maze of pipes and conduits. 'Take us out of orbit and put us on course for the Graveyard.'

'As you instruct,' replied a frigid voice.

I immediately felt the vibration through my feet as the fusion engines fired up. The thing inside that tank, which might or might not have been the usual ganglion of a press-ganged prador first- or second-child, could take over.

Everything fell into stillness aboard the *Coin Collector* during U-space jumps. Without orders, the thetics just became somnolent, without action and prey to hunt, Harriet spent her time dozing or following me about like a lost puppy. On this occasion, she was in lost puppy mode, easily keeping pace with my scooter as I drove through the ship, finally pulling up beside yet another massive diagonally slashed elliptical door that opened ponderously as I dismounted. Just outside this door, I surveyed twenty thetics standing ready clad in impact armour with pulse-rifles shouldered. They were somnolent but at a word from me would wake and be ready. In two more U-jumps, I would give that word as we tracked down yet another possible element of the farcaster. I bit down on my frustration. When would the Client finally give up and summon me back? When could I finally end this? I walked through the door.

The cauldron was a pale pink glass sphere twenty feet across supported in a scaffold of gold metal extending from the floor to the ceiling fifty feet above. Across the back wall of the chamber were the doors to rows of chemical reactors. Catalytic cracking columns stood guard to one side while, on the other, squatted an object like a mass of stacked aluminium luggage woven together with tubes. Each case was a nano-factory in itself and the whole generated the smart-plasm fed into the cauldron – the distillation of a billion processes. Gazing upon this set-up, I felt it just did not seem sufficiently high-tech, but looked like something Jules Verne might have dreamed up in a moment of insanity.

I lowered my gaze to the rows of moulds bracketing the catwalk leading to the cauldron itself. The ones to my right were closed, like sarcophagi, their contents incubating. To the left, half of them were closed, a robot arm running on rails to inject plasm into each. The others stood open to reveal polished

171

interiors in the shape of humans, a thetic peeling itself up out of one of them assisted by two more of its kind. Meanwhile, thetics from the other open moulds stood in a group behind, observing the whole procedure with blue eyes set in milk-white faces, mouths opening and closing as if miming the speech they were incapable of producing.

'I wish we could extend their lives,' I said.

'Why?' asked Harriet, completely baffled.

'Four years and two days seems to be the point, beyond which returns diminish,' I replied. 'I wonder if that limitation is why the Polity scrapped the idea?'

'The Polity?' wondered Harriet, her thinking even slower in these periods of inaction.

The thetics had been an attempt by the Polity to produce large quantities of disposable soldiers – a project with which I felt sure the Client and I had been involved during the war. Or perhaps we weren't? There had been other researchers, scientists and experts of every kind on that ship sent to that first meeting with the Client, so perhaps the thetics were the result of some research by one of them? Perhaps when the Client had run, just after the AIs broke up the farcaster, it had stolen data and equipment too? How else had it obtained the samples with which to rebuild all this here? I shook my head, frustrated by the confusion. Where the thetic technology had come from and what my involvement had been were questions that would probably remain unanswered – they probably lay in that portion of my mind the accident had taken away.

Unfortunately, as well as the thetics' lifespan being limited, both the amount of programming they could take and the damage they could withstand was limited too. For the quick production of disposable hominids, smart-plasm was all very well, but on receiving damage under fire, its constructs tended to quickly revert to their original form, and crawl out of their uniforms like particularly nervous slime moulds.

'Golem chasses,' I said as I walked on through the cauldron room towards the back corner.

My own body was an amalgam of a Golem base frame, smart-plasm and an early form of syntheskin outer covering – as a whole a more rugged combination. I wasn't entirely sure what human parts I had retained: perhaps my brain, perhaps only part of my brain, maybe just some crystal recording from that original flesh. I wondered if it a bioweapon had taken away the rest of me, and wondered if I had designed it.

'Golem chasses,' Harriet repeated, with less intelligence than a parrot.

I decided not to bother making a suggestion I had made before, of giving her prosthetic Golem hands to replace her unwieldy claws. She wasn't interested when her mind was at a high point, and would be less interested now.

A smaller door at one rear corner of this chamber took me into my private laboratory. Here I felt the tension begin to ebb. It wasn't as if I could somehow be disobedient here, ignore the Client's orders or cease my endless search for farcaster elements, but somehow its grip on my existence seemed less rigid in this place. Perhaps because here I occupied those parts of my mind not concerned with that search – those being the parts wholly focused on my original interests so long ago.

Oddly, the effect here seemed the same for Harriet, though she had no alien entity controlling her mind. Her interest perked up as she surveyed all the complicated equipment, peered at nanoscope screens and clumsily tried to pick up objects made for human hands and not claws painted with shocking pink nail polish. I say oddly because elsewhere her interests didn't often stray into the scientific.

173

I checked on a brain worm first. Version 1056 had strayed a long way away from the parasite that forced ants to climb to the top of stalks of grass when a sheep might be strolling by, and thus pass itself on to said sheep. This particular beauty would make a prador suffer terminal claustrophobia, which was not so great for a space-faring species who wore protective armour. Not only would the victim want to get out of the ship, it would be unable to wear any kind of protective suit. Of course, prador could survive in vacuum for an appreciable time, but still the victim of this parasite would die. I'd yet to test it out, and didn't think I ever would.

The next bug caused a prador's carapace to grow as soft as sponge, and the next was a fungus that dined on their nerve tissue. I only checked on them briefly before moving on to the latest version of my favourite fungus – perfect now in every detail and perhaps a precise copy of a fungus that the Client possessed. Thus I occupied my spare time pursuing my interests in parasites and biological weapons. Thus, by pursuing the lines of research I had followed with the Client, I tried to restore some lost memory. Staring at the latest nanoscope images and latest computer models of the function of this last fungus, in all its different genetic settings, I tried to remember seeing them before, but there was nothing.

'The gun?' queried Harriet.

'One day,' I said.

Really, it I should test it, but I needed some victim deserving of such an end. Perhaps, during this latest search, if all the data were correct, I would find such.

The Graveyard lay in the intersection point of two spheres of interstellar occupation, everything beyond its edge being called the Wasteland or the Reaches, or having no name at all. As the

174

Coin Collector heaved out of U-space, I knew we had arrived upon sensors picking up high amounts of space debris across many light years and upon gazing at a screen image of the devastated world called Molonor. This world possessed its own orbital ring of debris that had once been space stations. Also orbiting was a small moon half subsumed by a base that seemed a conglomerate mass of those same debris. I eyed the ships scattered about that moon, along with the various ground-based coil-gun emplacements then, after a short contemplation, focused in on one of those ships. Here sat an in-system cargo hauler the shape of an ancient rifle bullet, sitting in a U-space carrier shell like a hexagonal threaded nut. I pinged it and got a confirmation of identity: the *Layden* – one of Gad Straben's haulers. Straben was my target now – the Client had made that abundantly clear during one of our frequent drops out of U-space to let the *Coin Collector*'s engines cool and realign.

'Harriet,' I said, opening com. 'Where are you?'

'The Cauldron,' she replied.

'I'll be with you shortly.' I considered how, like a dog about to be taken on a familiar walk, she had rushed ahead, then I experienced a moment of puzzlement. Harriet didn't often get this far ahead of me, usually stayed by my side, so she had to be *very* eager. I shook my head, dismissing the thought before inputting a course to take the *Coin Collector* down into close orbit, conveniently close to the *Layden*. With that done, I stood up and headed out of the captain's sanctum, finally arriving at the door outside the Cauldron.

'Gad Straben,' said Harriet, dancing from clawed foot to foot. 'The gun!'

I nodded solemnly, perhaps so. Gad Straben was evil enough.

Through its various other contacts about the Graveyard, the Client had learned that, after the disappearance of a black AI called Penny Royal, salvagers had finally plucked up the courage to venture to the AI's original home base. This was a wanderer planetoid wormed through with numerous tunnels. As always, they had gone there for technology and, before some event burned up everything inside that small world, it was rumoured that Gad Straben had managed to obtain some objects of value, things that might be elements of some wartime weapon, and he had begun to put out feelers, make enquiries... The Client wanted them. The Client hoped at last to obtain pieces of the farcaster.

'But scraping the barrel,' Harriet opined.

I studied her carefully. It must be one of her good days because she was showing a lot more intelligence than usual.

I nodded. After searching for so long it seemed increasingly unlikely we would ever find any part of the farcaster, or that it even existed at all. The items supposedly obtained by Gad Straben might be our last shot and the Client might recall me at last. My hand strayed down to my hip, fingers tapping there for a moment. I noted Harriet watching closely and quickly withdrew it.

'Yes, we are,' I agreed. 'The Client has less chance of finding what it wants now than before.' I paused for a second, then shuddered, feeling a little stab of the Client's influence over my mind. It was time to start acting.

Straben's organisation was a criminal one, salvage being a mere side line, and he was as paranoid as all who ran such concerns in the Graveyard had to be, if they were to survive, so I had to both act fast, but take care. There were risks associated with getting too drastic in the Graveyard. It might be styled as a kind of anything-goes no-man's land but that wasn't true. It was a volume of space in critical balance, a buffer zone between the Polity and the prador and both sides watched it intently.

'Do we have enough for Hobbs' Street?' Harriet asked.

I nodded. 'One hundred ready to go,' I surveyed the twenty thetics in the corridor, now no longer somnolent but not really showing any inadvertent movements associated with real life.

'Have you spoken to John Hobbs yet?' she asked.

I looked at her again. She had suddenly become a lot more coherent, a lot more intelligent, just like the Harriet I used to know. She was asking the right questions now when all I had come to expect of her was child-like demands for her version of fun.

The Molonor moon base, until thirty years ago, had been essentially lawless, but then one salvage hunter became much annoyed with protection costs and damage to his operation by the constant squabbles between the criminal elements there. After a particularly rich find, he used his newly acquired wealth to hire in some hoopers to make the place more amenable to his operation. After a brief year of chaotic readjustment, which resulted in many crime lords ending up processed into fertilizer, John Hobbs became the ruler there. He allowed criminals to come and do business, spend their wealth there, establish their bases, but did not allow them to bring their fights with them.

'He was surprisingly helpful.'

She tilted her head slightly to one side, waiting for an explanation.

'He could have been a problem, but for his hoopers and our old association,' I explained. 'Hobbs tolerates a lot, but some of the criminals down there he doesn't like at all. He's only too willing to turn a blind eye to anything that might happen in Straben's headquarters.'

177

Still that tilted head.

'Coring,' I finished.

Harriet straightened up. 'I see.'

'Meanwhile,' I continued, 'we might not have to go to Hobb's Street at all, since a less risky opportunity has presented itself. I'm taking us into orbit close to one of Straben's ships, the *Layden*, which is here.'

'Sphere Two?' Harriet suggested.

'Certainly,' I nodded, then stabbing a thumb towards the twenty thetics. 'These are programmed for basic obedience and combat – nothing fancy. They'll do.' I now turned to face the thetics. 'Automatics should have the rest ready for Hobbs Street should we need them.'

The thetics hadn't been humanized, but that was not necessary for what I intended. I checked the coloured bar codes on their combat armour then selected the commander of this unit.

'Bring your men with me,' I instructed.

The commander, unable to speak, dipped its head in acquiescence. When I mounted my scooter and set off the whole unit turned neatly as one and broke into a jog to keep up. By the time I reached an access tube to Sphere Two, they were panting and their white skins sheened with sweat. Harriet wasn't out of breath at all. I dismounted and walked over to palm the control to the tunnel door. As it slid open, I stepped to one side and again addressed the thetic commander. 'Enter and secure yourselves in the acceleration chairs.'

The thetics trooped inside.

'Are they necessary?' Harriet asked.

'Straben's carriers usually have a crew of between five and ten.' I glanced at Harriet. 'I know that's not too many for you, but I want to be sure. Also, if we don't find what we're after here this can act as a test of this new batch so we can be sure of them before we hit Hobbs' Street. You remember the last time?'

Harriet dipped her reptilian head in acknowledgement. I'd sent a group of armed thetics against a single prador first-child – one of the many renegade prador in the Graveyard – guarding a store said to contain a Polity weapon, from the war, as usual. The moment the first-child fired on the thetics, they had collapsed into a bubbling mass. Unstable plasm, and a perfect demonstration of why the Polity might have dumped this technology. I took out the prador with a particle cannon blast from the *Coin Collector*, but it had all been yet another waste of time. The Polity weapon had been the carcase of some insectile war drone – its mind burnt out long ago.

I turned away from Harriet, glad she had bought the lie I had just told her. The reality was that I didn't want her going first into that ship. She might be fast and deadly, but armed only with claws and teeth she might well end up on the bad end of a pulse-rifle in such an enclosed environment. It hadn't happened before, but the feeling I had that things were somehow coming to an end was making me more protective of her.

Moving aside, I now gazed through the slanting windows overlooking the bathysphere bay. Bathysphere Two – the *Coin Collector* had only two of these vehicles – had first been adapted for inter-ship travel, its line detached and chemical boosters affixed all around its rim. Its second adaptation had been mine: a big metal mouth extending around its main door, a leech-lock. This could attach to the hull of any ship, its rim digging in with microscopic diamond hooks and making a seal. It had come in very handy over the years.

Harriet followed the thetics in, and after a pause, I followed too. Inside, the thetics were, as instructed, sitting down in the concentric rings of seats and strapping down tightly, their rifles slotted into containers beside them. I headed over to the single seat before the adapted prador controls, sat down and hit the release button. Even as I secured my own straps, the bathysphere jerked and set into motion. I turned on the screens and observed the space doors opening, then laid in the correct course. Harriet, meanwhile, squatted down beside me, her claws clenched around the floor grid.

'Shouldn't be too bumpy,' I said.

'One I've heard before,' Harriet replied.

In a moment, we were out in vacuum, the chemical rockets firing to put us on the pre-programmed course. I glanced over to the door leading into the leech lock, hit a control and the door irised open. Within this, running on rails around the inner face of the lock, was a robot cutter that wielded a carbon-titanium thermic lance, tubed for feed-through of laser heating, oxygen, peroxide and catalytic nano-spheres. It was the fastest way to cut through just about anything. I closed the iris door again. It was also messy, producing thick searing smoke and poisonous gases.

'Approaching vessel, what is your purpose!' a voice demanded from my console.

'I've got something for Gad Straben,' I replied, now calling up an image of Straben's hauler on my array of hexagonal screens.

'Identify yourself!'

I turned on the visual feed and gazed at an unshaven face displayed in just one of the hexagons. A half-helmet augmentation partially covered his head, and the one eye I could see widened in shocked recognition.

'I'm Tuppence,' I said, just to be sure.

'Gad Straben is not here,' said the man.

'Not a problem – I'll leave his gift with you.'

'You are not to approach this ship. I will not allow docking!'

I lined up the boost and paused with my finger over the control to operate it. 'Don't be so hostile. I'm sure Mr Straben will be very interested in what I am bringing him.'

'I know exactly who you are, Tuppence,' replied the man. 'If you approach any closer you will be fired upon.'

Of course, many in the Graveyard knew of me, even though I'd been away for a couple of decades. Many who had dealings with me had suffered, while others had gained. The likes of Straben had generally been the former kind.

'Oh well,' I said, and hit boost.

The sudden acceleration tried to lever me sideways out of my chair, but I locked my body in place. Behind me, a couple of the thetics made an odd warbling sound. At the same time, I saw the *Layden* fire up its own engines to move away and two flashes on its hull marking the departure of two missiles. I watched them curve round and head towards Bathysphere Two their drive flames growing in intensity like angry eyes.

'Incoming,' I stated.

'No shit,' said Harriet.

G-forces now tried to throw me into the screens as the bathysphere turned to present its thickest armour to the missiles. They hit one after the other with shuddering crashes. The screens whited out for a second, then gradually came back on with sparkles of burning metal shooting past. It would take a lot more than what the hauler had available to penetrate even ancient prador armour. The *Layden* was now up very close, still trying to accelerate away but just having too much mass to shift quickly. I pointed at the screens with one finger and drew a target frame over part of its hull just behind the carrier shell.

'Impact in three, two, one…'

The force of the crash bent the supports of my chair so it hung sideways. A thetic, emitting a short squeal, slammed against the curved wall opposite the leech lock then, as the bathysphere rocked into stillness, dropped to the floor with a soggy thud. I checked on Harriet and saw she'd torn up some of the floor grid, but had still managed to hang on. I unstrapped myself just as the thermic lance kicked off behind the iris door, roaring and hissing like some trapped demon. Standing, I checked on the rest of the thetics. One of them was reverting, its face now a shapeless mass, one of its gauntlets on the floor below and a white worm oozing from the sleeve of its combat armour. Another of them had completely deliquesced. Its suit was empty, a milky pool scattered with pink offal around its boots.

'Unstrap and prepare your weapons,' I instructed the remainder.

As they obeyed, the thermic lance finished its work and a loud crash ensued. That was the hydraulic hammer smashing a disk of hull into the ship beyond. I reached down and hit the control for the iris door and it slid open to release a cloud of stinking smoke, slowly clearing as air filtration ramped up to a scream. The interior of the other ship was devastated: a burned and melted mess of interior walls, crash foam and fire retardants snowing, some fires still burning.

'Thetics,' I called, while pointing into the other ship. 'Go in there and secure the ship, try not to kill the one you saw me speaking to.' They had just about enough intelligence to follow such an instruction. If there weren't any survivors it wouldn't matter too much – would just mean a bit more work inspecting the cargo, and checking the ship's log and other data stores.

In good order, they moved into the other ship, silently passing instructions between themselves and splitting into two parties, one heading forwards and one to the stern. Just a minute later I heard a laser carbine firing, then pulse-rifle fire in return.

'Not too bad,' said Harriet, now standing at my side and eyeing the two thetics that had failed, then the one that had smashed into the wall and was now slowly oozing from its suit.

'Standard ten per cent,' I agreed, moving towards the iris door. I meant the two failures – the one that smashed into the wall I counted as a casualty.

'What are you going to use?' Harriet asked. 'Demolition charges?'

'In good time, Harriet,' I replied. 'We're here after information and, if we're lucky, maybe even the item salvaged from Penny Royal's planetoid – I want to check up on the cargo first.'

Grav was out inside the *Layden*, so from the leech lock I propelled myself inwards to find my way to a central dropshaft. The cargo area on ships like this usually sat ahead of the engines, so I turned right, soon having to push aside a floating corpse that could have served as a sieve. Shortly after that, I observed a group of four thetics heading back towards me, and pulled myself to one side to allow them past. Further on, I found two of their number leaking out of their suits, then another member of the crew – most of his head missing.

'In there,' said Harriet, pausing at a side tube and sniffing.

I entered the tube and eyed the palm-locked doors, then drove my fist through one of them and tore it out of its frame and tossed it aside. The room within was racked out, the plastic frameworks filled with simple aluminium boxes the size of coffins. On seeing these, I first felt disappointment, then a growing anger. There would be no salvage aboard this ship for its cargo was of a very different kind. I dragged one of the coffins out, pushed it down against the floor and tore off its lid.

Inside lay a naked woman, her body marked with circular blue scars and her head bald. Her eyes were open and she was breathing gently, but she showed utterly zero response to me. I slapped her face, hard, but all she did was slowly return her head to its original position. I reached in, cupped the back of her neck in one hand, and hauled her up into a sitting position to study the scars on her head.

'Fully cored and thralled, I reckon,' said Harriet.

'So it would seem,' I replied, releasing the woman and watching her slowly lie back like a damped box lid closing.

I pulled out another box and checked the contents of that, shoved it back in the rack and moved on to a square box at the end, pulled that out and opened it. This contained hexagonal objects each the size of a soup bowl, prador glyphs inscribed in their upper surfaces.

'Thrall control units,' I said tightly, pausing to look at the number of those other coffin-sized boxes around me and wondering if the same number lay behind each door. 'Let's see if our thetics managed to get us a captive.'

Making my way up to the bridge of the hauler, I noted another two thetics down and returning to their original form but accompanied by two more of the crew, riddled with pulse-rifle fire. Finally, entering the bridge, I found four thetics pinning their captive to the floor, others milling about aimlessly, while three of their kind floated through the air, partially dismembered and reverting – obviously having run afoul of their captive's laser carbine before they could bring him down.

'I want two of you to remain here to restrain the captive,' I instructed. 'The rest of you go back to the bathysphere, now.'

The milling immediately ceased and the most of the thetics departed.

'Get him up off the floor,' I instructed the two remaining. The fight seemed to have gone out of him now, probably because of the shots to each of his legs and his right biceps. He was obviously in a great deal of pain.

'I have some questions,' I said.

'Fuck … you,' the man managed.

'My first question is: does your cargo consist of fully cored humans only? That is, are there any included who have been spider thralled.'

'Why the hell … should I answer you?'

'Curious question to which I'm sure the answer must be obvious,' I said. 'If you don't answer me I will torture you until you either do answer me or you die. Harriet.' I beckoned with one finger and Harriet turned away from a deliquescing thetic she had been sniffing. 'His right hand do you think?'

Harriet walked right up to the man, nose to nose, then sniffed down his right arm, pausing for a while at the wound in his biceps them moving on down to his hand. She licked his hand, then lifted her head back up to gaze into his eyes.

'Crunchy,' she said, exposing her teeth.

'Why do you want to know?' the man asked, trying to focus his gaze on me.

'Why do you want to know why I want to know?'

'I don't want to die.'

I smiled tiredly and turned away, heading over to the ship's controls. As I began to search for the ship's log and other data storage, I said, 'All you need to know right now is that if you do not answer my question Harriet here will bite off and eat your right hand.'

185

I glanced round in time to see the man brace himself and pull himself upright. Returning to the controls I found myself puzzled by the lack of security. Quickly locating the ship's log I transmitted it to the *Coin Collector,* receiving confirmation a moment later.

'The customer for this shipment ... did not want spider thralls used because after a period of time they can be rejected by the body.' The man paused, then continued in a rush, 'I'm just the pilot – I'm not involved in the rest of it.'

Ah, here's something, I thought to myself as I uncovered a number of encrypted files, then feeling slightly impatient, turned back to our prisoner.

'The customer presumably being a prador ... So let me clarify,' I said. 'Each and every human being in your cargo has suffered the removal of both the brain and a portion of the spinal cord so is essentially just technologically animated meat. They're all dead.'

'Yes ... it's best ... they don't suffer.'

'I see.' No one here to rescue then. I had done some questionable things in my time but what Straben was doing here lay utterly beyond the pale. I'd known his organisation was involved in the coring trade which was why I'd had no reservations about sending the thetics in like I had, and now I had complete confirmation.

'Next question.' I held up a finger, then brought it down on the touch controls. The encrypted files refused to transmit. I stared at them for a moment, then banished them from the screen and called up a ship's schematic. 'What did the salvagers find in Penny Royal's planetoid and where will that find be located now?'

'I don't know ... I don't know what you're ... talking about.'

186

The schematic showed the location of this ship's mind – a second-child ganglion that was barely sentient. It merely acted as a data processor and stored none at all in itself. However, it had to store it somewhere. After a moment, I had it. Smiling, I reached down and tore off the panel in front of my seat. In there I located a series of crystals plugged in like test tubes in a rack. I detached optics, switched the rack over to its own power supply before detaching the external power feed and pulling the whole thing out. I now had the ship's collimated diamond data store. I could try to break into the files it contained and sort through the data myself, but there were terabytes of it here. Best to hand it over to Tank.

'You don't know about some item or items obtained from Penny Royal's planetoid?'

'No ... I don't.'

The man seemed to be telling the truth and, really, I didn't feel I had the time to check. Hobb's Street had to be our next target and we needed to move swiftly.

'Thank you.' I dipped my head in acknowledgement, then patted a hand against my left thigh. I could try out the *other* gun now, but that seemed mean, since Harriet hadn't seen much action here. I relented. 'Harriet, you may kill him now.'

The man shrieked as I stood up with the ship's data store and headed for the door glimpsing, as I went, Harriet pulling on something like a dog worrying a length of bloody rope. As I headed back towards the bathysphere I decided that first I would have the prador mind removed from this ship and transferred over to my own – a useful replacement should that thing in the tank finally expire, or should I, for whatever reason, want a ship mind that did not owe its loyalty to the Client. The best option then would be a kiloton thermite scatter bomb, on a timer set to go off sometime after our visit to Hobbs Street. It would completely gut this ship, burn up its cargo and destroy its workings, including its U-drive and fusion reactor. The ship would then only have any value as scrap and one portion of Straben's organization would be defunct – and during this mission, I would have cleaned up at least a small portion of the crap scattered about the Graveyard.

Hobbs Street smelled odd, damp and sweet. This wasn't due to the residents here, but to a mushrooms. An odd mutation of a terran honey fungus had spread throughout the moon colony, running its mycelia through air vents, electrical ducting or any other opening available, sucking nutrients from spillages on the floors of hydroponics units or out of the soil of private gardens. I paused in my study of a clump of honey mushrooms sprouting from a crack in the foamstone pavement and considered the workings of coincidence. I had decided that here I would use the *other* gun, and there was a connection…

  I looked up as an ancient hydrocar motored past. It was the cops, and I was surprised to see them. The car, a by-blow of flying saucer and Mercedes, had an assault drone like a huge grey copepod squatting on its roof. The white vehicle had fluorescent blue circles decorating it – a colour scheme that had come to mean much the same as the black and orange stripes of a wasp: danger. The driver and his mate, respectively a hulking man and an equally lethal looking woman, eyed me as they passed, the blue ring-shaped scars on their faces visible in the streetlights.

  'Probably here in the hope of picking up any strays,' I said.

  'There won't be any,' said Harriet.

'They would probably like to join in,' I continued. 'John told me that he had some trouble dissuading his hoopers from contacting me and offering assistance.'

Harriet dipped her head in acknowledgement. 'Understandable, considering the history. Jay Hoop, his pirates and their coring operation weren't very popular on Spatterjay.'

Weapons grade understatement, I thought. It surprised me that Straben had managed to keep his headquarters here at all.

'Here they come,' said Harriet.

Hobbs' street was crowded, it being one of the most popular thoroughfares here, and now becoming even more crowded. The thetics were clad in a wide variety of clothing and concealed their faces with syntheskin, but they hadn't managed to suppress their inclination to march along in neat squads like the soldiers they were meant to be. There were five street doors to Straben's conjoined buildings, which extended five floors up with the chainglass street roof attached across on top of the fifth. Fifty thetics were in the street, ten to each door, while a further seventy thetics clad in light space suits were, even now, moving into position up on the building's roofs, which were exposed to vacuum.

I watched, through the eyes of my artificial body and through pin-cams the thetics all wore in their clothing. I saw those up on the roof avoiding the heavily secured airlocks, consulting building blueprints and selecting areas over which they glued down atmosphere shelters, before beginning to cut through below, thus making their own airlocks. They would be inside within five minutes. Meanwhile, those down on the street were moving in on the doors with sticky bombs or sausages of thermite, depending on the design of door concerned. I began walking.

189

'So, Harriet,' I said. 'You seem a lot more coherent lately.'

She glanced at me, her reptilian face unreadable. 'Do I?'

'Undoubtedly,' I said, watching her.

'I've never been incoherent,' she argued.

'Not as such but –.'

I couldn't take that further because a loud bang ensued, the explosion as bright as a welding arc and a gust of smoke blowing out into the street and then rising up towards the glass roof. People started yelling and running. It might have been thirty years since John Hobbs took control but still there had been incidents, and the people here knew when best just to run. I noted that one of the doors had disappeared just as thermite flared further down the street and two more explosions ensued. I watched thetics pouring into three of the buildings, pulling short wide-blast sawn-off pulse rifles from under their coats. I saw thermite burn in a fast ring around an armoured door then a central charge blow it inwards. Just one more...

I glanced over towards the door concerned as a machine gun began firing in short bursts. An explosion took out the door, but from a stone-effect arch above it, a lumpish ugly security drone had dropped on a pole and begun firing a miniature version of the Gatling cannons prador favoured. I saw thetics torn apart, even one civilian who had been a bit tardy running for cover. I reached down and flipped open the patches on my trousers, drew my QC laser and plugged in its power lead, then I drew the *other* gun, noting Harriet now watching me intently. Meanwhile a thetic opened out a telescopic launcher, shouldered it and put a missile into the door arch. The drone arced into the street and smoking bounced along it.

'Harriet –' I began, but didn't get to finish as she shot off and went through the door concerned. Obviously, the most

190

secure doorway was into the building I most wanted to enter because, if my data was correct, Gad Straben himself had entered here just a few hours ago. I now entered, greeted by the sound of gunfire and the commingled screams of pain and terror, which were the usual result of Harriet's presence. It occurred to me that she might have been uncomfortable about my questioning and that was why she had gone ahead, but why this occurred to me, I don't know.

Through pin cams on their clothing, I observed the thetics in the other buildings moving from room to room and killing anyone who resisted, just so long as they weren't Straben. It was brutal, but then Straben's organization was brutal and any working for it had to know they were culpable in mass murder. Those on the roof were now in too and working their way down – just as efficient and methodical as those working up from below – but also just as indifferent to personal survival. I reckoned on walking away from here with maybe just twenty or so surviving thetics. The rest would crawl off and die completely to become food for the honey fungus, or else turn into something nasty in the drains.

Directing my course by pin-cam feeds, I climbed the stairs since the building's dropshafts were keyed to staff ID tags and wouldn't work for anyone else. Most of the action was now taking place on the third floor. At the second floor, some man in businesswear carrying a heavy flack gun charged down, skidded to a stop on a landing and took aim. I raised my other gun just as a flack round exploded against the wall behind me and peppered me with shrapnel, then changed my mind and raised my QC laser, a short while afterwards stepping over the burning corpse.

By the time, I reached the third floor it was all over. The main data room looked like an abattoir and over in one corner Harriet was tearing chunks off some rather corpulent individual

191

and gobbling them down. Many of the consoles were smashed and smoking, holo-displays flickering through the air like panicked spectres and flimsy screens seemed to burn with internal blue fires. Over to one side a chainglass window overlooked all this, plush office space inside and there, working a console in frenetic panic, sat Gad Straben. I ran over to the door – armoured of course – kicked it hard then swore as my other boot went straight down through the floor and the door remained in place.

'Get me a charge!' I shouted, heaving my leg back out of the hole.

Only two thetics had survived the fight in here, and were guarding two women and a man who lay face down with their hands behind their heads.

'You three,' I said, brushing debris from my trousers as I walked over. When they looked up I continued, 'Get up and go,' and stabbed a finger towards the door. They slowly stood up, eyeing me as I replaced my weapons in their holes in my legs and closed them up, then took off just as fast as they could. They were probably only temporary employees of Straben, since they hadn't resisted, so whether they lived or died was a matter of indifference to me. I turned to the two thetics.

'I want an explosive charge to get through that door,' I said concisely, since neither of them had understood me the first time.

One of them went over to one of its fellows, quietly deliquescing in a corner, pulled some sticky bombs from his belt and returned with them. I stared at them for a moment then went over to the dead thetic myself and checked its belt. There – just what I needed. I detached a circular object like a coaster and took it over to the office window, slapped it against the chainglass and hit the pressure button at its centre. With a whumph the chainglass turned to white powder and collapsed to the floor. I stepped over the ledge and into the office, seeing Straben simply stand and hold out empty hands.

'You move quickly,' he said.

Straben, a slightly fat man with a bald rounded head, was clad in businesswear and looked like some Polity executive styling his appearance on some antediluvian fashion. I ignored him for a moment, carefully studying my surroundings.

A glass-fronted case along one wall contained a variety of ghoulish antiques: a spider thrall and a full-core thrall, a couple of slave collars and an old automatic pistol. These were all the kind of objects you could obtain from dealers out of Spatterjay. I watched a nano-paint picture transit to its next image – a painting of a hooder coming down on some man in ECS uniform. Then I strolled over to the desk, then round it, and stood facing Straben.

'I move quickly?' I enquired mildly.

'You arrived in the Graveyard only a few days ago,' said Straben, then with a shrug, 'I didn't expect you to act so quickly.'

I looked at the desk, noting a flimsy screen up out of the surface and the holographic virtual control Straben had been using a moment ago. The screen was blank. I tried my hand in the control but it wouldn't respond to me.

'It's genetically coded to me,' he said.

'I could always cut off your hand,' I suggested.

'That won't work either,' said Straben, for the very first time showing some sign of anxiety.

I gazed at him for a second, then waved him out into the main office space. He nodded congenially and walked over to where the window had been and stepped through.

'Questions now?' he asked.

'Yes, questions,' I replied.

Straben halted and turned towards me, tilted his head irritatingly like Harriet, and waited.

'So,' I said, 'was it your intention to try and seize the *Coin Collector*?'

Straben gazed at me in apparent puzzlement. 'Certainly not. It was my intention to sell you some valuable artefacts I have obtained.' He turned slowly to survey the wreckage around him. 'But it seems I was mistakenly under the impression that you were a reasonable man I could do business with.'

I fought down another surge of irritation. We couldn't stay here much longer. John Hobbs might have decided to look the other way but he wouldn't do so for much longer. There would be reports going in of an incident here and he would have to respond.

'From Penny Royal's planetoid?' I suggested.

'Yes,' said Straben. 'I have them in a secure location and, despite this unfortunate mess,' Straben gestured about himself. 'I am still prepared to do business.'

'So which of your vessels salvaged them?' I asked.

'The *Cadiz* – it got there before Hobbs or any of the other vultures.' Straben smiled as if in pleasant recollection. He was certainly a cool customer and was now growing more confident. 'The objects concerned seem to be part of something larger and certainly contain U-space tech, though precisely what they are for is a puzzle.'

The objects sounded precisely like what the Client was seeking, which was beyond suspicious. It was also the case that before coming down here I'd thoroughly checked the relevant details Tank had taken from the *Layden*'s data store. Straben was lying, though to what degree and precisely what his aims were remained unclear.

194

'Wrong answer,' I said. 'The *Cadiz* was in the prador Kingdom at the time.'

Straben hid his shock well, but it was evident. 'Do you honestly think I keep *precise* records of my ship itineraries?'

'Possibly not.' I shrugged. 'But apparently you shut down your salvage operation decades ago.' I paused contemplatively for a moment. 'In fact, as I understand it, John Hobbs would be the best to ask about artefacts from the planetoid since it seems his salvagers were the only ones that went there before everything of value was obliterated by some sort of chain reaction, and that the artefacts he did obtain were routed directly to the Polity.'

'So John Hobbs might tell you,' said Straben, obviously thinking quickly now. 'He was trying to nail down the market – make it exclusive.'

He paused, searching for further excuses and lies, so I quickly interjected, 'Perhaps you could tell me about the warehouse you've been renovating – the one located on an asteroid in this system.' He definitely couldn't hide his shock now. 'Perhaps you might like to tell me why you felt the need to kit out the place with so much armament along with a hardfield caging system?'

'How can you –'

'You set the bait and that's the trap,' I said.

Now he was lost for words. I gave him a little while, but he lost the struggle as Harriet moved up to stand beside him, leaned her head down and gave him a long sniff.

'No more lies,' I said turning to Harriet. 'Usual method: if he lies again I give you the nod and you bite off his right hand.'

Harriet danced from foot to foot, champed her jaws then as usual licked round her mouth with her long red tongue.

'Now,' I continued, 'what exactly is all this about?'

Straben just stood staring at Harriet for a long while. He shrugged, then sighed.

'It's about the reward,' he said.

'What reward?'

'I will need guarantees,' the man replied.

'You can guarantee that if you don't answer my questions Harriet will first eat your hands. If that doesn't work she'll start on you from the feet up.'

'You are rather brutal and uncivilized in your dealings,' Straben observed primly.

That was it. That was the limit. A man who cored and thralled human beings to sell the prador was calling *me* uncivilized? I reached down to my thigh, opened the patch in my trousers then mentally unlocked the hatch in my leg there. I took out the *other* gun and weighed it in my hand. Harriet, noting this, look a pace back. It didn't look like much – just a heavy chromed revolver.

'Your last chance,' I said mildly.

Straben could obviously see I was feeling a bit testy. He quickly said, 'A fortune in any form required, a Polity amnesty for all crimes *and* a free fifty year pass into the Kingdom ratified by the King himself.'

Puzzling. The Polity never gave amnesties to the likes of Straben, and that the Kingdom and the Polity had agreed on some joint reward seemed just as unlikely.

'There's some heavyweight action behind it,' Straben continued, now taking a step back and resting his weight against one of the desks here. 'I couldn't believe it at first but it really checks out.' He gestured vaguely upwards. 'Polity agents out there and direct confirmation from one of the watch station AIs. The King's Guard are involved too. I don't know what you are involved in but both the prador and the Polity desperately want to get hold of you.'

'It is feasible that such rewards might be offered to negate some very serious threat.'

It took me a moment to realize that Harriet had spoken. I eyed her carefully. Once we were back aboard the *Coin Collector* I felt we needed to have a long talk, and I needed to scan what was going on inside that reptilian skull of hers. However, I knew precisely what she was implying.

'I need to talk to the Client,' I said.

'Yes, I think you do,' Harriet agreed. 'Shall we finish up here?' She tilted her head slightly, directing her gaze towards the gun I held.

There was nothing more to be learned from Straben. I returned my attention to the man and fired once, the kick jerking the barrel up and the shot going into his stomach and flinging him back across the desk. Even so, I'd dialled down the impact of the bullet to suit the human form, since this gun had been designed to punch bullets through a prador's natural armour.

The man lay gasping, then abruptly jerked, stretched out flat and went into convulsions. Black threads spread across his skin and his flesh started swelling. He emitted a gargling scream then slumped into stillness just as brown sprouts broke out of his skin like spear points, then began to swell at their tips. These swellings, each rapidly growing to the size of a tennis ball, turned a darker brown and acquired widely scattered black scales.

'Fascinating,' said Harriet. 'So it doesn't take control of the host – just kills quickly?'

'It's weaponized,' I replied. 'There's no advantage in spread by it keeping the host alive since that comes with sporulation – and at a point of growth the host cannot survive.'

Harriet glanced round at me. 'But sporulation has been retarded I presume?'

'It has – I don't want to kill off the whole colony here.'

She nodded thoughtfully, then asked, 'I am right in assuming that this is based on *ophiocordyceps unilateralis* or as it is known as on Earth, the 'zombie ant fungus'?'

'It is,' I said, slightly stunned by her sharpness.

'And that is just one of your bullets?'

'Yes.'

'Fascinating,' she repeated.

This sharp new Harriet would be, I thought, fascinated to know that this particular weaponized parasitic fungus would also be an effective way to kill another creature, a multiply renewing one. But that wasn't something I wanted to think about too much, especially with another *conversation* due with the Client…

Upon returning to the *Coin Collector* I delayed and delayed, but the Client was not to be denied – always testing its connections to my mind, always *pushing*.

Time.

The stabbing sensation in my head told me I had delayed too long. I closed my eyes and began numbing all the nerve connections to my artificial body, highlighting the other intrusive connections in my skull. The link, running via the thing sitting in the tank to the ship's U-space communicator, opened up. And all at once I returned to hell.

Rage and suspicion came first, with that always-present undercurrent of loss. I stretched a hundred feet tall; a conjoined chain of insect forms reaching towards the roof of the deep volcanic chamber, a boiling wind blowing across the nearby lake of lava raising the temperature just enough. Hive creature and hive, perpetually dying and giving birth, immortal, the Client clung now to ersatz trunk of a giant tree being fashioned of silica crystals by one of its exo-forms – a thing like a giant horseshoe crab suspended from the roof by a long jointed tail. It read me, and peeled its upper section from the tree in its fear, emitting a pheromone fog, distributing it with the beating of glassy wings. Exo-forms down below like manta rays on spider legs, hoovering up and crunching down old fallen husks from past renewals, bleated and bumped against each other in bewilderment.

Synaesthetic interpreters finally cut in as I contained a scream in my skull, and turned complex organic chemicals to something I could truly understand. Then came a pause, with a scene replaying in my mind: my killing of Gad Straben. I felt avidity, then came words.

'It is time for you to come to me,' the Client told me, a whole avalanche of meaning falling in behind the words. 'The danger is too great.'

The connection faded. Time passed and I reconnected to my artificial body. I sat for an hour in my chair feeling as if on the point of death and slowly, ever so slowly, brought myself back to my world.

'Harriet,' I said, my voice grating.

'I'm here,' she replied from very close.

'It seems our search must end because the Client thinks the danger from the Polity and the Kingdom is too great,' I said, testing the words aloud for their veracity.

'The search is over,' said Harriet, and there seemed a lot more meaning behind her words than plain parroting. She then asked, 'You have the coordinates?'

I looked around at her. She was standing right beside my chair and seemed far too eager and interested for my liking. I suddenly knew, with absolute certainty, that to supply her with those coordinates would put me in immediate danger. How did I know? I'm not sure, but it seemed to me the old Harriet was right back – the one I trusted to complete a mission for pay, but no more than that.

'The coordinates have been sent, but not to me,' I lied, and sat upright. 'Tank has them.'

Harriet swung round to gaze at the object concerned and seemed about to say something more when the drag of the ineffable took us, and the *Coin Collector* entered U-space. I stood up, Harriet swinging her attention back towards me. I did not know how far we would have to travel to reach the Client's location but, this being an ancient prador vessel, I knew it would probably have to drop out of U-space to cool off, and I felt that on those occasions I would have to watch Harriet very closely.

The first time the *Coin Collector* surfaced from U-space, I was prepared, but Harriet seemed to go into that childlike lost puppy phase and showed no sign of acting against me in any way. I even gave her some very dangerous openings – ones that might have resulted in me ending up in pieces on the deck, but she ignored them. Perhaps I had been deluding myself about her? Perhaps I was so used to what had seemed to be her mental decline that my suspicions had only been aroused by it ceasing and reversing? I decided thereafter to take some simple precautions when around her, like always carrying my two weapons, but no more than that. She deserved at least some of my trust, and I had work to do.

The Client had summoned me to it and perforce I had to go, but its orders were no more complex than a summons and that gave me some freedom of action. I started with the thetics, wiping their base programming and designing something of my own. I needed them to be able to carry out certain instructions and, most difficult of all, I needed them to be able to continue carrying out those instructions even if I ordered them to do otherwise. The simple reality was that at close proximity, the Client would be able to seize complete control of my mind and thus, through me, the thetics. I needed them to continue, to give distraction, to give me a chance...

The second time we surfaced from U-space Harriet came and found me in the Captain's Sanctum, deeply internalized, trying to gauge what resistance I had to the Client's control of me, if any at all. She could have killed me then because I was completely vulnerable what with most of my nervous system shut down. Instead, she just walked over to stand before me and, as I returned to a normal state of consciousness and responsiveness, she spoke.

'There's something you need to see,' she said.
'What?' I asked.

She just turned around and headed back towards the door. I weighed pros and cons as I stood up, then I decided to follow her. It struck me as unlikely she was leading me somewhere she could attack me, since she could have done the job just then. She waited outside the sanctum beside the scooter I had last used to get here, dipped her head towards it, then turned and set off along the corridor. I mounted up and followed and, with a glance back, she increased her pace. She led me into the cargo section of the ship, a place I did not often visit, then to a wide square door into a particular hold space. As I dismounted, I recognized this door at once, but kept my own counsel as she nosed the control beside it to send it rumbling and shuddering to one side.

I followed her in and surveyed my surroundings as the lights came on. The cargo the three hundred feet square space contained had not changed much over the years since I had last been here. The large first-child, who had been the captain of this ship, rested in one corner like a crashed flying saucer, most of its limbs still intact but now one of its claws having dropped away. A short distance from this prador corpse, second-children had been stacked like, well, crabs on a seafood stall. This stack had collapsed on one side and noting some movement there, I walked over. As I approached, an eight-inch long trilobite louse scuttled out, heading straight for my legs. I kicked it hard, slamming it into the wall above the stack of second-child carapaces.

'It's because of the ship recharging with air,' I said. 'There must have been ship louse eggs somewhere, and moisture in the air must have reversed the desiccation of these.' I gestured to the dead before me, including a mass of third-children and smaller prador infants piled in the further corner

I hadn't seen anything but dead ship lice aboard when I returned to consciousness here a century ago. Then the ship entire had been almost in vacuum, and when I first ventured down here the erstwhile crew had been vacuum dried. Gradually the ship's automatic systems had recharged the whole vessel with air, but it had taken decades.

'The lice are unimportant,' Harriet intoned, her seriousness undermined when she had to kick away a louse trying to crawl up her leg.

'I've seen all this,' I said, gesturing about the hold. 'I know that the Client slaughtered the prador aboard. So what, the prador slaughtered its entire species.' I didn't mention how the way the corpses had been sorted and neatly stacked always bothered me. Had the Client kept these as a food source? Could it actually ingest this alien meat?

'You've seen all this,' Harriet parroted.

She abruptly turned away and paced across the hold. I sighed and walked after her, but as I drew closer, I suddenly realized that there was another square door in this far wall. I paused, scanned about myself, then realized I had never spotted it before because I'd never felt any inclination to walk this far into this dim mausoleum. Harriet nosed a control beside this new door and, rumbling and shaking, it too drew open. I followed her inside.

More dead, I realized, and more ship lice. I gazed at the neat heap – stacked like firewood – for a couple of seconds before reality caught up with me. These weren't prador; they were human corpses. I stood staring for a long drawn-out moment, then forced myself into motion and walked over to inspect them more closely. The corpses here were also vacuum dried and many of them had suffered the depredations of ship lice, which in places had chewed them down to the bone. I turned my attention to one nearby that had obviously been dragged from the stack by lice and completely stripped of flesh. The lice had ignored the uniform, obviously getting inside it to dine on the meat. I recognized the uniform at once. I was looking at the skeleton of an ECS commando.

Moving closer, I saw further uniforms, but also a lot of casual dress, a high proportion of clean-room labwear and the occasional spacesuit and vacuum survival suit. There had to be over a hundred people here.

'You've seen this?' Harriet enquired.

'No,' I replied.

'Do you remember?'

I turned towards her. 'No, I don't.'

I felt slightly sick as I turned away. It must have been a wholly psychological feeling since my artificial body was incapable of nausea. So why had Harriet brought me here to see this? I didn't know, all I did know was that I was standing beside the entire scientific team – plus ECS security personnel – that had been sent to liaise with the Client. Now turned around I saw what lay beside the door. I eyed a glittering stack of crystal fragments, and ten human corpses untouched by desiccation or decay because, of course, they weren't human but Golem androids. Beside them rested two huge metal beetles, motionless, no light gleaming in their crystal eyes: war drones. It seemed the Client had killed the AI complement of that mission too.

I headed out of the hold.

The moon was highly volcanic because it was one of many similarly sized moons irregularly orbiting an ice giant. While the giant they orbited tore at them gravitationally, they also tore at each other. Running a model of the system, I saw that at least two of these moons would shattered in about a hundred thousand years, thereafter it would stabilize as an asteroid ring – the remaining moons being shepherds.

'Do you have something you wish to tell me?' I asked Harriet as I gazed at the images displayed in the hexagonal screens.

'I have nothing I can say to you yet,' she replied.

Was that because we were too close to the Client now? I could feel its influence reaching out to me, demanding, dictatorial. Coordinates sat clear in my mind as the *Coin Collector* lurched under fusion drive, dropping lower and decelerating. Even if I wanted to stop this, to go away and never head for those coordinates, I couldn't, for Tank controlled the ship now.

The world was mostly black, etched with red veins and red maculae, white at their centres with hot eruptions, smears of grey ash spread equatorially from these. It drew closer and closer, the great ship's engines roaring and it shuddering around us.

'Why are we landing?' Harriet asked.

The question was obviously rhetorical.

'Perhaps,' she continued, 'the bathyspheres are not large enough to convey what needs to be conveyed.'

I had never described the Client to her, so was she guessing or did she know? It was true, nevertheless, that if the Client wanted to move itself and its multitude of minions aboard this ship, then the ship had to land. What did this then mean for me?

Soon the horizon was an arc across the whole array of screens before me and we seemed to be coming down on a relatively stable plain before a range of mountains like diseased fangs. Scanning gave me a cave system deep in those mountains, precisely at the location of the coordinates in my mind, while the *Coin Collector* aimed to land to one side of them. I stood up and headed for the door, Harriet as usual close behind me. As I mounted my scooter, I then sent orders from my artificial body – orders I hoped I could not rescind.

While heading down into the bowels of the ship I turned to Harriet, pacing easily at my side. 'The air out there isn't breathable.'

She flicked her head once. 'It doesn't matter – I ceased to need breathable air long ago.'

'So you underwent more modifications than I know about?'

'Some,' she replied.

Lower down sulphur laced the air in the ship and it was hot. It ceased to be breathable for a human being, or any creature that needed oxygen, on the lower level, as we approached a massive open door with a ramp extending from it to the charred ground below. I parked my scooter beside the door, hoping I would be able to return to use it, but doubtful of that, and I began walking down. My artificial lungs had now ceased to process what they were breathing and my body had gone over to power cells and stored supplies.

'What are they?' Harriet asked.

I peered out across the plain at the four creatures approaching. They looked like manta rays hovering just above the ground as they swept towards us, but upping the magnification of my eyes I could then pick out the blur of insect legs moving underneath them.

'Exo-forms is what we called them,' I replied. 'The Client is a hive creature and a hive all in one, perpetually conjoined, being born and dying all in one and able to meddle at genetic levels with its parts. It is a natural bio-technician, geneticist, and makes forms like this to interact with environments outside its preferred one. It was a form something like these that acted as a translator.'

'So your memories are clearer,' Harriet suggested, as we proceeded on down.

I realized they were, and I remembered the terrible anger of the Client when the AIs shut down the project, though the results of that anger were unclear but for those corpses in the hold, just as were details of the project itself before that, and precisely how the AIs had closed it down. How could the AIs have broken up and scattered the farcaster when the Client had slaughtered the whole team, including its AIs?

The ramp was shaking – perpetual tremors transmitted from the ground and through it to my feet – but the new rumble was something else. As I stepped off onto a surface of shattered and then heat-fused chunks of obsidian, I turned.

'Here they come,' I said, and stepped aside.

The thetics were already a quarter of the way down the ramp, over two hundred of them now. They were all clad in hard shell spacesuits of a combat design that enabled them to move quickly. They came down in good order at a steady trot, in neat rectangular formations. At the base of the ramp, they spread out, utterly ignoring me, following their orders. Two groups of them then went down into firing positions and pulse-rifle fire cut through the poisonous air towards the approaching exo-forms. Two of them immediately went down, ploughing into the ground like crashing gravcars. Two more swept to one side, but then a missile from a shoulder launcher hit between them and sent them tumbling. The thetics then moved on at a run, heading for the coordinates in my mind.

The Client was very very disappointed in me and I now expected punishing pain, which I felt sure, I could now resist for long enough. I followed the thetics out, my mental defences as tight and as ready as they could be. But the Client did not attack and, in those parts of my mind where it had its grip, all contact slid into something completely alien – beyond my understanding.

'It's a good plan,' Harriet opined, 'but for the Client's defences and its absolute hold on you.'

'What do you mean?' I asked, now breaking into a fast loping run.

'I mean,' said my troodon companion, easily keeping pace with me. 'You ordered the thetics to go in after the Client and attack it, and then you disconnected yourself from them so you could issue no further orders, so the Client could not force you to order them to desist.'

'And?'

'You hoped that if they didn't kill it they would at least keep it distracted enough for you to get close and use the weapon you designed specifically to kill it.'

'You seem to know rather a lot,' I suggested.

A battle now raged ahead of us, at the foot of the mountains. We reached it just as it was terminating, exoforms like giant horseshoe crabs turned over and smoking like wrecked tanks, thetics reverting in the grip of long white worms, others pouring out of suits torn apart by ice-pick mandibles. But many were left, all funnelling into the wide cave mouth ahead. I followed them in.

At last, said the Client, perfectly understandable.

The cave sloped down, ever darker, then lit with a hellish glow. The chamber seemed to have no limits. It seemed I had walked through some Narnian doorway out onto the surface of a hotter brighter world. Ahead of me, I saw thetics keeling over, one after another and I couldn't see what was killing them. I kept walking; found I could not stop walking. I stepped over and past hard shell suits and observed dissolving faces behind chainglass visors. Harriet was still beside me and I glanced across at her.

Kill me now, I thought, but couldn't say.

'It's killing them with the farcaster,' she said, dipping her head to indicate what lay ahead.

The Client was wound around its crystal tree, large wasp-like segments conjoined in a great snake hundreds of feet long. At its head was the primary form, which I could see was an adult some days away from death and yet to be cast away like those husks scattered on the ground all around, to allow the next creature-segment take over. At its tail its terminal segment was giving birth to another, which would remain attached and in its turn give birth. The whole cycle – the time it took for the terminal form to reach the head – was just solstan months long. Meanwhile, all those segments fed, chewing down an odd rubbery nectar exuded by the crystal tree, which in turn extracted the materials to make it from the ground below, and from the husks the exoforms fed to its nanomachine roots. But there was something else about that tree too. It fed the Client, supported the Client, and was the totality of its technology and, near its head, a crystal flower had bloomed: the farcaster.

Soon I was circumventing the husks of former head segments. Reaching the base of the tree, I saw the last of the thetics collapsing around me, and I went down on my knees. I don't know whether that was my own impulse or an instruction from the creature rearing high above me. I managed to turn my head slightly, searching for Harriet, just in time to see her huff out a haze of smoke, slump, and then sprawl beside me.

I'd let her down. I'd been careless. I felt a surge of grief immediately followed by a dead dark hopelessness. What was the point now? What was the point of ... continuing?

Give me the gun, said the Client.

The farcaster was here and my search had been a pointless one. I just couldn't understand, I just couldn't ... and then I saw it.

The human body lay inside some kind of pod at the foot of the tree, almost like a flower yet to open. Through crystal distortions I could see it nestled in white snakes, some attached to it, small ones around the gaping wound in its skull, a large one entering its mouth, others attached here and there around a body that had been broken and torn. And through crystal distortions I recognized my own face.

Give me the gun. It wasn't an instruction in human language but a need, a chemical pattern, a chain of pheromones perpetually renewing. Somehow, I found the strength to resist, and saw the snakes wriggling about my doppelganger lying under crystal ahead.

No, I managed.

It could send one of its exoforms to take me apart and thereafter seize the gun. I knew with absolute certainty that it had finished with me. I was a tool it had employed and all its tools died when their usefulness ended. I knew with utter certainty that I was going to die. I just did not want to die in ignorance.

Explain, I tried.

The Client at once understood that I accepted defeat and death, and relented.

The pressure came off and I found myself deeper in the Client's distributed mind, ever dying and ever renewing. Chemical language offered itself and I accepted. I was both myself and the Client again, and its memories opened.

I soon understood what had killed the thetics and Harriet: energy dense micro-explosives no larger than spores but detonating inside with the force of gunshots. The Client had farcast such explosives into the prador aboard the *Coin Collector*, draining its limited supply of energy and those same explosives, before escaping aboard that ship so long ago, while the worlds of its kind burning and tearing apart under prador kamikaze assault.

Why not all, I wondered.

It could have made more of these explosives and steadily annihilated every prador in existence, surely? No, because there were trillions of prador and each first-child or second-child, as the Client had learned, could not be killed with just one such explosive. And here was the complete killer of that idea: it needed to know the precise locations of its targets. It needed help; it needed spotters to locate prime targets like father-captains, like the king of the prador. And it needed a weapon that once farcast into such a target would then wipe out all the prador around it – it's family. That's where the Polity came in, and that's where I came in: one of the Polity's prime biowarfare experts.

I felt the rage again. The orders had been explicit: nothing was to remain. Even as I hit the destruct to turn all my computer files to atomic dust and burn up my samples in thousand Watt laser bursts, the micro-dense explosives tore me apart, and I knew nothing. Now, however, I understood how little trust the Client had of its allies, how it had targeted them all, killing all the humans in the team, shattering the crystal minds of all the AIs. Then, realizing its mistake, it had come for me, and incorporated me – drawn me in like a damaged but still useful exo-form.

But the journey, why the pointless search?

The Client needed me separate from it because as an exoform close to it I could pick up on some of its thoughts and might uncover the lie, and learn that the farcaster was intact and that it wanted the bio-weapon I had destroyed. That separation, maintained by the first-child ganglion in the tank and U-space communications, it could shut down in an instant. With our minds so close, why could it not take the design of that weapon straight from my brain? It couldn't, because it wasn't there – it was lost with a large chunk of my brain. However, my skills remained and I was capable of remaking it.

It took the Client many years to build my avatar. It used one of the Golem whose mind it had destroyed, it used elements of the thetic program, which had been the product of one of the research team it had killed, and it did the best it could. It needed me motivated to rebuild that weapon. My motivation was an ersatz freedom, maintained by my ostensible separation from the

Client and the firm knowledge that the bioweapon would work as well against it as against the prador. I responded as predicted. I remade that weapon, it resided aboard the *Coin Collector*, and it resided inside the bullets in the gun inside my thigh.

Give me the gun.

I realized that the action of handing over that weapon wasn't the main thing the Client required, but its consequence. By handing over the gun I would unlock the knowledge inside me.

Trillions of prador. I didn't like them very much but such a genocide appalled me. The Client had its farcaster – had never been without it – and shortly it would have the weapon to annihilate them all. How it intended to target them I didn't know, but it could find a way for it had the time of an immortal and the utter certainty of purpose. I put up futile resistance and agony filled my skull, not the one in my artificial body, but in that one over there, wrapped in worms and entombed in crystal. My vision was blurred as I stared at the seared ground and fought for, I don't know, at least some redemption from what was to ensue. Then my vision cleared a little, and I saw a strange thing.

Ten objects lay scattered across the ground in front of me. They were, colourful curved spikes, shocking pink.

I gave up, simultaneously sending the signal to open the hatch in my thigh while reaching down to tear aside the canvas flap. My hand closed around the butt of my fungus gun and I withdrew it, all the knowledge of what its bullets incorporated riding up inside me. I really wanted to aim the weapon at the Client and pull the trigger, but that was utterly beyond me. I turned it, rested it in the flat of my hand and presented it. Already the Client was looping down, both mentally and physically multiple wings roaring to support its weight, its wasp-like leading segment reaching out with four limbs terminating in hands that seemed to be collections of black fish hooks, black hooks in my skull too.

But it was the hand of a reptile, sans claws, that took the gun.

'Tuppence,' said a voice, but I was still in that moment.

I saw Harriet aiming the gun with a dexterity she had seemingly not possessed in many decades. One shot went into the Client's leading segment, into its thorax, which in turn partially melded to the head of the segment behind. I second shot went in two segments back from that. Then another two shots went in widely spaced, one after another. The hooks withdrew from my mind but I was rigid with agony, the Client's agony. I managed to turn my head in time to see Harriet flung aside by a detonation in her side. It tore a hole, but this did not reveal gore but something hard and glittery. She rolled, came up again and fired the remaining two shots.

'Tuppence.'

A roaring scream filled the cavern as of a whole crowd thrown into a furnace. The Client reared back and wrapped itself around its tree, black lines rapidly spreading from the bullet impact sites. It shed its forward form, birthed behind, sucked on the crystal tree suddenly turned milk white as it filled with nutrient. It birthed and shed in quick succession, its discarded segments falling about me not as dry husks but soggy and heavy as any corpse. I saw one issuing brown sprouts, spore heads expanding. The Client fought on for survival, tearing at its tree, crystal began to fall and shatter then like the dried wings of its husks once had. Around me, I now saw exoforms, but there was no coherence to them – they were just running, crashing into each other, crashing into the walls of the cavern.

213

'Tuppence.'

At last it ended, the Client freezing round its tree, final segments infected, one newly born freezing halfway down its birth canal, a last head segment falling. The Client died sprouting a fungus, which in its original form, killed mere ants. I died too. Under crystal I saw black threads spreading then all sight of my body blotted out as a spore head exploded in there.

'Oh will you snap out of it!'

I opened my eyes. I was aboard the *Coin Collector*, in my chair, facing my array of screens. The Client's world was there in vacuum and, around it, I could see the flash of fusion drives and the distant bulks of ships.

'Why am I alive?' I asked, peering down at my battered artificial body.

'You're not,' said Harriet. 'You're dead.'

I turned to study her. She had put her artificial claws back on and had painted them bright custard yellow, even applied some eye shadow of the same colour. It occurred to me then that I should have wondered, what with her supposedly being so inept with her claws, how she had always so neatly applied the nail varnish and other make-up. Transferring my gaze to her side, I could see no sign of her injury, just clean scaled skin.

'What do you mean I'm dead?'

'The Client used stock memcrystal for the processing in your avatar. That crystal has more than enough storage to contain a human mind. You're a copy and even though your human body is dead, you live. You are you, Tuppence.'

I wasn't quite sure how I felt about that.

'Are you Polity?' I asked. 'Are you a Polity *agent*.'

'No, completely independent,' she replied cheerfully.

'I'm confused.'

214

'Understandable – it's been a trying day.' She paused while I stared at her, then relented. 'Okay, you hired me and I got thoroughly screwed. The damage was bad and it was way beyond the reward you gave me, or the facilities available at that hospital. That war-drone made a real mess. Then, while I was in the hospital, I received an offer I couldn't refuse. They'd pay to repair me. They'd bring in the expertise. They'd pay to turn me into what I am now –'

'And what are you now?'

'I'm practically indestructible, and more machine than lizard.' She paused. 'And with a mind distributed about my body so it couldn't be killed with a single farcaster shot.'

'Right,' I said. 'Please continue.'

'I was to stick with you, and lead them to the Client.' Harriet paused. 'However when I worked out what you were up to, I went for the bigger reward – the one for offing the Client.'

'The Polity,' I said, feeling slightly disgusted.

'Polity technology, certainly, but not the Polity or its AIs.' She pointed a claw at the screens. 'Them.'

I stared at the screens for a long moment, then reached out and upped the magnification. They weren't Polity ships out there swarming around the Client's world; they were prador dreadnoughts.

I wasn't sure about how I felt about that either.

'What now?' I asked.

Harriet raised a claw up in front of her face.

'The yellow was a regrettable mistake, I think.'

Just then the *Coin Collector* shuddered, and I realized something large had just docked. I guessed the prador were bringing her reward, and wondered if that might be regrettable too.

END

BIOSHIP

The sea is a deep umber, carrying peaty silt in every wave. Flashes of pink and white break through like wounds in dark skin, where multi-legged beasts squirm and feed in the laden water. Easily breasting the swell comes the ship. Two rudders like flippers jut from the rear of this inverted turtle hull. A gaping manta maw hoovers muddy water and squirming crustaceans, which the ship filters out, jetting wastewater from its stern to boil the sea and drive it ever onward. On a deck of glittering oyster-shell nacre, Sian Simmiser stands with Tom John Cable and gazes with slot-pupilled eyes at the horizon. Cloud, like a steel cliff rises up into the lavender sky.

'And so the season rides upon us like apocalypse,' says Sian.

'Poetic,' replies Tom John. 'But fifty days of rain holds no poetry to me.'

Sian smiles at him and wonders if he realizes that everything he says holds a kind of poetry to her. She turns at the sound of the cabin door popping and tries not to glare at Captain March.

'Two days and the hold'll be egg-bound,' he says. 'Leastways we'll be back in port for the worst of it.'

March chews at his lip tendrils and stares speculatively at Sian, who turns away, annoyed at this attention from him she has had over the last few days, further annoyed that Tom John does not give her the same. She glances beyond the Captain to the high bridge where many of the crew watch the coming storm through transparent shell.

'The ship could do with a rest. Seas have been thick here,' says Tom John.

'She'll work until the last or know the consequences,' the Captain replies.

Sian pretends not to be needled by that. The Quill is asexual so should never be referred to as 'she'. This particular Captain's cruelty to his bioship is also something that both disgusts and frightens her. She has seen the results in the Quill's almost obsequious manner to him – the way it opens doors and extrudes hull steps whenever he approaches, and has biolights scuttling to keep up with him when he patrols the lower hull.

'Best I check below. Make sure she's ready to close up,' says Tom John.

'I'll come with you,' says Sian – anything to get away from the Captain's piggy gaze and wet mouth.

'You know, you should be careful,' says Tom John as they cross the deck.

Sian glances back to the Captain who strolls to the rail with his hands clasped behind his back. Careful? Should she accede to the Captain's obvious lust when that is the most she wants to avoid? Careful because of some other nebulous threat?

The hatch comes up with a ripping sound as the resinous seal exuded by the ship breaks and Tom John leads the way down into the dim luminescence of the hold. Sian follows as he reaches the bottom of the ladder, conscious all the way down of his presence below her, hoping he is watching her descend. She wonders what it will take to get through to him finally. Must she walk naked into his cabin? Today she wears a toga with no undergarment. She wonders if the draught she is getting is worth the effort. Halfway down the ladder she looks down and sees Tom John staring up. She smiles at him. He blushes and swallows and moves quickly away from the ladder. Sian feels a satisfaction at a chase well begun.

Captain March stares at the sea and wonders just what Sian's game is. Over the sensory link from her cabin to his, she has shown him what she wants: provocative and posing naked. He has signalled his agreement, but she seems not to notice. Perhaps it is time for a bit of coercion? She must know what he is, so that must be what she wants. He needs to get her alone, but Tom John seems to have a limpet-like attachment to her. So thinking, March abruptly turns from the rail spines and heads for his cabin. The Quill, sensing his approach to his own quarters unseals the shell door and swings it aside on hinge muscles, and inside extrudes a sleep-clam, which it opens to reveal scarred and lacerated flesh. March moves past the clam to where a nerve node protrudes, with veins extending from it across the glistening wall. He hammers the node with his fist and the whole cabin shudders. With a sucking inhalation, Quill abruptly retracts the clam, then forms a sensory manifold out of the surface of the node: a complexity of tubes and a single squid's eye.

'Now I have your attention,' March says, interlacing his fingers and stretching them against each other. He is about to reach out to the manifold when he notices a web of flesh blistering out from the wall between two veins.

'Did I ask for this?'

His reply is a flickering of random pixels in the surface of the flesh, which slowly resolve into a picture. This picture is one he knows Quill has built by sonar imaging, as its source is utterly lightless. He sees a smooth surface breaking into ripples around an area where a snakelike form has attached. Here then is his solution: remoras are Tom John's field of expertise.

The motors are spliced from bivalves and their action produces a sound as of huge wet sex. Tom John is utterly conscious of this as he connects nutrient sacks to the huge pulsating bodies. Each sack weighs twenty kilos and the work of bringing them from the refining organ is making Sian sweat, in the dark warmth of the hold, and this sweat is sticking her toga to the curves of her body. And Tom John is aware of this too. With his wrist spur, he punctures each bean-shaped sack before pushing it into the feeding receptacle of each motor and, at each motor, he presses his fingers into the sensory pits of the nearby wall to bring biolights scuttling across the ceiling to gather above him. The creatures cling with black spider legs as tic-like they attach to the ship-flesh ceiling and cast down blue luminosity from their sugar-bag bodies. He feels somehow safer with this light about him – less susceptible to Sian's obvious intent. Increasingly he is wondering why he should deny himself. The Captain's claim that she has chosen him does not seem valid.

'That should keep them through the storm,' says Sian, as he takes the last sack from her and pushes it into its elastic receptacle. Tom John nods and surveys the length of the water arteries to the clustered spherical filtration and refining tanks at the fore. The sucking roar from beyond these is now diminishing and the tanks suck and groan with less vigour.

'Closing up,' he observes.

'Then there's nothing more we need to do down here,' Sian replies.

Tom John turns to look at her, and she regards him, waiting.

'Nothing we *need* to do,' he says.

Sian lets out a slow and heavy breath and shakes her head.

'There is something I need you to do,' she tells him.

How ignorant can he pretend to be?

'Someone might come,' he says.

'I want you to come,' she tells him.

They move face to face and he reaches out a hand to her. She takes his hand, brings it up to her mouth and chews at the palm before sliding it down to rest it on her neck, his wrist spur at her throat. Gently trapping his hand with her chin, she undoes the belt and stick-strip of her toga and shrugs the damp fabric to the shell-scaled floor. He notices how her 'daption is not at odds with the smooth lines of her body. Her wrist and ankle spurs carry the mauve pigmentation of her skin, her stomach ribbing runs in a smooth curve from below breasts that seem just the final peak and fold of that ribbing, and her red slotted-pupil eyes and black hair are in perfect complement.

'Here,' she says, pulling him by his hand to one of the water pipes. Guided by her he turns at the last with his back to the pipe. She opens his shirt then trousers and while holding and rubbing his penis, pushes him back so he is sitting on the pipe. In his excitement, he has almost slewed the resinous seal on his glans. She smoothes it away with her thumb, before straddling both him and the pipe. He reaches around one taut buttock to find her seal is long since slewed away, and soon she is sliding onto him. They move to the rhythm of the motors and soon exceed it. The Captain walks out of the darkness to them when they are dressed and ready to return to the deck, and Tom John knows by his flushed look and bitten lip tendrils that he has been in the hold for longer.

Sent like a child to her cabin because a remora has penetrated the hull. Pressured to come here when she objected, because of her infringement of ship's law. And that look the Captain gave her, head to foot, greenish slime on his upper lip from an obviously faulty seadaption – why else the ugliness of lip tendrils and chitin on the palms of his hands, why else the barb

221

on his tongue and his pointed teeth? Sian fumes as her doors rips open accommodatingly and her sleep-clam extrudes and after a moment opens. She ignores it as she discards her toga and pulls a sponge with its trailing stalk from the wall pit. As she swabs herself down and the fluid from the sponge slews down her body to be absorbed by the floor, she swears quietly, and does not notice the squid eye – the sensory link she has no knowledge of – closing in the wall for the last time. Someday, she tells herself, she will have her own ship and no longer be at the beck and call of such a man. Finished washing, she returns the sponge to its pit then flings herself down on the soft wet flesh of her sleep clam. She has shut her eyes when that softness closes down on top of her and gently muffles her screams.

As he moves into the lower hull, Tom John is worried at what the Captain might do, but knows that for the present the remora must take precedence. In a chamber with the shape of a heart, he strokes a nerve node with the back of his hand and steps back so the two biolights that have followed him do not cast his shadow is across it. To his surprise, the node extrudes a sensory manifold before blistering up a map to show the location of the remora penetration. He gazes into the squid eye and wonders why it must sense him before providing what he needs. He glances aside at the cache-bladder down to which the veins from the node, like tree roots, spread.

The long coffin-sized bladder splits with a faint popping and Tom John stoops over it to take out the short bony harpoon he usually uses for this chore. There is another surprise: the weapon revealed to him is a stinger – rather excessive for dealing with a remora. It consists of a tube of ribbed muscle the length of his arm, with two handgrips, and a magazine of stings slung underneath. The pit-trigger in the forward grip he operates with his wrist-spur. He takes up the weapon and holds it so the nearest biolight illuminates the translucent magazine sack. There are four stings inside and he sees that three of them are a different colour from the first to be loaded. He again gazes up at the ship's sensory manifold and the eye gazing back at him is lidded and tightened, before opening again. Squeezing the first of the stings up into the launch tube of the stinger, he goes off in search of the remora, uncomfortable with the fact that the Quill just winked at him.

Beyond the heart chamber, the ship opens out, braced by bony struts between hull divisions. The biolights, keeping with him, are now many metres above. He walks quickly to the rear of the ship, water arteries and food canals revealed in the floor and ceiling. At the appropriate place, he turns to the port and heads for outer hull. Soon he sees that the remora's point of penetration has been accurately located for him, as here is a healed wound, bulbous with tangerine scar tissue. Strangely, it is not a recent wound. He studies the floor and sees the slime trail heading, inevitably, to the rear hold, and follows it. This trail too, is not recent – it is greyish and glutinous as are all old trails on shell where the ship cannot absorb them.

Soon Tom John sees mounded spherical eggs, each large enough to contain a man, bound to the walls of hold by lattices of hardened resin. Over one such mound is poised a wrinkled ovipositor spurring from a thick ceiling artery. It is motionless now that the ship no longer harvests the protein of the sea to convert it into this mounded product. At the first mound, Tom John sees the remora.

The creature is a giant lamprey, but one with ridged chitinous blades on its head stretching back from a triangular mouth filled with red cutting disks. It has penetrated a ship egg, has obviously been feeding for some time, and is now bloated with this unaccustomed bounty. Sensing Tom John's presence, it rears up from its gluttony and indolently swings its head round to face him. Tom John feels no fear as he walks in close enough to be sure not to miss, then aims and triggers the stinger. The weapon contracts in his hand then spits out the loaded sting: a barbed glassy spike with two poison sacs attached. The sting penetrates below the remora's mouth and the sting sacs pulse as they drive the poison into the creature. The effect is electric – the remora flings itself into the air then comes down convulsing and thrashing. After this, its body pulls into a tight arc to the sound of crunching vertebrae, and slowly the creature ties itself into a tight fleshy knot. Tom John turns away and trudges back the way he came, as already the floor is softening around the dead creature, in readiness to draw it down.

The heart chamber is open to him when he returns to it, but the bladder cache inside is closed. The ship's eye regards him and opens up an organic screen.

Sian gasps gratefully at clean air as her sleep-clam opens, and realizes that the air is fresher and colder than usual. She sits upright and sees that her door is open on a wall of grey cloud and drizzle-laden air, and Captain March. She quickly steps from her clam in fear that it might close on her again and stands to face the Captain.

'Simmiser, Simmiser,' he says, and licks at his top lip with his barbed tongue.

'What do you want?' she asks, knowing the answer.

The Captain steps through the doorway, and the door hinges closed behind him. 'I've come to take what you offered and should have given.'

He leers at her nakedness and slides his thumb down the join of his shirt and to the top of his trousers. When he drops his trousers and steps out of them, she sees that in his seadaption what she should have seen long before: he is made for sadism. His barbed penis is erect and the hooked scales on his thighs glitter in the blue light.

'I made you no offer,' she says.

'You could have closed the sensory link any time you wanted,' he tells her.

She backs up, but there is nowhere to go and soon he pins her to the wall. 'What link?'

'Enough of your games,' he mutters, his words slurred.

She fights him but he is hideously strong and quite obviously enjoys her struggles. Soon he will enter her in one way or another and she knows then that the agony will begin. She fights all the harder as he spins her and throws her face down on the clam. But suddenly he bellows with rage and has released her. Sobbing, she turns and sees that he is now facing the wall. A nerve node has appeared there and extruded a manifold and unblinking eye. Why does an unrequested sensory link anger him so? March drives his fist into it, once, twice, then again. The Quill rocks with the pain of his blows and the cabin door springs open to give access to the storm. The howl of the wind and the roar of the sea nearly drown out three sucking thuds. March is screaming and groping for the three stings that pump venom into his back. On the floor he thrashes and groans and squirts green chyme from his mouth. He knots foetal, hands and feet clenched to fists, and the only movement on him the still-pumping stings. Underneath him, the floor softens as the Quill prepares to take him down.

'The ship wanted this,' says Tom John. 'And a rapist deserves no less.'

Sian Simmiser does not reply as she teases the Captain's hook scales out of her thigh and paints finger patterns on her

225

mauve skin with her red blood. She glimpses up at the watering squid eye that regards her.

Hides her fear, her knowledge.

ENDS

SCAR TISSUE

Condensation dewed the cold metal surfaces of the escape pod's interior. He did not want to admit the truth, and damned Jayne's stubbornness as he cradled her. He should have forced her to accept implantation of a doctor mycelium. Her refusal of such invasive measures was illogical, since she had undergone more drastic surgery had been used to install her gridlink. An insentient mycelium would have sufficed. She did not need the kind that spoke. Damn her, damn her... Only hours later did he finally release her. The huge surge of inductance during the attack had turned her gridlink white hot inside her skull, and he realized even a doctor mycelium could not have repaired the damage. It might have kept her body alive, but what is a body without a mind? He never cried, and the unfocused rage that had been the driving force of his genius, focused, and became something frigid.

Dis remembered too, but then Dis was there as well.
> `They think you mad and in their way, they treasure you. You are their relic.`
> *Then everything is as it should be.*
> `Yes: mad Bailey and his dead wife.`

Bailey allowed himself a bitter grin as he gazed out through the bridge window.

The ship had once been a carrier for the fragrant mineral oil pumped from the under strata of Nineva. It retained its name, the *Amoco*, but not its purpose or much of its original appearance. The interior accommodation was now all curved glass and pastel metals, the deck golden with photovoltaic cells, and the bridge had been moved forward to make room for a landing pad. The hull remained the same, but was partially obscured by the floating hotels anchored either side of this five

227

kilometre-long behemoth. These structures glinted with myriad windows and from their lower walls folded out jetties for the mooring of small craft and easy access to the sea. From his padded leather seat, Bailey observed the activity on the jetties. The concessions he had sold there were doing well, as were all the businesses in the public sections of the ship. When he departed, a corporation he had personally funded would take over maintenance of the *Amoco* and more of the private sections would be opened out. He did not want this to happen yet. He did not want people too close to him for what was to come.

The aircar was a small private carrier with the bland look of officialdom. Bailey watched it land and wondered, for the nth time, if this was it.

Give me x50.

There was something like an internal nod from Dis, and Bailey felt the muscles contract around his eyes. Now he could focus on who got out of the car. The woman was certainly no tourist and he had her down as ECS immediately.

`She is Earth Central Security. She asks to speak with you - a request just came through the Foraster marine AI. Low level.`

It would be low level. They wouldn't want it getting about. I'll meet her in the mausoleum

She was determinedly hiding her nervousness by closely studying Jayne's body in its armoured cryopod. As he walked into the dim chamber, Bailey noted the pause while she gathered her resolve, and how when she turned to face him, her determination slipped a little.

`They expect you to look like a madman.`

I know.

'What can I do for you?' he asked pleasantly.

The woman stepped forward and smiled. Her clothing consisted of a monofilament coverall and desert boots. Round her waist she wore a utility belt at which was holstered her pulse gun. An augmentation sat behind her ear, partially concealed by her straight brown hair. Her face was not pretty in the classical sense, but there was strength there.

'Linda Forlam, ECS. Pleased to meet you Mr Bailey,' she said.

He shook her hand, found it warm and damp. The palm of his hand twitched in response, but he reined Dis in – not allowing any invasion. A spasm of disappointment not his own washed through him.

After an embarrassed pause, Linda went on, 'The *Boletus* has been found.'

Bailey did not allow anything to show in his expression. He remembered the wrenching crash of the hit and the pain as the inductance surge fried his aug behind his ear. Through watering eyes, he saw Jayne just dropping bonelessly to the starship deck, and remembered how even then he had known she was unrecoverably dead. Then the scramble for the lifepods, the booms as those pods were ejected, a momentary tilted vision of the *Boletus* hanging in space while a ship like a wedge of midnight closed in, then the blinking distortion as what remained of the ship's AI dropped the *Boletus* into underspace.

'Where?' he asked.

'Out-Polity, about as far out-Polity as you can get. The AI was dead, but it had managed to put a fifty year delay on realspace entry.'

'And the cargo?'

'By the time an ECS ship got there the *Boletus* had been cut open and the cargo snatched. I think there is little question about who now possesses it,' she informed him.

Bailey turned from her to study the flash-frozen corpse of his wife. People felt it was a tragedy how he sought ways to rebuild her mind, how he sought to resurrect his love. They understood so little, because he had not allowed them to understand.

'Thank you for telling me this,' he said, 'but it was not necessary for you to come.'

'I've come to take you into protective custody.'

Bailey smiled and nodded to himself. 'And why should you want to do that?'

'Isn't it obvious? If they manage to utilise that cargo they'll stop Polity expansion in its tracks. Can you imagine what a terrorist could do with those things? They'll want you, and if they get hold of you ...'

Bailey felt a momentary frisson at the thought, and quickly suppressed it.

He glanced back to this woman from ECS. 'I neither want nor need your protection.'

She stared at him for a moment before speaking. 'I'm afraid it's not that easy,' she said, and of course drew her pulse gun.

'Does ECS kidnap its citizens now?' he asked, taking a step closer to her.

Dis, dispersion through the floor.

`As you will.`

Bailey stood with his legs braced. He felt the tightness in his feet as the mycelium punctured the soles of his boots and rooted into the ceramal floor

'It is usually the Separatist excuse. But this is for the greater good. Please come along with me,' she said.

'I think not,' said Bailey.

Linda glanced to Jayne's corpse. 'We'll bring her, of course.'

Bailey shook his head. 'You fail to understand. Really, I don't need ECS protection.'

'Then I'm sorry,' said the woman.

Her pulse-gun flared once. The energy burst hit him in the chest and would have knocked him to the floor had not Dis made his body as of stone. Small lightnings laced his skin and wisps of smoke rose from his clothing. The energy bled away into the deck.

'You see?' Bailey asked.

Perhaps she did see, for the setting of her gun was higher for the next shot, probably remote adjusted from her aug. Bailey stumbled back and fell against the cryopod. His chest felt as if it had been hit with a spade and blackness encroached on the edges of his vision. Looking down he saw the burn where the pulse of ionized gas had burnt into his chest. He allowed himself to go limp and slid down.

You ready?

I am ready.

Pulling a fresh charge cartridge from her belt, the woman walked over and squatted beside him. Bailey reached out and grabbed her wrist. The cartridge clattering away, she gaped at him in blank shock.

'These were your orders?' he asked, air driven up from his undamaged right lung to operate his vocal cords. She tried to pull away.

Now.

The woman winced and with a puzzled expression stared at his hand. An abrupt widening of her eyes signified that she knew what was happening. She tried to pull away, took one gasping breath, then convulsed before dropping unconscious to the floor.

They would risk killing me because of what I know.

This surprises you? asked Dis, his doctor mycelium, as it extracted itself from the woman's body.

They were quick. He gave them that. But then he suspected they had arrived on the *Amoco* not long before or after the ECS agent. Moreover, laden as he was with the armoured cryopod containing his dead wife, he left an easy enough trail to follow. The man wore a long coat with a hood up over his head, and Bailey had no doubts as to what that hood concealed. He brought his own car down before the Hilton and unloaded Jayne with an AG trolley. Observing his tail climbing out of a taxi not far behind him, Bailey noted how little effort the man made at concealment. He supposed they were confident of snatching him before anyone could intervene. After taking the dropshaft to his prebooked room, he settled the cryopod on the thick carpet before settling himself on the sofa. Only moments later the door slid aside again and the man stepped through.

The interloper halted at the threshold for a moment as the door closed behind him. He pushed his hood back to reveal a shaven pate to which clung an augmentation like a huge crystal slug. His eyes were blank metal spheres.

'Well you're the mouth and the mind. Where's the muscle?' Bailey spat.

Seconds after, the window exploded into the room, and in drifted the martial half of this partnership of machine and men. This one bore a human face and torso, but that was all. Its lower body (it not being evident if it was male or female) melded with a transparent sphere, so it appeared this cyborg floated on a large soap bubble. At the centre of the sphere, hanging like genitalia, clustered unidentifiable hardware. From its left shoulder sprouted a heavy manipulator arm ending in a grab, and from its right shoulder extended a smaller arm ending in a complex hand. Below this arm rested yet another, smaller, arm and hand of intricate complexity. Attached to the rear of its skull was a box twice the size of its head, supported by metal struts running down through its back to the sphere, so the flesh part of this individual looked like bait threaded onto a hook.

'Do I have to guess what you want?' asked Bailey.

'You have no need to guess,' said the one with the metal eyes, and gestured to the floating half of the partnership. Bailey turned and saw mechanisms twist and reconfigure in the bubble. A holographic targeting grid snapped into existence, slightly off-centre, between the floating cyborg and the cryopod containing Bailey's wife.

'No, no that won't be necessary,' he said quickly.

A point of light ignited before the floating cyborg's head. Something whispered and, to one side of the pod, a coffee table exploded into a disk of splinters, which collapsed to a point and disappeared with a sound so brief and intense Bailey felt it in his guts. Now the point of light bloomed again, and the grid centred on the cryopod.

He dropped to his knees. 'No!'

'For your information,' said iron eyes succinctly, 'I am Fetch and my partner is Thanos. You will come with us. Your wife will come with us. When you have done what we wish of you, we shall allow you to return.'

Bailey nodded agreement, unable to take his eyes off Thanos.

They distance themselves from humanity and forget how to read humanity.

They are dangerous.

233

Yes, and stupid.

The ancient Japanese man walked like a young man. In the gloom of the mausoleum, he spotted the figure of Linda, prone by an oblong area clear of dust. He studied her for a long moment, his expression unfathomable, moved over to squat beside her, and reached out to press a gnarled hand against her face. When he withdrew his hand, she opened her eyes and sat upright with a gasp. In a moment, she had her breathing under control.

She glared at the old man. 'He could have killed me, and who would have blamed him? I apparently tried to kill him.'

The old man nodded.

'Then tell me why. Why was that necessary?' she asked. 'Couldn't we have slipped it into his morning coffee?'

'His doctor monitors most closely those points where his body ends and the world begins. It watches in his gut, his lungs, and at his skin. We could not have put it in his coffee,' replied Horace Blegg – agent Prime Cause of Earth.

'His clothing?'

'They would detect it.'

'Why not a long shot then? Was it necessary for me to risk my life'

'He believed your intention was to capture him, and if that was not possible, then to kill him.'

Linda stooped and picked up her pulse gun, then the cartridge. 'A distance shot would have been for a kill.'

'Precisely,' said Blegg. 'He knows that we have some idea of his capabilities, and now believes that we merely underestimated them. The ruse worked.'

She grimaced at him.

After that first exchange, the twinned cyborgs quickly got to work. Using its heavy arm in a casual demonstration of power, Thanos loaded the cryopod into an AGC transporter set on hover outside the hotel window.

As it did this, Fetch questioned Bailey. 'Why is this cryopod so heavily armoured?'

'I value her higher than anything. Have you forgotten what it is to be human?'

Fetch did not reply for some time.

'Acceptable,' he said, eventually, then gestured for Bailey to enter the transporter before him.

Once they were all inside, the vehicle shot straight up into the sky. The acceleration slammed Bailey to the floor. When it finally eased, he pulled himself to the hull and rested his back there. Listening to the sounds of seals closing all around him, he knew they were just about to go extraplanetary.

'I take it you snatched the cargo of the *Boletus*?' he said.

'We did,' replied Fetch.

'And you want me to show you how to use it?'

Fetch said nothing for a moment, then turned his head to study Bailey like someone would with real eyes. 'You will show us how to use it. You will open the canister for us, give us all the necessary programming tools, and any other assistance we might require.'

'You're very confident of that,' said Bailey.

'You will do this willingly. If you do not I will destroy your wife's cryopod then put you in a cell with her body while it decays. I will then mind-ream the information out of you before killing you.'

Nothing if not direct.

They will want to mind-ream and kill you anyway.

You state the obvious.

Acceleration dropped off and Bailey felt his weight leaving him. He grabbed a duct running inside the hull and held himself in position. Fetch and Thanos did not move at all; Fetch probably wearing stickboots, and Thanos no-doubt holding position, hovering in the middle of the transporter bay, with micro air jets. They remained thus for an hour. Bailey felt a touch of space sickness; immediately negated by Dis. More manoeuvring, gentle this time, then the sound of docking clamps. Seals cracked and the door opened. Thanos revolved in the air and fixed Bailey with bloodshot eyes. Bailey stood and walked from the transporter with the two cyborgs close behind him.

'You have the cargo here?' he asked.

'We have not,' said Fetch.

The ship bay was wide and circular. Bailey wondered if this vessel was the one that had attacked *Boletus*. It was possible, though he knew that these *people* possessed many such ships. They also owned a station somewhere – he was very sure of that. When he halted to study his surroundings, unsure of where he was supposed to go, steel claws clamped his biceps, something snaked around his ribcage, and sharp fingers clamped his head solidly.

'Do not resist,' Fetch instructed.

Online.

Ready.

With no attempt at care, a needle drove into his hip. He flinched and gritted his teeth, but Dis was on the pain in a second.

Nanocyte tracers.

Can you handle them?

There is nothing to handle. They merely collect information.

236

I don't recollect arrogance as being one of your programmed traits.

You gave me sentience. You must expect that I come to know myself.

Yes, quite.

Fetch moved round before Bailey. The cyborg's crystal aug sparkled with internal light. 'You contain a mycelium.'

'It's only a doctor mycelium – nothing for you to worry about,' said Bailey.

A long pause ensued. The lights in Fetch's aug glowed brighter. 'Confirmed.'

Thanos released its hold on Bailey.

Mass was difficult conceal no matter how advanced stealth technology became, so the craft, *Trapdoor*, was small and cramped. Ensconced in a control chair with consoles and monitors jammed close all around her, Linda gazed through a wide front screen consisting only of a simple chainglass/LCD sandwich. The craft needed no armour or displaced viewing. If an enemy detected it, only speed might work – otherwise she was dead.

'How close are we?' she asked.

Trapdoor, the small ship's AI, was quick to reply. 'Not close enough, and we have a problem.'

On the screen, small numbered lights blinked into existence. Every now and again one of the lights would shift, very quickly, to a new position.

'Micromines,' said Linda. 'How's our vector?'

'Our vector is fine for their present position, but as you just observed, they are randomly shifting,' said Trapdoor.

'There's no such thing as random.'

'The limitations of human language are not my fault,' the AI informed her, a note of distraction in its voice. It was the distraction that reassured Linda. The AI would not have diverted processing power to alter its voice like that if facing grave problems. Trapdoor would sort it. AIs were almost as good at this sort of thing as they were at sarcasm. After a long pause, it spoke again, the distraction still evident.

'There will be an explosion. Do not concern yourself.'

Immediately the screen blacked out. There came a hiss of static and the rushing thrum of coolers as the ship lurched to one side. The temperature inside very quickly rose a few degrees. In a moment, the screen lost its opacity and Linda was able to watch flecks of red hot matter drifting with the ship, and cooling.

'An explanation would be nice,' she said.

'Pattern prediction did not work. The mine that closed on us I detonated at a safe distance with a kilogram of asteroidal rock I carried for just that purpose. Hence, the debris you see. I also used the cover of the explosion to alter our course somewhat. If you look up and to the right ...'

Linda jerked her head up, but for a moment could see nothing. Eventually she realized that up there no stars were visible. She soon resolved the shape of the other ship.

'Big,' was all she said.

'But primitive,' Trapdoor observed. 'You'll be glad to know that we are now detecting the signal from the beacon you so delicately implanted in Ian Bailey's chest.'

'His doctor mycelium didn't find it then,' she said.

'Nor his enemies,' Trapdoor added.

'How long will it take us to reach it?' Linda asked.

'At this speed it will take ten minutes to reach the hull.'

'Any sign of engine start?'

'Their ion drive is heating up. This is what we want, as it will give us cover for deceleration.'

'How fortunate.'

'The shock absorbers would have taken it ... just,' said Trapdoor.

Linda grimaced to herself. She was aware that this craft could take a lot more punishment than its passenger could, and didn't pursue the matter.

The luxurious cabin, in which they installed him, possessed a spa area, panoramic window, automated bar and kitchen, and a huge bed. The bar, kitchen, and spa did not work, and the huge bed still contained its last occupant – a dried-out husk curled foetal under rotten blankets.

Seems they neglect their passengers.

`I do not understand the purpose of this.`

Nothing much to understand really. They just don't care. Aesthetics are irrelevant to them, as is a sense of smell. They don't expend energy on what they would consider a pointless task. Clearing this cabin would be such, as would be making any of the utilities work.

`Why have such a cabin at all?`

I would guess it was cut from another ship. Maybe for me, more likely to get hold of him.

Bailey stared at the corpse for a moment longer, then moved to the panoramic window.

You know, Dis, people were confined to wheeled chairs and other machines because their severed nerves would not heal. Scar tissue got in the way. Now people who interface with machines have the gene, that forms scar tissue, turned off. Scar tissue fouls that interface, blocks the connections, cripples them.

`I knew there was a purpose. Now I fathom it.`

Yes, I knew you would. You are very much like your twin in all but function.

`Human viruses need human cells to procreate.`

239

Yes, yes they do.

`Won't they be suspicious?`

What, of mad Bailey and his dead wife?

Bailey smiled to himself then turned when the door behind him ground open. Fetch walked in while Thanos hovered in the doorway. Fetch stepped to one side and Bailey found himself blinded by intense green light. He felt his face tingling. That tingling spread down his body.

`Nanocytes active again. Also some kind of active scan. Your DNA is being damaged. I am repairing it. Not yet critical.`

Suspicious cyborgs.

The tingling ceased and the green light went out.

`Nanocytes going quiescent. Active scan ceased. I am still repairing damage.`

'Where are your weapons?' asked Fetch.

'I have no weapons,' said Bailey.

Fetch turned his head to one side. Lights flickered in his aug. Perhaps he was receiving instructions.

He said, 'You hate us. You consider us responsible for the death of your wife, and should want us dead. Did you expect us to give you direct and unsupervised access to the cargo canister?'

Bailey shook his head. 'No, I never expected that. But I do have an agenda, my friend.'

'What is this agenda?'

'It's quite simple really. My wife is dead and all Polity technologies will not resurrect her. You, with your advanced cyber technology, could resurrect her. Do this, and I'll open that canister for you and give you that military mycelium with all the programming tools you'll need. I'll release Orcus into your hands and damn the Polity. They did nothing but get Jayne killed.'

There was a long pause and much flickering of lights.

'We will consider your proposal,' said Fetch, eventually. Thanos backed out of the way to allow Fetch to pass, then moved back into view fix Bailey with its bloodshot eyes while the door ground shut.

`They'll swallow that?`

They will. They'll use every lever at their disposal. I'm their only way into that canister.

The little composite craft hit against the pitted hull of the larger vessel. Shock absorbers took the impact and claws bit into the black metal to hold the craft there like a tick. After a couple of minutes, Linda allowed herself to relax a little. If they had been detected, she would have perhaps known about it for the microsecond prior to them being turned into a spreading cloud of debris.

'Now we wait,' she said.

'Not for long,' replied Trapdoor. 'The ion engines have started.'

'How long for this hulk to get up to UE?' she enquired.

'Twenty minutes on ion drive, another twenty on ramjets, then underspace engines will engage. This is presupposing they use maximum all down the line.'

'You'll bet they will for this little operation,' said Linda, then lay back and closed her eyes. Jesu, there was so much riding on this. You didn't get a personal encounter with Agent Prime Cause for an operation unless it was critical, and by critical she meant obliteration of planets critical. That conversation on the asteroid … all very cryptic at the time, but now beginning to make sense…

The star field shot overhead like a speckled belt, since the life bubble lay directly adjacent to the axis of rotation. If you

241

looked at the sky for too long you started to get nauseous. It was best to concentrate on either the floor or the rockscape beyond the transparent walls.

'Sometimes there are useful tools in Pandora's box. We have to take them out, use them for a while, then put them back. This will be the place. Earth Central called it Elba, which doesn't bode well for us closing the lid. You'll bring him here.'

The ensuing conversation with Blegg hadn't made much sense until they got onto mycelia and what Bailey had been working on aboard his ship, the Boletus, *but thereafter she began to realize what she might be dealing with, which, of course, was how Blegg wanted it – he wanted his agents to think. Later, Trapdoor related the myth of Pandora and the history of Elba. She'd not known.*

All the evil in the world.

Mycelium: the filamentous body of a fungus. The thing you saw on the surface of the ground was only the fruit. The plant itself spreading its filament body underground. Bailey's Mycelia lived inside human beings, mostly, and bore strange fruit indeed. They could be defined as artificial intelligences, complex nanomachines, life, even. Doctor mycelia could keep a human practically immortal and alive in very bad circumstances. Military mycelia where enough to give nightmares to the most hardened pessimist. As Blegg implied: some things should go back in the box.

Linda opened her eyes for a moment as the red haze of ramfields opened across hundreds of kilometres of space.

'Wake me when we're there,' she said, and closed her eyes again.

Bailey finished eating the dry block these cyborgs called food. It was all taste with its vitamins and proteins and fats, but it was

242

the taste of marmite and oranges and something else gone putrid. He washed down his meal with one of the cartons of tepid water they also provided. The window changed from underspace grey to starlit black, with a hint of light to one side from the ion drive. There must be something here but Bailey had yet to see it. The ship would not be back on ion drive if there were still any distance to travel.

He crunched up the carton and cast it onto the bed with the rest of the empties, then studied the touchpads on the window sill. They bore pictographs, but none he really recognized. He touched one and the stars took on a hint of violet.

UV I guess.

He persevered until obtaining what he wanted: a gravity map, a picture requiring no light. Now he saw they were approaching a dark orb, from behind which a coin-shaped space station was coming into view. He clicked the view back to normal and now observed lights glinting on the station.

Interesting that they should be in orbit round a dead sun.
Why?

Because it means they probably have a fusion generator on board, rather than use solar power.
I still do not see the interest.

Let us say it would be of more interest to your brother.
Ah.

The door began its laborious grinding and Bailey turned as Fetch and Thanos entered the room.

Bailey remained by the window. 'Do we have an agreement?'

'We do,' said Fetch. 'We will resurrect your wife. As you requested we will even do this before you open the canister for us. Be sure to do what you must do.'

'Oh I will, I will,' said Bailey.

He again gazed out at the station. It wore a circlet of the wedge-shaped ships like a crown, so it seemed most of the bastards were here for the party.

And that makes both of us liars.

`They will try this?`

They will, and it will be the obscenity that will start their downfall.

As the ship drew closer to its destination, unnoticed by Bailey or his captors, a small stealth craft detached from its hull and drifted away. The larger ship docked in its place and completed the circlet over the station. Bailey walked, ahead of Thanos and behind Fetch, down a ramp into the vast interior. Here thousands of cyborgs sped about their duties. Many were like Thanos and Fetch, but more esoteric designs were evident, and others without any trace of humanity – what scraps of it remaining being sealed in metal and crystal. Bailey observed a cyborg that appeared to be human head on a platter. It zipped by to one side of him, while a thing like a giant beetle lumbered past on his other side. When this second mechanism turned he saw it bore a human face. The face seemed to be screaming while the beetle continued its work; in this case the unloading of Jayne's cryopod. Bailey moved towards her, but a steel claw closed on his arm and drew him to a halt.

'When she is ready she will be brought to us,' said Fetch.

Bailey reluctantly followed his captor.

The inside of the station bore little resemblance to a normal human artefact, there being a dearth of the usual elements of human construction like walls and ceilings. There were a few walkways for the likes of Fetch, but otherwise the interior contained open areas for flying cyborgs, and cramped masses of equipment.

Perfect environment.

Fetch and Thanos eventually brought Bailey to one of the cramped areas: a chaos of tight construction, of beams and plates and tangles of optic cables. Through this they led him eventually to a small chamber, at the edge of which stood a pedestal-mounted touch console of the kind to which he was accustomed. Before the console, a free-standing chainglass window revealed a chrome cube, thirty centimetres at the side, resting on the grid floor beyond.

'I need to see my wife first,' said Bailey.

'Your wife will be here soon,' said Fetch. 'We do not delay on these things. You must begin.'

Bailey stepped over to the console and studied the logic screens immediately above it. For a long time someone had been attempting to break the sequence. He snorted then placed his hand on a bioreader. It displayed a section of his genetic code on the logic screens. Flicking through it to a certain point he made one or two alterations, then called up something from the huge databank and hit the splicing sequences. An amusing conceit: his genetic code spliced with that of a poisonous mushroom. When the splicing completed he hit send and gazed through the chainglass window. The cube developed a black line, then slid open on polished rods to expose a white sphere.

'There that opens the outer casing,' said Bailey. He turned to Fetch and said no more for a moment. Standing beside the cyborg, Jayne looked warm and alive. They'd dressed her in a bodysuit.

'Jayne … oh my God,' said Bailey.

Jayne smiled at him. He moved towards her then stumbled to a halt when a targeting grid snapped into existence before him.

'You must let me go to her,' he said to Fetch.

'We can easily undo the work we have done,' said Fetch.

'I know, just let me touch her, just let me know she is no longer cold.'

The grid snapped out of existence and Bailey went to his wife to take her in his arms.

'Darling,' she said.

He pulled her close then kissed her. His mouth tingled. She was warm and soft – an environment easily invaded by mycelia.

What's her status, Dis?

`The virus is multiplying exponentially and has been since they thawed her. She has been spreading it in the air for at least twenty minutes.`

What did they do?

`They removed what was left of her brain and put in a simple cyber mechanism.`

Bailey released his wife and stepped back. He watched Thanos and Fetch.

'Now you will open the inner … inner … casing,' said Fetch.

Thanos, who until then had remained in position as if pinned in the air, suddenly dropped a few centimetres before returning to position.

How long now?

`Minutes only.`

With the weapons they possess, a minute can be a long time.

`The virus acts quickly to turn on those sections of the DNA controlling the production of scar tissue, but it takes a little time for that tissue to form and begin to affect the interfaces.`

Bailey nodded to himself and walked slowly over to the console. When he glanced back he saw the walking corpse, which had once been his wife, now swaying as if to some internal music.

She's going.

Massive viral production is destroying the corpse.

Bailey began work at the console, pulling up gene-based coding sequences, giving every impression that he was doing what had been asked of him. He pretended not to see his wife's corpse abruptly fall over. He glanced round when Thanos' targeting grid snapped on then drifted up and aside. He moved carefully to put the console between himself and the cyborgs. Lights were incandescing like fireworks in Fetch's crystal aug. The face once expressionless was now puzzled, an expression that remained as Fetch took a pace forwards, then fell sideways on the gridded floor. He lay there mouthing like a beached fish until eventually the words came.

'Reply … reply …reply,' he said.

Thanos had no reply. That cyborg drifted towards Bailey, passed over his head, bumped gently against the window then slid down to the floor. Bailey stepped over to this half human and watched as its skin turned blue and fluids started to seep from the junctures between flesh and metal.

'Just too many connections,' he said aloud, then peered at Fetch. 'He could be saved, if anyone wanted to save him.' Stepping over the body of his wife, Bailey walked to the side of the window and looked back. What had happened to her here was justice. She had initiated death, but her death he had accepted long ago.

'I'm getting some strange signals from the station,' said Trapdoor.

'What kind of strange?' asked Linda, gazing up at the representation of station and the dead sun displayed by the LCD sandwich of her screen.

'The kind you get from extremely logical beings trying not to panic,' observed the AI.

'Then it's started. How long will it take?'

'Minutes only ... oh shit,' said the AI.

Linda sat up straighter. The AIs voice had gone flat. Trouble. 'Automated defence system activated. Missiles coming our way.'

On the last word the little ship lurched as it accelerated under huge G for which the internal gravity could not wholly compensate.

'Launching chaff.'

The ship lurched again and Linda caught something silvery flashing past the screen. Intense light hit the screen and it blacked. She frantically checked controls as acceleration pressed her into her seat. Was there anything she could do to help Trapdoor?

She checked their position. 'Defence system. How old?'

'Archaic. Many missiles, though,' replied Trapdoor.

'Take us to the sun's surface. Their motors won't pull your G,' said Linda.

There was another lurch. The screen came back on and Linda got a view of silvery missiles in a geometric swarm. A low humming came from the little craft's motors as they wound up to full power. The missiles dropped to one side of the screen then out of sight until a secondary screen popped on to show the tail view. On the main screen now was a lightless orb picked out by graphics.

'So, we have the whole pack of them after us,' said Linda.

With intonation returning to his voice Trapdoor replied, 'Yes, they are like guard dogs. The intention is to drive prowlers from around the station – probably launched by some failing automatic system. If we jumped now we could easily escape.'

'We don't want to do that. How long until we can lose them?'

'Minutes.'

'A lot can happen in a minute,' Linda noted.

Bailey stepped around the window edge.

The illusion of security.

I do not understand.

They didn't need to seal the canister away. They just needed enough of a screen to prevent me from rushing to get my hands on it. After all, Thanos was here and how could I possibly get away from … it?

Once behind the window he walked across gridded floor and squatted by the canister. The two halves of the chrome cube he pulled apart. The half without the rods he turned on its side, then picked up the sphere and dropped it back into this.

The canister itself is palm-keyed to me. I've no doubt they'd have taken my hand off at the wrist to use it, rather than risk me opening it for them.

There was no reply from Dis, and Bailey smiled to himself. Of course, the doctor mycelium was nervous, since this was an important moment for it. He reached down and rested his spread hand on the surface of the sphere. When he took his hand away a circle appeared in that surface, and the section it enclosed sank into the sphere before sliding to one side. Inside there was movement – something nacreous shifted and expressed rainbow light.

'Dis, let me introduce you to your brother Orcus,' said Bailey, and plunged his hand into the sphere.

For a moment his hand felt merely cold, then something grabbed it and held on. He heard Dis let go something like a scream, or a sigh. It receded, merged into a growing mechanistic roar. Cold cracked up Bailey's arm. Something wrenched at his elbow, his shoulder, his back, then was soothed. He closed his eyes and listened to the roar inside him. Dis he felt as a cobwebby presence in his muscles and in his bones. This other thing was a steel hawser hanging in his flesh, secured by razor hooks that did not hurt, but were on the edge of tearing him apart. He opened his eyes and glanced back to the window, through which he saw Fetch pulling himself upright, blind, drool running from the corner of his mouth.

'Like you and Thanos, are Dis and Orcus: two halves, a partnership. Dis is the healer and Orcus ... Orcus is like Thanos: he provides the muscle, the firepower. Now they are one.'

Fetch tilted his head and Bailey wondered if he had heard a word.

Are you there now? Are you ready?

WE ARE ORCUS. WE ARE READY.

Good.

Bailey withdrew his hand from the sphere and placed it on the gridwork deck.

Orcus, you know the situation because Dis knows it and now you are one inside me. But it is your nature that you must be ordered. Orcus, I order you to destroy this station, all its occupants, and as many of the docked ships you can reach. The cryopod in which I brought my wife here I want you to leave intact, as myself. It is your return point.

AS ORDERED.

250

Around Bailey's hand the grey gridwork turned glittery and crystalline. This effect spread in a slow star, then one arm of this star sped toward Fetch. The cyborg jerked upright and screamed, rainbow light filling his mouth, then he imploded and a sheet gore and metal fell out of the air. In his place sprouted a rainbow tree, which after a moment sank back into the deck. Next to it the window crazed and broke into finger-sized shards. That arm sped on, and other arms sped in other directions. Metal broke, plastic shattered and chainglass turned to powder. By the time Bailey was on his feet he could hear screams and explosions, and smell burning flesh.

Your brother is most efficient.
`It is how you made him. Must he return to us?`
I'm afraid so. He cannot be left loose.
`I prefer to be myself.`
I know. I'm sorry.

Bailey walked through glittering shards. Thanos was now nothing but a spreading pool of gore in which a few unidentifiable components lay. As the chaos rapidly spread, Bailey walked out the way he had entered. Flying cyborgs were dragged out of the air by cast webs of filaments. He observed the beetle cyborg split in half and ooze circuitry like lava from a volcanic vent, its human face no longer screaming, but grinning insanely. The head on a plate hovered high out of reach while a rainbow cone grew below it. He did not wait to see the result of that encounter. The cryopod lay next to the broken beetle, as they had not thought to put it anywhere safe, or yet to dispose of it. They did not think like that. Bailey opened it with a touch and climbed inside.

Wake me in a thousand years, Dis.
`Really?`
A joke, old friend.
`I am all out of humour, Bailey.`

251

Silver specks dropped towards the sun and were just gone. Linda felt a tugging even with internal gravity at maximum compensation.

'I hope AG isn't faulty, Trapdoor,' she said.

'If it was faulty you wouldn't be asking that question,' replied the AI, all its sarcasm back.

'What am I feeling then?'

'Tidal forces. That dead sun still has quite a spin to it.'

'Oh,' said Linda, feeling stupid.

The sun shifted to one side of the screen. Now the drone of the engines contained an ominous hollow note. Linda ignored the stress indicators and all the other glaring displays. The craft would handle it or not. There would be no in-between point.

'We are at perihelion. Beginning break away in thirty seconds,' said Trapdoor.

'Is this to make me feel like I'm involved,' Linda enquired.

'Touchy touchy.'

Thirty seconds passed. The droning note changed and the sun slipped farther sideways. The noise ceased and slowly but surely the station swung back into view.

'Jesu! Look at that!'

'I am looking,' Trapdoor replied grimly.

The station was falling apart. Explosions were blowing out panels and scattering debris around it in a glittering orbital cloud. Internal fires burned behind blackened and distorted beams. Rainbow light flared here and there.

'A ship is leaving,' said Trapdoor.

'Now that's not so good. Any get away and you can forget containment.'

One of the wedge ships lifted from the station on a flare of blue and began to peel away. Something like a streak of rainbow lightning flickered up at it then went out. A white light flared near its engines and the ship burned like a sculpture made of fuse paper.

'Catalytic fire, interesting,' Trapdoor noted.

No more ships managed to detach, but Linda observed a cone of rainbow light snap out from the station – the merest speck of matter propelled at its tip. Then the cone retracted into that speck drawing, in an instant, all signs of that rainbow glow from the massive station.

'Is that–'

Suddenly the screen blacked out protectively. When vision returned it was to show a spreading cloud of debris and nebulous flame – all that remained of the station.

'Fusion generator,' Trapdoor explained.

A blinking light appeared on the screen and expanded into a square. It tracked the expansion of the debris cloud as it focused on one small piece.

'I think it would be incredible if he were alive,' said Linda, as she manually steered the craft towards that dot.

'He was vengeful, not suicidal,' said Trapdoor, bringing the system controlling the towing grapple online.

Bailey opened his eyes to a starfield that shot overhead like a speckled belt. There was a muted roar inside him and he felt too full and too dangerous. He sat upright in the now open cryopod, and gazed around. A life-bubble enclosed him on a small asteroid. There was little inside the bubble, and a no-doubt limited supply of oxygen.

Exactly how I would have done it.

WE CAN ATTACK.

There's nothing to attack, Orcus.

Bailey glanced at the canister on the floor. It was spherical, white, and open in readiness, and it rested in one half of an armoured box that was twin to the one on the station. He climbed from the cryopod and observed the spacesuit lying next to it. It was probably made to measure.

'Can anyone hear me?' he asked.

'Yes,' replied a woman's voice.

'Do I know you?' he asked.

'We met. I shot you and your mycelium stung me. It was a brief affair.'

Bailey smiled and walked over to the sphere. He put his hand inside.

Orcus, I order you to get inside this vessel, and, when I have removed my hand, I order you to seal yourself in.

OPENING CODE REQUIRED.

My DNA and hand print, as before.

Bailey closed his eyes and felt the hooks pull free inside him. It was not gentle, but the Dis half was there to mend things. His spine crackled. There were thumps at his shoulder and elbow, like shocks from a welder. He opened his eyes as cold flowed from his hand.

He is gone.

Bailey nodded then removed his hand from the sphere. The little hatch slid across, pushed out into position and sealed. The sphere became perfect. He tipped the half box, containing this, up to its other half, and pushed the rods into their sockets. Stepping back he watched the two halves of the box draw together – sealing the sphere away. He turned to the spacesuit.

Should I bother to put it on?

Why do you ask this?

In their position I would throw away the key.

Perhaps they are more forgiving.

Perhaps.

Bailey shrugged to himself then set about donning the suit. When he sealed it, he walked out through the airlock of the bubble and that temporary building collapsed behind him. Under the belt of stars he waited to be picked up.

Or not.

ENDS

THE VETERAN

Cheel had nearly escaped when she saw the man take off his face. She was sure she'd lost Croven's boys on the loading dock, but hid amongst plasmesh packing crates long enough to be certain. As a further precaution, she took a roundabout route to the terminal, to catch the ferry to the Scarbe side of the river. And there he was:

Seated on a bollard, the man contemplatively removed his pipe, as if to tamp it down or relight it. Instead, he placed it stem down in the top pocket of his shirt, then reached up and pressed his fingers against his cheekbone and forehead. His face came away from his hairline, round behind his ears, down to a point just above his Adam's apple. The inside of his mouth and much of his sinus were also part of the prosthesis, so only bare eyeballs in the upper jut of his skull remained – the rest being the black spikes and plates of bio-interfaces.

Cheel gaped. From another pocket, the man took some sort of tool and began to probe inside the back of his detached face. He put the prosthesis in his lap, then took up his pipe and placed it in his throat sphincter. Smoke bled from between the interface plates of his cheeks. His bare eyeballs swivelled towards Cheel then back down to the adjustments he was making. She suddenly realized who this must be. Here was the veteran who worked on the ferry. Here was one of the few survivors from a brutal war between factions of dense-tech humans. Not understanding what was impelling her, she walked out on the jetty and approached him.

The veteran ignored her, until after he removed his pipe from his throat and replaced his face. The prosthesis engaged with a sucking click. Perhaps, without his face, he just could not speak?

'And what is your name?' he asked patronisingly.

'Cheel.'

With the same tool he had used on the back of his face, he contemplatively scraped out his pipe. After repacking it with tobacco from his belt-pouch, he ignited it with a laser lighter. Puffed out a cloud of fragrant smoke.

'What can I do for you, Cheel?'

She didn't know what to say. She wanted to ask about dense tech, about star travel, if it was true he was over two hundred years old, and if it was true that the Straker nova, which grew in the sky every night, was the result of a star his kind detonated during a battle. But there was no time.

'Hey Cheel!'

She felt a sudden flush of horror. Stupid to walk out on this jetty. Stupid to allow this momentary fascination to delay her escape. She turned and saw her original pursuers blocking her escape from the jetty. Glancing aside at the water of Big River, she saw a suderdile swimming past. Unusually for a girl raised in the river town of Slove-Scarbe, she could swim. She had learnt out at the coast, when Grand Mam had been alive, but that skill would not help her here. Town residents didn't learn to swim because the survival rate in the river was less than thirty seconds.

'What do you want, Slog?' she asked.

By his expression, she guessed he wanted more than her immediate death. Discovering his cache of jewels missing, Croven must have quickly worked out that she had finally left him, and let Slog off the leash. But what the hell did he expect? As his sickness progressed he became increasingly violent and unpredictable, and she did not want to die with him when one of his lieutenants finally took him down.

'You've been a really naughty girl, Cheel.'

Slog, Croven's second, had killed three people that Cheel knew about. She looked behind her, hoping for some escape route, maybe a boat. The veteran was gone, though why he should hide she had no idea – he was one who had nothing to fear from Slog and his kind. She drew her shiv and began to back up. Maybe if she lured them down this side of the jetty she could escape past on the other side, or across the top of the packing crates? Then more of Croven's gang arrived and she knew there would be no escape. Suddenly the horrible reality hit home and she wanted to cry. They would rape her, all of them and for a long time, and if she that didn't kill her, they would feed her to the suderdiles. She backed up further, came opposite the bollard on which the veteran had been sitting.

'What did you do?' asked the face lying on top of the bollard.

Cheel just stood there for a moment with her mouth moving and nothing coming out. Eventually: 'I was just trying to get away from Croven.' She neglected to mention Croven's cache of jewels in a hide roll hanging by cords from her shoulder.

'And what will they do to you?' asked the face.

'Rape me, then kill me.'

'What's that, little bitch?' Slog directed others of Croven's gang to cover every way off the jetty. Beyond him she saw Croven arrive – the lanky black-haired figure was difficult to mistake, especially with that wooden gait and unnatural posture. Could she appeal to him after her betrayal?

'Nothing,' said Cheel. 'Nothing at all.' She glanced at the face.

It winked at her then said, 'Pick me up and turn me towards them.'

What did she have to lose?

As she snatched up the prosthesis, Slog drew his Compac airgun and aimed it low. He wasn't going to kill her, just smash a kneecap if she put up too much of a fight. She'd seen him do that before. His expression was nasty, grinning, then suddenly it changed to confusion when he saw what she held.

'What do you think?' the face asked, vibrating in her hand. 'Slog is a pathetically descriptive name for him.'

'I don't–' Cheel began.

Something flashed, iridescent. A sound, as of a giant clearing its throat, rent the air. Slog froze, a horizontal line traversing down the length of his body, searing him from head to foot. Then he moved and flame broke from pink cracks appearing in his black skin. His air gun burst with a dull thrump, took his hand away. He held the stump up before his liquefying eyes and started screaming. Croven came swiftly up behind him, turned him and shoved. Slog screamed in the water, his blackened skin slewing away. Cheel didn't see the suderdile that took him. One moment he was splashing in reddish froth, then he was gone.

The face vibrated in Cheel's hands. 'Croven, the girl is coming with me to the Skidbladnir, and that was in the nature of a warning to you and your gang.'

Croven stared in horror down into the water, then at his glistening hands. Next, seemingly jerked into motion, he made a circular signal in the air with the point of his finger. Gang members began retreating from the jetty, heading away.

'Why her?' He suddenly turned to stare at the face. 'Is that part of you not prosthetic as well?'

'Ah, Croven,' said the face. 'The thing about power is that you don't have to justify what you do with it. Surely you know that already.'

Croven nodded, turned away briefly, then turned back to gaze directly at Cheel. 'I wasn't going to kill you. I love you.'

Cheel believed him, but was very aware of his use of 'wasn't'. Now, her causing Slog's death even if indirectly, Croven would not be able to back down. He waited for her to say something, and when she did not, he headed away.

'What now?' Cheel asked when all of the gang were no longer in sight.

'Now, carrying my face, you walk to the ferry.'

Cheel began walking, realising as she did so, that in engaging so completely with the talking face, she had momentarily forgotten it was only the veteran's prosthesis.

'Where are you?' she asked, as she reached the end of the jetty.

'Never you mind. Just keep walking to the terminal. I was right to assume you were heading for the Scarbe side?'

'You were.'

Cheel saw no sign of Croven or his gang, but knew they were very likely lurking nearby. Ducking her head down, and tucking the prosthesis under her arm next to the jewel roll, she hurried towards the looming shape of the skid ferry, or the Skidbladnir, as the veteran called it. She half expected a slug from an air gun to slam into her at any moment, if not vengefully from Croven then from one of the others, but none did. Sensibly, no one was attacking while the veteran remained invisible close by. Why did it have to come to this?

Time and again she had pleaded with Croven to live out his remaining time on the coast with her. With his cache they could have lived comfortably for some time and then, as it ran out, she could have found work. She would have looked after him, nursed him to the end. But his choice to stay where ruthlessness and physical violence were the measure of a man

260

meant there could be only one ending. It was all right for him to choose a bloody end for himself. He had no right to choose it for her too.

Soon she reached the ferry ramp, where she groped in her pocket for her token, but it seemed the veteran's face was token enough and the guard waved her aboard. Avoiding the restaurant deck because of the delicious smells and her lack of funds suitable to purchase what was sold there, Cheel went all the way up to the roof deck and there, leaning against the balustrade, she kept an eye on the boarding ramps. A hand tapped her on the shoulder, and she turned to the faceless veteran, holding out his hand for his prosthesis.

'How is it you're not seen?' Cheel asked.

'Chameleonware.' His face, its mouth still moving, again seated with that sucking click. Eyes now in place where before there had been none, he gazed up at the sky and continued, 'But in making myself invisible down here, I've made myself all too visible elsewhere. Though admittedly the proton flash was what attracted attention.'

'Slog?'

'Yes.' He turned to regard her. 'The weapon I used to burn that piece of shit.'

Cheel glanced up to where he had been gazing, and raised a querying eyebrow.

'Friends,' he said. 'Though I find it difficult to think of them as such. They let me rest to salve and repair what remains of my humanity, but by using my weapons to kill, I've told them I'm ready to take up my duties again. I don't think a quarter of a century is enough, but then I don't think any time is long enough.'

From below, she heard the clack of ratchets and loud clangs as the crew raised the ramps and secured them to the side of the vessel. Deep in the belly of the Skidbladnir, big diesel engines started rumbling.

'What will happen?' Cheel knew she would have to get away from Scarbe as quickly as possible. The veteran had saved her, and right now protected her, but that would not and could not last. And Croven would come after her.

'They'll send a tral-sphere with tac updates and new mission parameters.'

Cheel just nodded. She understood none of that but did not want him to stop speaking. He was talking dense tech here, stuff about the war, and about technically-advanced humans killing each other.

In steel cages behind them, vertical shafts began turning. These drove the big shiny grip wheels clamped on the thick ship-metal cable reaching from the Slove pylon behind them to the Scarbe pylon a kilometre across the river. The ferry began to ease out of dock. Dispersing suderdiles surfed a white water wave away from the bows. Cheel turned to gaze across the river to their destination.

'When will this tral-sphere arrive?' she asked.

The veteran smiled. 'That you ask indicates you have no idea what I'm talking about. The tral-sphere is, of course, already here. And so is the war, and so is the enemy, and so already is my plan.'

A crewman saw him leap aboard, but showed no inclination to chase him down into the dank lower holds of the ferry. In the dim light admitted by a filthy portal into a long steel corridor, Croven drew his air gun from his belly holster and checked the load. He noted that his right hand was shaking – the added stress of the situation exacerbating the symptoms of his neurological disease. Damn Cheel for forcing this on him. Slog had quickly detected her inept theft, otherwise Croven could have let her go. But Slog and the others knowing, meant Croven had to order her immediate capture. For her theft from and betrayal of him, the minimum he could get away with, whilst retaining his status, would have been her humiliation and beating. Now, after what happened to Slog, he must try to kill her and the veteran. But Croven did not want to kill Cheel and doubted he could kill the veteran.

The gangs of Slove had long known that the veteran was untouchable. But this was the first time he had actually used one of his dense-tech weapons to kill. Before, it had always been one of his invisible visitations. Some offenders he gave a beating, others he threw in the river. Quite often they were like Croven: gang members who lived by a code allowing them to admit no fear. The veteran had killed Croven's lieutenant, and for that Croven must exact vengeance. That going up against the veteran meant death did not excuse not making the attempt. Perhaps Croven should have listened to Cheel.

When she had first suggested leaving Slove and heading out to one of the coastal towns, Croven had given the idea serious consideration. He had been bored and here was a chance at a fresh start, new challenges. But the shakes had started about then, and medscan confirmed something was wrong. He'd paid a researcher to find out what. After only a few hours of delving in the public com library the researcher laid it out for him. Croven had a reversion disease: one of those ailments long considered the province historians by the bulk of humanity, but returning to primitive colonies like this one. Prognosis: no cure on this world.

Now the drugs that had alleviated some symptoms of his Parkinson's were becoming less and less effective. He estimated he had a year as gang leader before someone took him down. He would have lasted longer in one of the coastal towns but, after Cheel had grown bored with his sickness and left him, probably have starved to death in the end. Croven preferred the idea of going out bloody. Perhaps now was the time.

'Croven.' The voice had a metallic quality that made him think for one insane moment that the ferry was speaking to him.

'Veteran,' he said at last. The man must have seen him board, and had now come after him in the invisible form. Croven turned sharply towards the length of corridor it had issued from, and fired half his ten-shot clip into the shadows. The slugs smacked and whined down into the darkness.

'I am not the veteran. I am his enemy.' The voice grated in Croven's ear.

Then, suddenly, the ferry dipped and shuddered and some force picked Croven up and slammed him against a steel bulkhead. Now, with a reverberating clang a curving black surface appeared, intersecting the floor and wall of the corridor. Croven saw that the portal had been shattered and realized that what held him had probably saved him from injury. He could hear yelling out there, screaming. A hatch irised open in the black surface to reveal gleaming tight-packed and squirming movement.

'Choose,' the voice hissed.

Something had slammed the thousands of tons of iron and steel of the ferry to one side and now it was groaning as it dragged back into position under the cable, and huge waves slapped its sides and washed the lower decks. The abrupt motion would have flung Cheel over the rail and into the jaws of the suderdiles had not the veteran wrapped an arm around her.

'What?' she gasped.

'That was fast,' he said. 'But not well-positioned.'

A thunderclap now, and suddenly they were in shadow. A sphere had appeared. It was twenty metres across, jet black, and only three or four metres above them, its surface intersecting the grip-wheel gearboxes and the ship-metal cable. When it shifted slightly in relation to the ferry, severed cable snaked out of the clamping wheels, slammed down on deck nearby, then slithered off the back of the ferry taking most of the rear cast-iron balustrade with it.

'I guess I could have done better as well,' the veteran observed.

Two of them, two of these tral spheres, Cheel realized. But where was the other one? She saw that the visible one had sheared the ferry's gearbox clean through. Thick gleaming oil slopped out and a couple of hypoid gears bounced across the deck. As she looked around, she guessed the location of the other one. People were screaming, some of them thrown into the water by cataclysmic arrival of that first sphere inside the ferry. In horror, Cheel watched a woman trying to hold a baby up out of the water, away from the approaching suderdiles. Disconnected from the cable, the ferry was now turning, carried downstream by the strong current.

'There are people in the water!' Cheel exclaimed.

'Yes,' the veteran shrugged. 'People die.'

Cheel stared at him in disbelief. She had discounted his previous callousness. He was two hundred years old, an advanced human, and she had thought he would be better than, something more than, people she knew.

'You don't care?'

'Of course he doesn't care.' Cheel turned as Croven stepped up on deck. 'We are primitives to him.'

265

There was something seriously amiss with Croven. His skin was uniformly white and somehow dead, and only as he drew closer did she see his eyes seemed plain steel balls.

'Ah, the automatics picked you up,' said the veteran. 'They always make an assessment and choose one who is willing for conversion. What swung it, Croven, your pride and gangland honour, or the promise of a cure for what's eating out the inside of your head?'

Croven ignored the jibe. He concentrated on Cheel. 'I've been recruited and now, knowing I could kill you in an instant, am certain I don't want to.' He now looked at the veteran. 'I know the enemy.'

The air between Croven and the veteran was taut, telic, as something invisible probed and strained it. The feeling began to grow unbearable.

'Move aside.' The veteran touched Cheel's shoulder.

The ferry was now hundreds of metres downstream from the crossing point and there were no screams from the water anymore, just spreading red where grey suderdile flukes stirred and broke the surface. The visible sphere continued to hang like a balloon above the ferry. Then, a crashing from below and the deck tilted. Cheel grabbed a drive shaft cage to stop herself sliding over. The other two remained upright, both now standing in mid air, where the deck had been. A hundred metres out the other sphere folded out of the air with a thunderous crash. A hole opened in the side of it revealing gleaming movement.

'Had I not been your enemy before you stepped into that tral-sphere, I would be now.' The veteran shrugged – a strangely out-of-place action from somcone floating off the deck. 'It's how you've been programmed.'

The steel deck below them was rippling, intersecting shear plains, nacreous sheets and lines, appeared in the air

266

between them, kept rearranging as if struggling to form some final complete shape. Cheel smelt burning and saw oily smoke gusting up the side of the ferry towards her. There was more screaming, some from inside the ferry and some from the water. Glancing down the tilted deck she saw a life boat drifting past, people struggling to board it, even though it was tangled in broken rope and half tipped over by the weight of a suderdile, its jaws closed on the legs of a bellowing ferryman. This latest disaster, she realized, had been caused by Croven – by him shifting his sphere outside the ferry. He and the veteran were as bad as each other: the ferry and those aboard it meant nothing to them.

'It can't be settled here – you know that,' said Croven.

The veteran smiled humourlessly. A column of intersecting fields, looking like stacked broken glass, stabbed down from the sphere directly above the ferry, enclosed him, folded him away. Resistance removed, the deck before Croven split in a thousand places, peeled up and blew away in a white-hot storm, sparking and glittering from the ferry. This exposed a maze of rooms and corridors packed with people struggling in bewilderment through smoke suddenly dispersing. Croven turned to face Cheel, then the same weird distortions stabbed across to him, and folded him to his own sphere. Cheel wondered if they had taken the battle elsewhere to save lives, if Croven had peeled up the deck to give air to these trapped souls. She wanted to believe in some altruism on the part of dense tech humans, old and new. But when the ferry tilted further, evidently sinking, and the smoke down below turned to fire, there was no room for that belief. As the steel deck grew warm below her, she watched the battle in the sky.

Between the two spheres, now dots many kilometres apart, those same shear planes and lines crazed the sky. The two seemed to be employing forces so immense they stressed and fractured existence. Light flashed across one of these planes towards one of the spheres, and something slapped it down. Over the horizon rose a storm of dust as from mountains falling. Another such ricochet sent a two-metre wave down the river from some distant destruction, bucking the ferry and changing its angle of approach to the bottom of the river. Then, out of the sky, some basin of force scooping. Cheel clung to the cage as first she was pressed hard against the deck and felt it collapsing underneath her, gouts of fire issuing from where it had been torn away nearby. Then she was flung sideways, her body fully away from the steel and legs flailing in the air. The ferry beached with a crash, slamming her to the deck again.

Croven was losing. Around him, the veteran's attack program was sequestering machines at an exponential rate. In the time it took him to calculate how much longer his control would last, it was gone. He expected to die then, not in some spectacular manner as the veteran's single enemy, but in the same way that the crew of a destroyer would die – almost irrelevant to the destruction of the machine itself. But his elevated awareness remained, and he realized the veteran had held back from destroying the structures built inside Croven's head, and allowed him to live.

Haitus.

Croven opened his eyes to sunlight, on a ridge above a mud bank where suderdiles would normally bask. The river was turbid and none of the creatures in sight. There was dust in the air and a smell as of hot electronics.

'Why did you choose me?' Croven asked, already guessing the answer.

The veteran, seated on a rock nearby, replied, 'They always place an autosystem near where one of us has become inactive – ready to counter us should we activate. But such cyber systems require a human component.'

'I'm already aware of that,' said Croven bitterly.

The veteran stared at him coldly. 'The human component is first programmed, then given control. However, if the human component is faulty, more control reverts to the system. I can destroy such systems with ease. It is the random human creative element that can be dangerous to me.'

Croven sat upright. He felt fine, better than fine. 'So you wanted someone dumb like me in control.'

The veteran shook his head. 'It was time for me to activate again – to reveal myself. I'd already chosen to do that by killing Slog, knowing that would give you reason to try to kill me, just as the enemy system, detecting me, came online, its routines guiding it to you. A human with substantial neurological damage made an easier opponent for me, because there would be less of the human in the system. But I was also watching the situation, and Cheel's theft and attempted escape from you, was too good an opportunity to miss.'

'I don't know what you mean.' But Croven did.

The veteran went on relentlessly. 'Your own actions would put in danger someone you love, and made you doubly vulnerable. Shifting the ferry like that was enough of a diversion of resources. It's why you lost, Croven.'

Swallowing dryly, Croven asked, 'What now?'

The veteran stood. 'I'll leave you with your implants. They'll keep you functioning for another ten years. Beyond that,' he shrugged, 'I have other battles to fight.'

The veteran turned away, space revolved around him and he was gone. Above, a black sphere accelerated straight up, receded.

In the background, the ferry lay broken-backed over a hill. It was still burning, and the survivors gathered in stunned groups, not knowing what to do or where to go. The enduring image imprinted in Cheel's mind was of a man squatting on the ground holding his burned hands out from his body, whilst behind him a little girl whacked, with a length of metal, a beached and dying suderdile. Other denizens of the river and drifts of weed were scattered in the vicinity. That bowl of force had snatched them up along with the ferry and much of the river. Lying in the dirt were fish, disjointed crustaceans, pink river clams. Cheel was uninjured, and in that she was one of the few. The fires had caught many, but she had avoided them by climbing down ladders on the outside of the ferry. She had been able to help only a few of them. Pulling up handfuls of weed from a nearby pile, she approached the man, and wrapped strands of it around his burned hands – the best she could do to cool the injury.

'Come away now,' she said to the girl, when the suderdile made a gasping attempt to snap at its tormentor. The girl ignored Cheel and now tried to poke out one of the creature's yellow eyes.

'A novelty that cannot be ignored.'

Cheel spun round to face Croven, inspected him from head to foot. His skin now bore a more healthy hue, but there was still something metallic about his eyes.

'Did you kill him, then?' she asked.

'No, I lost, and he spared me.'

'Remiss of him to leave scum like you alive.' Cheel rested her hand on a nearby rock. Croven was not carrying his air gun, but she knew what he could do to her with only his hands.

'You don't really know me at all, Cheel.'

'I know that you can't let me live, after what happened to Slog.'

He gestured to the ferry. 'I saved your life, and the urgency I felt, which made me what I was, is no longer with me.'

Cheel glanced round at the ferry. Either he or the veteran had lifted the craft out of the river and deposited it here on the bank. He claimed it was him.

'And how am I supposed to react to that?' she asked.

'Come with me to the coast.'

Cheel again took in the surrounding ruination and gripped the rock tighter.

'Go to Hell,' she said.

Croven stood utterly still for a while, then he nodded once and walked away.

ENDS

AND END ALL!

Printed in Great Britain
by Amazon

57557469R00163